DEATH ON THE LINE

A Judith Spears Mystery - Book 2

Sam Oman

DEATH ON THE LINE

THE SECOND JUDITH SPEARS MYSTERY

Copyright © 2024 - Sam Oman

All rights reserved. No part of this publication may be reproduced, distributed, or transmitted in any form or by any means, including photocopying, recording, or other electronic or mechanical methods, without the prior written permission of the publisher, except in the case of brief quotations embodied in critical reviews and certain other non-commercial uses permitted by copyright law.

Cover art: Wilkes Design

Chapter One

There is something supremely tranquil about an autumnal evening in the flaxen English countryside. The clean azure sky, dabbed by cotton wool smears, did little to betray the bitterly cold breeze that had stirred in the morning and tussled a liberal layer of frost crowning the fields. It was a warning that autumn was verging on an unseasonably early winter.

For Charlie Walker, the rolling hills surrounding Little Pickton always put him in mind of a classic painting. A Wainwright or... some other bloke he couldn't remember. His usual exhaustive list of painters was entirely informed by regularly watching *University Challenge*, a television quiz that he religiously watched, but seldom got a single answer correct.

His stout black boots crunched the semi-frozen mud track as he hurried to keep up with Reeta, a podgy black Labrador he was walking for the owner. He was in dire need of exercise and a drastic reduction in treats, as was the dog.

Charlie was already gulping in lungfuls of air and felt his heart pounding beneath his wax-coated Barbour jacket.

"Oi, Reeta! Get that tail back here!" He called out, ending each word with a tired exhalation that curled like smoke from his mouth. He held up the leather lead that was coiled around his hand, as if it would summon the dog back. Reeta didn't give a damn. Once he'd unclipped the leash as they entered the forest, she had launched ahead with her nose ploughing through the leaves as her senses came alive. She was allegedly something of a star, according to Mrs Ply, who had regularly employed *Charlie Walker Walks* over the years. According to her, Reeta was once a prize truffle hunter in Tuscany, where she still had a villa they summered in - which meant Charlie looked after the hound for the month she was away. Why she had returned to England was anybody's guess. Charlie thought it had something to do with mafia involvement. Perhaps she was on the run. Why else would anybody choose Little Pickton over the Tuscan sunshine?

"Reeta!" he yelled again, as the dog sprinted around a turn in the track. He'd taken a different path through the woods just for the sake of variety. He wasn't worried about losing his charge. The hound always did this, and he always regretted he didn't have the energy of youth to run after her.

The track turned to the left, forcing him to stoop under some low-hanging branches that indicated few people had come this way over the year. A few yards further on, he noticed the trees were thinning, revealing the railway line cutting through the forest like a surgical scar. He hadn't realised they'd walked that far west of the village. Tufts of frosty grass poked between the sleepers along the single line track, and Reeta had paused to sniff at a bundle of twigs, her nose leading her in circles. Charlie wasn't too concerned about walking on the track. The line had been officially closed for a decade, although the occasional freight wagons made a pilgrimage along it. It was more often used by the local train Society, that had lovingly restored an old steam train and ran it for tourists along the eleven mile stretch between Little Pickton and Denzel Green. Not that either town boasted any tourists, unless they were lost. He suspected the club had deliberately chosen the route, so they effectively had their own private railway they didn't have to share with the general public, despite obtaining a lot of National Lottery money for the renovation. Or perhaps they were running drugs? He'd read about the notorious county-line gangs, although he hadn't the time to read up on the facts. The name said it all.

He shook the lead and was about to call the dog, but the action triggered Reeta to give a single bark, then sprint down the line with her nose zigzagging between the tracks, and the twigs clamped in her mouth like a prize.

"Bloody hell, Reeta! Give a bloke a chance, will you?"

Once again, he was forced to hurry in pursuit. His foot slipped twice on the icy sleepers, forcing him to step on the uneven gravel in between. It crunched and shifted underfoot, slowing him down while the dog bounded enthusiastically up the track. He aborted several attempts to call her because his breath wheezed between his lips and his heart was hammering in his chest. The track bore to the right, tightly framed by ancient oak trees. He could hear Reeta's excited yapping. Charlie decided that if she'd found a valuable truffle, then it would be worth a potential heart attack. Although he wasn't sure what the odds were of finding one in winter, in England.

He focused on each step as he power-marched along the track and only looked up when Reeta's barking became louder. He stopped in his tracks... and on the track, when he saw the polished green locomotive standing ahead, with Reeta barking a warning at it.

"Well done. You've found a train on a rail track." He moved forward slowly, hoping not to provoke the mutt into sprinting away. It was odd that they'd stop the train in the middle of the forest, unless it had broken down, which occasionally happened. There was no smoke rising from the stack, but nevertheless, when he caught up with Reeta and slipped the leash back on, he nervously hopped off the line just in case it started up again.

"Hullo!" He called as he circled around the tank engine. He'd approached it from the rear, and only now realised that the passenger carriage wasn't attached. The society had been rather proud of the 1920s carriage they had found on a scrap heap and lovingly restored. They seldom ran one without the other. "Hello?" He called again.

Silence greeted him. Even Reeta had shut up and munched on her twigs. He was sure that it took more than one engineer to run the train. If it had broken down, why would they leave it unattended? Not that anybody would steal it.

Now level with rungs leading up to the open-sided driver's cab, he could see there was nobody inside. Reeta whined and tugged on the lead, her nose firmly pointing to the cab, as if a prize truffle was nestled inside. Charlie was intrigued, more so because he had always wanted to drive a train, but the idiots who ran the Society had never even allowed him to stand in the cab. He glanced around, in case the driver had nipped off for a pee, then secured the end of the lead around the vertical handrail at the side of the ladder, and climbed inside.

He felt like a giddy child again, sneaking somewhere he shouldn't. He scrambled up with a sudden flush of youthful energy, which was abruptly tempered when he saw a pair of legs. It wasn't so much the dirty denim dungarees and sturdy metal toe capped boots; it was the fact they were sticking out of the open boiler door. The macabre sight froze Charlie.

It was seconds later that a smell struck him that would put him off barbecues for life.

Chapter Two

The clattering cup and saucer resonated like castanets.

Well, thought Judith, if they sound like castanets, that certainly means it's not Timothy's fine old bone china. Probably Ikea's best, she mused, wherever that was made. It's probably more on the plasticky side. At least the coffee was genuine enough to keep Charlie focused.

Judith Spears leaned back in a chair and gave a warm smile to the still-terrified Charlie sitting across from the table in the village's watering hole: *Tea For Time*. It was late afternoon, and he'd recounted his journey through the forest, his grisly discovery in the train, and the subsequent police haranguing he'd had to endure before returning the dog back to its worried owner.

"Why is it always dog walkers who find corpses?" said Charlie. "It's a health hazard. Happens all the time in my profession."

Judith ran her fingers through her fine red hair, which remained vibrant into her fifties. "Dog walkers find these things because they're always out and about enjoying the countryside."

"Always poking around places other people just simply can't be bothered to go, and in all sorts of weather," observed Maggie Tawia, who was sitting to the side of Charlie, eyeing him suspiciously with her arms folded across her bosom. "There must be a statistical likelihood that a large portion of dog walkers are serial killers." Her smooth Gambian accent would ordinarily be quite relaxing, but her words set Charlie on edge even further and the castanets upped tempo. Judith rolled her eyes.

"Come on, Maggie, that can't be right." Although Judith thought her friend had a point. Maggie had worked for over a decade for the HMRC, investigating fraud. Statistics were her bread and butter. "It's the woods. People do all sorts in the woods. That's why Charlie was there with Reeta." She patted his arm. "Little Pickton's number one dogger."

Charlie almost spat out his coffee and put the cup down with a thud. He looked forlorn, more concerned about Reeta's welfare than the victim he'd found. Judith looked sideways at Maggie. Despite her stern countenance, it was clear Maggie appreciated the man's affection for his beloved dogs.

That was something else to think about another time. Perhaps Maggie had been alone for far too long and was becoming attracted to sociopaths. Although Charlie was far from the worst person in Little Pickton, Judith wondered if she'd set her sights a little too low.

"Tell me again what happened, but this time, focus on the small details."

Charlie didn't look up. His gaze bored into the table. The tearoom was the first place he'd come after the police had allowed him to leave the crime scene. He'd ventured inside to meet Reeta's owner, exchange the poor pet who was long overdue her lunch, and then sat down before accidentally bumping into Maggie. After a quick exchange about what happened, Maggie summoned Judith with the power of a simple text message.

"Poor Reeta." Charlie sighed again, slowly shaking his head side to side.

Judith watched, bemused. He was feeling sorrier for the animal than he was for himself.

"She was sniffing away, zigzagging down that track, straight to the train like a guided missile," he said with a sigh. "She's a prize truffle hunter, y'know. Barking away, knew something was amiss. And then, when I climbed up, there he was. Poor old Herbert. Legs sticking out the furnace. A real goner."

Herbert Holland was the co-chairman of the LPRS – *Little Pickton Rail Society*. The man who had helped pull a couple of rusty rails from the ground, raised money from private backers and lottery funding, to produce a first-class steam train experience running from the middle of nowhere to the end of nowhere. Still, it was a mighty endeavour, and Judith couldn't deny it brought great pleasure to many people, even if steam trains were not quite her bag.

"At first, I thought it might be suicide," said Charlie, finally meeting Judith's gaze.

Judith gave a small shrug. "That was one heck of a way to go, throwing yourself headfirst into the fiery furnace of a steam train". But she couldn't rule it out. People had done far worse.

"That's what I told the police," Charlie said. "I thought

poor old Herbert had done himself over. They looked sceptical."

Judith nodded in understanding. She'd messaged DS Raymond Collins the moment she'd heard there was some skulduggery afoot. He'd simply replied with a single message:

NONE OF YOUR BUSINESS!

It had amused Judith. Of course, it was none of her business. It wouldn't be fun if it was her business. Still, the body was only freshly baked this morning, so she'd give the police a little time to see if they needed any help. Judith had garnered a bit of a reputation for being an amateur sleuth in Little Pickton. Something she vehemently denied when asked. Yet, it was a point of pride she couldn't help but enjoy when it was mentioned. Although she doubted very much the police would be drumming their way up her garden path for any assistance. Not that she had any to give. In fact, since she'd been a resident of Little Pickton, she'd never travelled on the railway itself so had no knowledge about it. Sure, she'd been present a few times when the train had been used for a pageant or church fete. But she'd never actually been on board the thing.

"Did the police give you any indication of what they thought had happened?" she asked.

Charlie shook his head. "Nah, I don't think they thought my suicide idea was particularly useful. But who knows?"

"Was there any sign of foul play?" Judith inquired.

Charlie's head bobbed as he thought. "Can one person can run a steam train on their own? There's always two of them on TV. One pumping the coal and the other peeping the whistle."

"An important job to be sure."

"But maybe you can? I mean, Herbert got it three miles

out of the station and brought it to a halt before popping his head into a thousand-degree furnace." Charlie looked thoughtfully towards the ceiling and then picked up his coffee to take another long slurp. His hand was still shaking, but detached from the saucer. At least it was a relatively silent act. "I reckon there must've been somebody else, maybe, but I can't think who. Herbert had no enemies. He never said a bad thing about anyone; he was a good 'un."

Maggie nodded in agreement. She'd been a resident at Little Pickton far longer than Judith and had a deeper understanding of the community. Her judgment on people was generally quite solid, at least solid enough for Judith to respect her opinion.

"I'd say he's a pillar of the community," said Maggie in agreement. "The poor man, he did good. They even gave the kiddies free rides on the train during the holidays. He loved that line. It meant the world to him. I've met the others at that Society. They're a little bit of a cult."

"You said *cult*?" Judith clarified.

"You know the type. When you get all these engineers in one place and they start talking about sprockets and pistons and stuff like that," she ended vaguely, betraying a true lack of understanding about mechanics.

"You mean that they all get together and start nerding out?"

"Exactly! Herbert was nice. I mean, he was boring, but he was nice."

Judith glanced at Charlie, who was nodding in agreement.

"Aye, as boring as sin," he acknowledged. "The whole lot of them."

Judith sucked her teeth, thinking, "Well, it seems even the most boring people are worthy subjects for a killer."

"I still think it's suicide."

Judith gave a small hum, indicating that she wasn't at all in agreement. Instead, she sipped her tea and murmured politely, "I'm sure you're right."

Of course, Judith Spears didn't believe that; she was a naturally suspicious person. A person who had every right to be suspicious, especially because of her own conduct throughout her life, wasn't exactly, oh, what's the polite way of saying it? Above board? Legal? All the above.

Still, Judith made a point of never setting out to judge the bad in people. On the contrary, she always tried to see the good, and along the way, she tried to have a good time. And while she bore no ill will to the poor old victim and any family, if indeed he did have a family, she couldn't deny that a murder made the chilly days a little bit more interesting than they ought to have been.

They lapsed into companionable silence. Charlie studied the infinite brownness of his half-drunk coffee, as he pondered the meaning of life and attempted to digest just what he'd seen.

The tearoom was relatively empty, considering it was one of the main social environments for the townsfolk to congregate during the day. The owner, Timothy, had kept it traditional and insisted on the food being homemade, which kept people coming. No day ever had quite the same menu. It depended on which cookery book he'd opened, or what TikTok page he'd stumbled over the night before. Some of his items occasionally strayed to the edge of *experimental*. Such as the banana and tomato tart Judith had impulsively ordered, but decided not to risk sampling.

She weighed up venturing out to the crime scene and blustering her way to have a gander at what had happened, although she doubted the police would give her access to the scene. Good old DS Collins would probably chase her away with a pitchfork, warning her to keep her nose out of it. After their last venture together, Collins had been a little cold since he'd put together a small file on Judith's background. A file they'd all decided would be best lost.

Her phone beeped. It was a text from DS Collins' number two, the lovely DC Sarah Eastly:

WE HAVE A MURDER!

It was followed by a winky face.

Judith looked up to see if Charlie had noticed the message. He hadn't. She sipped her tea again and gave a smug smile. Murder. Not a suicide. Well, for a Monday, it would not be as dull a week as she feared. Perhaps she should have a little saunter through the woods after all? She could dispense her indisputable knowledge about steam trains. She was already looking up facts on Wikipedia as she finished the last dregs from the pot of tea, said her goodbyes to Maggie and Charlie, and hurried towards her red Renault Clio.

The parking area was down a quiet country road, a few minutes' drive from the heart of the village. The train itself was a good ten minutes' walk through the forest, but Judith would not get close. The car park was filled with marked police vehicles. Judith pulled up on the road and approached the uniformed copper standing behind a sturdy piece of blue police tape. The sour-faced bobby folded his arms as she got closer.

"Constable Barry. How delightful to see you."

PC Barry's nose scrunched. "It's not such a surprise to see you turn up. Like a genie in the bottle. Or a persistently late Grim Reaper."

Judith angled her blue beret jauntily on her head. "I'm here to make all your wishes come true."

"Only if you bugger off. You're not getting in."

"Are you sure?"

"Two hundred per cent."

"Ah, I see. A crime against numeracy. How dreadful. Grammar will be the next victim."

"We don't want the likes of you here. Gossiping about murder and all that."

"Thank you for confirming it was a murder." She took delight in seeing Barry's eyes narrow.

"Well, that's what the boys are saying. There's a body and all, and the DS seems a bit stretched. He's been waiting on the forensic people who still haven't turned up." He checked himself, suddenly aware he was giving too much away. "And he happened to mention you by name. Specifically, like. He thought you might turn up, and he told us not to allow you anywhere near the crime scene whatsoever."

Judith nodded solemnly. "A very sensible precaution. And you're doing an admirable job." She flicked the police tape. "Nobody's going to get past that, are they? And you'll have to stay vigilant. I'm sure the Rail Society will be descending here like..." she struggled for an analogy. "Hedgehogs on milk."

"You shouldn't give them milk."

"Why ever not?"

"It's bad for them. Causes them to explode. PC Barry looked puzzled. "Or is that pigeons? You're supposed to feed 'em dog food."

"Well, you learn something new every day. Even if it is completely useless information."

They lapsed into silence. The cold air was getting to Judith's throat. She coughed to clear it.

"Well, if we both stand out here, we'll catch our death. And it sounds as if somebody's already beaten us to it." When PC Barry failed to crack a smile, she gave a little wave and returned to her car. "I'll be off then!"

Perhaps the rest of the day would not be as interesting as she had assumed it would be. She thought about calling Sarah Eastly to squeeze out some more information, but decided she'd gossip as soon as she could. For now, she had nothing to do but return home and maybe catch the latest quiz show before the news. Mid-fifties really wasn't an ideal time to retire if you wanted stimulation of any kind.

By the time she pulled up to her quaint country cottage, passing the blank sign on the gate, that declared it to be called *'Unnamed'*, spelled out without the use of any actual letters, a fine dusty sprinkle of snow began to fall. The bite in the air assured Judith that a *blackberry winter* was well and truly on its way. After the recent floods which brought glum misery, Judith had to admit there were few places she'd been that were more beautiful than Little Pickton draped in a veneer of snow.

She unlocked her cottage door and entered. Stomping her boots before hopping to pull them off. She then cranked up the digital thermostat and heard the boiler fire up in the kitchen. It was only a little after five and she'd already planned to fold into some warm pyjamas if she was going to spend the rest of the evening alone. However, such plans were quickly culled when she noticed a plain envelope resting on the coir floor mat. She picked it up. There were no markings, no address. She opened the flap, which had been tucked in as a hasty seal, and extracted a handwritten note. It simply read:

8.30 pm, CAR PARK - LION'S ARMS. I NEED TO SPEAK.

The script was florid, round, and distinctly female. The cursive letters were perfectly formed, which indicated a middle-aged lady from the village. Of course, that was just mild deduction to amuse herself. The mysterious author obviously hadn't noticed the motion-sensitive doorbell camera on her front door, so Judith had a high-resolution image of the woman who requested her help.

She tossed the letter onto a table next to the door and placed her keys on top. Her pyjama evening would have to wait. With luck, the invite would come with a complimentary drink.

Chapter Three

It was 20:45, and the sprinkling of snow had developed into a steady flurry of white flakes that cheered up the otherwise gloomy and dark pub beer garden.

What an awful place to meet, outside in the cold, thought Judith as she shivered, despite the thick, dark green puffer jacket, fur-lined boots, and a pair of blue woollen gloves. The idea of a complimentary drink quickly lost its appeal as everything the pub served would range from ice-cold to room temperature, and probably add to the inevitable hypothermia she was about to suffer.

She decided to give the mysterious letter writer five more minutes before she headed home. The last thing she wanted was to be stranded at the Lion's Arms overnight. The pub was two miles out of town, standing on its own at a crossroads. She peered through the windows at the locals huddled inside. She was pretty sure the topic of conversation would follow the inevitable speculation over Herbert's death. Judith was more interested in facts.

In the darkness, footsteps crunched the virgin layer of

snow across the frigid lawn beneath, drawing her attention to the car park. She hadn't seen a vehicle entering, but a figure was walking quickly towards her. It was a woman, in her forties, wearing a jazzy Christmas-themed bobble hat and a fleecy jacket that was far too thin for the cold weather. Her black trousers and comfortable-looking grey Sketchers were also not quite suitable attire for the weather. A red and green striped scarf covered her lower jaw, forcing her heated breath to mist her spectacles, which quickly cleared with each step. She recognised the woman from her doorbell camera.

"Mrs Spears!" she exclaimed.

"Ms," corrected Judith automatically. "Sorry, call me Judith."

"Ah, Judith. Thank you for meeting me," said the woman, glancing nervously around.

"Well, it sounded all rather melodramatic,' said Judith. "And cold,' she added pointedly. "Perhaps inside would have been a more fitting place. Close to the fire and with a cheery drink," she added hopefully.

The woman shook her head. "No, sorry, it's too public. I need to talk to you somewhere quiet."

Judith couldn't keep out a note of surprise. "Well, suggesting we meet in a pub was a rather unusual strategy for that."

The woman indicated the cars. "Ah, perhaps we should sit in my car? I've had the heating running. It's rather warmer."

Judith eyed her cautiously. "I must confess I'm not averse to climbing into strangers' cars." She flashed a tight smile. "You know, *stranger danger*, everything we tell the kiddies also applies to middle-aged stalwarts like me."

The woman gave a nervous laugh and shook her head,

loosening light flakes of snow clinging to her woollen hat like dandruff.

"Oh, I'm so sorry, of course, I'm Augusta, Augusta Calman. I need to talk to you about what happened today. I'm sure you've heard about Herbert Holland."

Her eyes strayed to the pub door as it creaked open, and two figures emerged, lighting up cigarettes and shivering from the cold.

"Why do you want to talk to me? I didn't know him."

"I need help." There was a pleading edge to her voice that was difficult to fake, unless she was a rather talented actress. "Before things get worse, I really need somebody who's proficient with certain... skills."

Despite herself, Judith was intrigued and indicated the car park. "I'm not sure how it can get any worse than death, but lead the way."

Augusta didn't say another word as she smartly turned around and led Judith to the far side of the car park, where her bright yellow Fiat 500 was parked. Again, for a clandestine meeting in a public pub, the choice of vehicle was hardly well thought out. Judith wasn't complaining, though. Inside, it was toasty warm. Judith assumed Augusta had been here the whole time. Why she had waited half an hour for Judith to freeze was anyone's guess. Maybe she was summoning up the courage to talk about whatever confession she was about to make.

"Okey-dokey, Augusta." Judith folded her hands in her lap. "I have absolutely no idea why you think I can help, but I'm always willing to listen."

"You have something of a reputation." Augusta began timidly. She glanced up. "I mean, a *decent* reputation, don't get me wrong. You're a woman who knows how to get things done. You know how to listen to people. To understand what makes them tick."

Judith gave a polite nod. After the bumbling compliment, she thought it would be rude to interrupt with a pithy comment about what a wonderful listener she was.

Augusta continued. "I'm part of LPRS, the Rail Society. I knew Herbert. We were among the core group that set everything in motion. Although, it was his dream, really. He had a vision of what the railway could become. He'd had a passion for trains since he was a little boy. It was a dream come true. You could see that in him every day." She sniffed. It was too dark to tell if she was sniffing from cold or emotion. After a brief pause, Augusta continued. "He's been murdered. I know that much. The police came around asking questions. We've all been advised to get solicitors. I'm frightened."

This time the silence stretched longer than felt comfortable. A fine sheen of snow had already turned the windscreen opaque. Judith prompted her.

"Frightened about what, exactly? That the killer may come for you?"

Augusta sighed. "About how bad this is all going to look. You see, I think I know why Herbert was murdered." Judith raised a quizzical eyebrow. It was a pointless action in the darkness, although Augusta appeared to get the hint. "Everyone liked him. He was always trying to do good, but that didn't mean he had no enemies."

Judith nodded thoughtfully. "Do you know who killed him?"

Augusta quickly shook her head. "Oh, I mean, it could be one of many people, I suppose, but whoever did it had an awful lot of motivation."

Judith frowned. "What sort of motivation?" The words were out of her mouth, but she already knew the answer. There were only a handful of those things people kill for: love, jealousy, money, hatred – and their complete opposites.

Augusta licked her lips nervously. "About two-hundred-thousand pounds worth of motivation." This time, when she met Judith's gaze, she didn't flinch. "That's what's been stolen from the Society's fund."

"Stolen?" Judith said in surprise. "Have you reported the theft to the police?"

"No. Herbert and Lloyd were worried what would happen when the news got out. They were more concerned about some land documents. I never got involved with the practical running of things."

"Lloyd?"

"Lloyd Groves. The other co-founder. He and Herbert were the only ones with access to the bank account. Other than me."

Judith was familiar with lengths people would go to for money. In the past, she had gone to unusual lengths herself. Although, in her case, violence was never an option, or at least never the preferred option.

"You're saying that somebody has stolen a lot of money. Herbert didn't want to go to the police, and other than the owners, you were the one with the bank access. And the police will know all this tomorrow?"

Augusta gave a jerky nod of acknowledgment. "Our computer was infected by a virus. I was the one who clicked on it. And when I did, the money vanished. What do you think the police will make of that?"

"Well, I suppose they're going to think that you stole the

money and killed Herbert Holland. But of course, I'm sure that you have a terrifically solid alibi."

The deep silence from Augusta answered that question.

Judith looked thoughtfully through the side window as the snow began to obscure that, too.

"I suppose the one thing I must ask is, did you do it?"

This time, the noise from Augusta was a heartfelt sob. "No! Of course I didn't. I could never, ever, ever. The Society was too special. And why would I?" She inhaled a watery snort through her nose. "I'm the obvious suspect! I don't know what to do!"

Judith regarded Augusta with curiosity. The woman was either a splendid actress or in great despair. The challenge lay in distinguishing which.

"Why should I involve myself in this?" Judith pondered thoughtfully.

Augusta avoided making eye contact. "As I said, you have a reputation, and I am quite desperate, Mrs Spears."

"Ms," Judith interjected automatically.

"I don't have any money to pay you. As daft as this sounds, I can only appeal to your good nature. And it's something of a mystery that might tickle your interest."

She finally met Judith's eyes with a pleading smile. Judith groaned inwardly. Augusta knew her weak spot. A damsel in distress, and Judith on the edge of boredom. That was certainly a combination that made her sympathetic.

Judith nodded thoughtfully. "Well, I'm not entirely sure what help I can offer, but I may poke my nose around." She heard a sob from Augusta, uncertain whether it was one of relief or angst. Automatically, she reached across and gave Augusta's mitten a comforting squeeze. "I believe DS Collins is leading the investigation. He's a fine man. He won't be bamboozled by red herrings or false leads. I think you should just tell them the facts. Miss nothing out. If you've done nothing wrong, then that's the Detective Sergeant you need on your side."

"I understand, but it's a relief to know you'll give it some thought. I'm terribly frightened."

"I'm sure you are," said Judith. "Things like this leave a ghastly taste in the mouth."

Inwardly, Judith was delighted to have something that would stave off the boredom, even if it sounded like a straightforward case of theft gone wrong. It shouldn't be too difficult to conclude.

Chapter Four

DS Raymond Collins was delighted by the unexpected delay. For once, he'd found joy in the understaffing of the police forensic team. The lean crew they had sent granted him more time to admire the gleaming olive-green tank engine. It was a childhood fascination manifested in a full-sized; a repurposed steam train that he had to interact with as part of his job. The dream-like experience, however, was marred by the dead body. But it was *almost* perfect.

Fortunately, the deceased had been removed, but due to the vast crime scene, forensics had to meticulously search the track and surrounding forest inch-by-inch for any microscopic piece of evidence, and that took an enormous amount of time. Collins sat on the engine's steps, with his feet dangling over the edge as he reminisced his boyhood ambitions. Train driver had been one of them. Along with astronaut and explorer. Thinking back, he had never once pined to be a police detective and now, in his early fifties, he was a Detective Sergeant. How had that happened? He cracked the stubble on his chin which, like the rest of his hair, had eased its dark brown sheen, and was now being invaded by a platoon of light grey follicles marching to the passage of time.

Fifty yards up the line, white-coated forensic officers meticulously combed the area, inspecting every lump and stone for potential clues. Their one-piece uniforms almost blended with the frosty morning. The chilly air caught the breath, but Collins didn't mind, wrapped as he was in a thick dark-green fleece jacket, as he pondered the unfolding mystery.

DC Eastly greeted him perkily. "Morning, Sarge." She handed him a plastic thermos cup of coffee she'd remembered to bring from home.

"Morning, Eastly. Fine day, isn't it?"

Eastly shivered, tightening her scarf. "Not for the victim, sir. How much longer do you think they'll be?" she inquired, nodding towards the forensic team.

"Another couple of hours, I suspect." Collins' joy was evident.

"I've already arranged with the Rail Society to set up preliminary interviews. We really should both be there." She wasn't sure if he'd heard, as he gazed dreamily into the middle distance. Eastly gave a sharp cough to catch his attention. "Network Rail has been inquiring about the engine's removal, too. They're very insistent."

DS Collins gave a quick snort of disapproval. The stretch of line was rarely used, other than by occasional freight, so he couldn't see what the fuss was about. He'd always liked the line as it snaked through the county. Despite regarding himself as a modern urban man, a small, repressed part of him thought it added to the area's charm.

"Heck of a mess," remarked Eastly, her gaze drawn to the

engine's furnace. Gruesome crime scenes didn't usually faze her, at least the ones she had seen on television and in training videos, but this one was the work of a particularly callous mind. Her eyes drifted over the engine, frost glinting from it. Trains had never intrigued her; her childhood exposure limited to a few episodes of *Thomas the Tank Engine*. As a teenager, motorbikes had caught her interest, and she'd managed to convince her mother to allow her to try Motocross. That endeavour had lasted a couple of months before she'd fallen off and broke her arm, bringing about an immediate ban from her parents. Now, as an adult, she often mused that it could be a fun interest to rekindle, especially if it helped find the mythical *right bloke*.

She'd grown tired of the tedious online dating scene and felt stuck in a loop of disappointment. She pondered if her high standards were the cause, although she couldn't help acknowledging the fact that living in Fulton, which boasted a single cinema and a new Nando's she refused to visit alone, hardly matched the exotic culture-capital where she envisioned her dream man lurked. And if she was being honest with herself, her standards were not really that high. Take Keith Lumley for example. The bar had been practically non-existent when it came to that dating travesty.

"Throwing the body into the furnace took a lot of strength," Collins said sagely. "And headfirst, too. He would have put up a lot of resistance, I mean, hands against the boiler, for a start. Resisting getting his head into the fire. Legs kicking out. I imagine it would be frightfully loud."

"We're in the middle of nowhere. Who'd hear?"

"Ramblers? Dog-walkers? We should put out an appeal."

"In our line of work, dog walkers are the fifth emergency service."

"The vic may have been drugged, or unconscious, or even killed before he went in."

"*Vic?* You've been watching too much telly, Eastly." He sipped his coffee thoughtfully. "Or there was more than one attacker."

"Assuming he was the driver - and so far, we've had trouble finding anyone in the county who can move one of these things - indicates he must have been killed just after the train came to a stop here."

"An argument perhaps?" said DS Collins.

"One so acrimonious that it caused him to stop the train in its tracks. Literally in this case. Then he got whacked, and the killer tried to get rid of the body in the furnace," Sarah concluded.

"Well, it's a definite line of inquiry. One I think you should certainly pursue during the interviews."

"Me pursue," said Sarah. "That's *your* role, surely."

On one hand, she knew her boss was trying to pass the buck, as he'd made it no secret that he'd rather be out playing with a train than taking statements. But on the other, Eastly felt a thrill of responsibility. As a lowly detective constable, it was her duty to do the grunt work, and it was a long road for promotion. Even though she and Collins had a respectable track record in the short time they'd been together, a little extra responsibility would always look good on her CV when the time came to move on to a force with fewer cows and local busybodies, and far more hunky young men.

"You'd like me to do the interviews while you supervise the crime scene?"

A broad smile cracked DS Raymond Collins' face. "Well detected, detective. That would be marvellous."

. . .

Detective Constable Eastly experienced a tremor of power when she commandeered Little Pickton's small village hall. The wattle and daub clad building stood between the church and the library and offered just enough space, tables, and plastic bucket chairs for the occasional bingo soiree or police murder investigation. A single uniformed officer called Kevin, whose acne-pocked cheek warned Sarah that he was probably too young for her, helped set up half a dozen chairs in an arc around a table with a wobbly leg. She secured a cup of tea from the common room and sat as the Rail Society entered.

Guiding them was a tall, slender man with round spectacles and a mop of grey hair that looked as if he'd just rolled out of bed, but it was meticulously styled. His thin face was moulded by fetching laughter lines. Eastly wouldn't be surprised if he'd modelled himself on Hugh Grant. Through a prior brief tour of the Railway Society's website, Eastly identified him as Lloyd Groves, the Society's charismatic co-chairman of the Society. His eyes were fixed to the floor, and he retained the visage of a haunted soul, or somebody who'd eaten one hot chilli too many.

He steered the group like a shepherd. Following him was Dawn Sanders. Unlike the concerned Lloyd Groves, she smiled and pleasantly tilted her head at Eastly. She was a small plump woman in her late thirties, with bobbed black hair. She wore dungarees over a red, long-sleeved top on which cartoonish pictures of cats peeked over the denim, and she clomped across the floor in bright, shiny Doc Marten boots. She was engaged in a hushed conversation with another man approximately the same age. He had a broad, stubbly face and his eyes were red from lack of sleep. His short, ruffled hair hadn't seen a comb for weeks and visibly dirty fingernails hinted at a rugged appearance. The name came moments later to Eastly: Derek Rivan. His eyes were fixed on the ground, only once glancing at the chairs but deliberately avoiding DC Sarah Eastly.

Augusta followed next, and Eastly couldn't help but notice the dark look she shot at the woman behind her as they jostled for a seat. Augusta made sure she sat next to Derek. The last woman, Barbara Dixon, had a fey appearance, with her eyes looming large behind black-rimmed round glasses. Her long brown curly hair was tied in a tight ponytail and was streaked with slivers of white. She had the type of face that was impossible to accurately age. Perhaps late thirties, but she behaved like a forty-something hippy. She conveyed an air of dignity and barely reacted to Augusta's silent provocation.

Last in line was a small Pakistani man of trim build, James Wani, who Eastly thought was impeccably dressed for an engineer. He wore blue jeans and a crisp white Ralph Lauren shirt. His black Oxford shoes had been polished to perfection, and Eastly noticed the heels were elevated. He calmly took in the room and was the only one who politely spoke directly to Eastly and the constable before taking his seat.

"Good evening," he said in a broad Scottish accent.

Eastly allowed the faint scraping of metal chair legs across the parquet floor to run its course before she stood up to address them. She smiled, thinking that a warm introduction would endear her to the group, but quickly she corrected herself upon realising that a cheery announcement about their murdered colleague might not be the best start. Just as she inhaled a breath to speak, the door creaked open, and Judith Spears entered. Although Sarah didn't recall Judith being part of the Rail Society, she wouldn't be surprised, considering the places Judith usually managed to infiltrate.

Judith flashed a pleasant grin at DC Eastly, then took a chair from the side and placed it next to the uniformed constable. He shot her a curious sideway glance but said nothing as she settled into her seat. Sarah suppressed another grin, inwardly recognising that the way Judith had positioned herself in front of the group implied that she was officially involved in the inquiry.

Sarah began. "Ladies and gentlemen, thank you for coming. I know you've all heard the news about Herbert Holland. It's my sad duty to confirm that he has been found dead."

"Was it murder?" Lloyd Groves interjected in a sharp, clipped tone.

Sarah hesitated and then nodded. "At this stage we suspect foul play, but this is an evolving investigation. Only those of us here are aware of it." She glanced at Judith in a silent warning. "So, we need to keep that confidential and remember not to talk to anybody else outside the room, especially not the press or family members."

The announcement prompted sighs of despair from the Rail Society members. James and Barbara both sobbed aloud, almost in coordination. Sarah caught Augusta glance at Judith with a look of recognition that Judith resolutely ignored.

James Wani sharply stood, knocking back the chair, which squeaked across the floor. "Who did it? Why was he murdered?"

"For God's sake, James," snarled Lloyd under his breath.

Sarah raised her arms to indicate he should sit. "All in good time, sir. The investigation has only just begun, and we're piecing things together. James Wani, isn't it?" He gave a startled grunt, clearly alarmed that she knew his name. He swiftly pulled his seat back in place and sat, folding his arms tightly across his chest. He cast a dark glance at the others.

"I know it's a difficult time and emotions are running high," Sarah said, marshalling her thoughts. "A statement will be taken from each of you separately. Tell me everything, no matter how irrelevant you think it may be, so we can start processing information together."

Lloyd Groves half-raised a hand for Sarah's attention, but started talking before she could prompt him. "Shouldn't we have a solicitor present for this?"

Sarah hesitated and gave a gentle shrug. "Of course, that's your prerogative, sir. If you feel uneasy and require the presence of legal counsel just to tell me you were down the pub last night, then by all means."

Glances were cast around the group, but they mostly avoided eye contact. Sarah forced her features into what she hoped was a reassuring expression.

"These are just cursory questions about where you were and your roles within the Society. I assure you, it's nothing uncomfortable. I'm here to try to offer reassurance that we're doing everything we can to investigate this terrible event. I also have many general technical questions, such as who in the group can pilot a train?"

Derek gave a mocking chuckle, then caught himself with embarrassment. "You don't pilot a train engine, love; you drive it. And it's a locomotive."

Sarah responded with a soft smile. "Exactly the reason I need experts like you. You see, Herbert was found on his own in the train." She refrained from disclosing graphic details about his condition. "Sorry, locomotive, which had stopped midway along the track. Am I correct in assuming that *driving* the train is a two-person operation?" A dip of the head from Derek confirmed that. Nobody else reacted, their stony faces gave nothing away. Was it shock? Ignorance? Or something else? "I assume you all know how to operate the locomotive?"

That received a sharp laugh from Dawn. "Not me."

"Really? What is your role within the Society?"

Dawn's voice rose with enthusiasm that reminded Sarah of the annoying know-it-all girl in school who kept answering every question to get the teacher's approval. "I am *integral* in fundraising and organising activities."

The room lapsed into silence. With nothing more forthcoming, DC Eastly directed them to a door in the corner of the hall.

"Feel free to ask me anything that is on your mind while I take you aside." She gestured towards the door in the corner of the hall. "We can have a private conversation in my office."

Derek smirked. "You mean the caretaker's office?"

"Which, for now, I have requisitioned for interview purposes," Eastly said tartly. "Don't worry. It won't be anything too taxing. You can be first." She was pleased to see Derek's smile vanish. "The rest of you stay here." She indicated to the uniformed constable. "If you require anything, please ask this young officer here. He'd be happy to help."

It took twenty-five minutes to process everybody. Primarily she collected their personal details and matching their faces to the staff printout she had taken from their website. Nobody was in a chatty mood as they recounted their movements over the last twenty-four hours. The details came with minimum syllable answers. The detective was careful not to spook anyone, so tactfully posed an innocent question about how well they knew the deceased. The responses echoed a similar sentiment:

Lovely chap. A respected co-founder, along with Lloyd Groves. He'll be sorely missed. I can't believe he's gone. Who would do such a thing?

It was all standard fare that left her wondering how much they had spoken together before coming to the hall. The Society members finally trundled out of the building, leaving Eastly free to talk to Judith. She was about to, when she noticed the PC was lingering like a keen hound.

"Anything else I can do for you, Detective?" he asked eagerly.

Eastly hesitated, quite taken by his smile, before she snapped herself back to the moment.

"How about putting the chairs and table back where we found them?"

The constable set about it with far too much enthusiasm for such a mundane task. He even gave a jaunty whistle and sneaked the odd glance in Sarah's direction.

"I hope you didn't mind me sitting in," said Judith with uncharacteristic humbleness.

"Mmm?"

"I hope you didn't mind me sitting in with Mr Buns of Steel," she repeated, snapping Eastly's gaze from the copper's backside.

"Not at all. I wasn't aware that you were a member of the Rail Society."

"A very recent member," said Judith. "For about two hours now, I suppose. I don't even have my membership card or free Matchbox train. What exactly happened to Herbert?"

DC Eastly gave an involuntary shudder. "It was horrid. He was shoved headfirst into his own engine furnace. While it was still on full blast."

Judith tried not to imagine how that would look. "That's quite a violent act."

"For that lot," agreed Eastly, nodding towards the car park outside.

Judith was thoughtful. "I suppose individually it would be quite a struggle. I imagine it would take a fair bit of muscle." She caught Eastly's quick glance at PC Kevin as his muscular arms flexed as he lifted a stack of chairs. "So, what do you think of them?"

"Nice." Eastly's dreamy tone snapped when she realised Judith was indicating towards the car park. She pulled a face. "I'm not sure. There was a tension in the room. Not the mass outpouring of grief I was expecting. I expect you know them."

Judith shook her head. "You know me, I like to keep myself to myself. I've seen most of them around the village. One tends to see the same faces on a weekly basis. And of course, Herbert and Lloyd are, were, pretty much the face of the Society. Even if Herbert shied away from publicity."

Sarah double-checked she had her phone and notes and started to walk towards the door, with Judith keeping alongside. "How did the behave while I was in the interviews?"

"Surprisingly quiet," said Judith. "They said little to one another. Odd for such a close-knit group. It felt as if anything that needed to be said, had been said elsewhere. Lloyd Groves looked in shock."

"Oh, I thought he was being arrogant."

"For most men, being in shock comes across as arrogance. Like when they realize they're wrong. Which they never admit, of course."

Sarah held the hall door open for Judith to pass through, and they stepped out into the freezing night air. The last of the group was pulling out of the car park in a battered white Volkswagen Beetle, but it was too dark inside to make out who. The others had already made a swift departure.

Sarah gave a thoughtful hum. "Not so eager to loiter around, either."

"We agree there are tensions within the group," Judith mused. "Whether that's current circumstances or ongoing feuds, who knows? Have you had a chance yet to get under the skin of the Society itself?"

Sarah shook her head. "The crime scene has taken up all our time."

"I'm sure DS Collins is having a whale of a time playing around with the train." She caught Sarah's look. "His absence is noted. Boys and their toys. I bet he hasn't even taken the time to visit the deceased's house, has he?" Sarah hesitated and shook her head. Judith gave a shrug. "I mean, that's the first place I would have gone. But then again, I've never really had a real train to play around with. I suspect it could be terrific fun."

Sarah's eyes narrowed. "That would be the next logical step, wouldn't it?"

"Of course it would. Such a shame that the lovely Detective Sergeant isn't available to show us lowly mortals how it's done."

Suitably rankled by the comment, Sarah gave an indignant snort that expelled a plume of vapour from her nose like an angry cartoon bull.

"Well, he isn't here, is he?" she said firmly. "And somebody has to do it."

Chapter Five

Herbert Holland's residence was a smart semi-detached house tucked in the south-eastern corner of Little Pickton. Here, archways of old oaks embraced a wide avenue of Edwardian houses. DC Sarah Eastly and Judith Spears arrived only to discover that Herbert lived alone, so there was nobody to allow them into the property. Normally, access would require a long, tedious wait for a locksmith to arrive and open the door.

Fortunately, the regular plod had encountered the same problem earlier that day when they'd come to inform any next of kin about his death. They had already gained admittance to the premises and found a spare key. Luckily, somebody had the presence of mind to ensure it remained in police custody and it soon fell into Eastly's hand.

Inside, the hallway and front room were neat and tidy, decorated with a lively red wallpaper that Judith would never entertain in her conservative bungalow, but somehow it worked here and didn't transform the house into a funky bordello. The small living room had a large television bolted on the wall, an Ikea sofa that was so firm it made the eyes water, and a coffee table crammed with magazines: mostly rail-oriented ones, yesterday's copy of The Sunday Times, which made Judith remark on how surprised she was that people still bought newspapers, and a Top Gear magazine. Likewise, the kitchen was spotless. Herbert Holland evidently valued personal hygiene. It possessed the unmistakable air of a bachelor pad.

Eastly tapped a picture attached to the refrigerator door by a Ffestiniog Railway magnet. Herbert Holland and two other men grinning in front of a ski lift station at *Baqueira-Beret*, smiling as they enjoyed a moment in life.

Judith felt a twinge of sadness about what the man had been forced to leave behind. The Rail Society had been the focus of his passion, turning what would be anybody else's hobby into a full-time job.

"Apparently, Lloyd Groves made a lot of money working in the city, a stockbroker or something like it. His family used to be well-to-do landed gentry types, but they lost most of it over the years. However, he made some serious money and moved out here to start a new life away from things. That's when he met Herbert, and the Society was forged. It's also because of the Society that he got divorced. Apparently, he is a workaholic."

Judith nodded sagely. She could identify with that. Her own dodgy past had taken her all around the world. Including from London to Scotland and eventually out here in the middle of nowhere. Little Pickton was a place where people settled when they stopped paying attention to the rest of the world. Or wanted the world to forget them.

DC Eastly pushed open the glass doors that led into the dining room. Whereas the rest of the house was immaculate, this room had been turned into a massive model train set. A hand-built plasterboard table filled most of the room with only a narrow gap around the edges for access. On top of it, Holland had built a highly detailed miniature Hornby-sized diorama.

"Wow!" Judith said, appreciating the craftsmanship of the small-scale model that included a detailed village station with several plastic people and a dog, a level crossing with working barriers, a viaduct with real water, an intricate interchange junction, and half a dozen trains and assorted carriages.

Sarah gave a snort. "Ah, he was a nerd, too." Her history of failed boyfriend projects was coloured by men who refused to grow up and still collected models, toys and God forbid, Lego. Even educated people in their thirties and forties. She suspected there was something in the water that prevented such men from maturing, but whatever it was, it annoyed the hell out of her.

Judith bent down, bringing her eyeline level to the miniature landscape. She closed one eye and imagined herself as a film camera drifting over a set. Even so close, the attention to detail was quite exquisite, and she couldn't help but be impressed.

Eastly wasn't so enthusiastic. "So, we're dealing with a Peter Pan who refused to grow up, built his own train set in the back room. Raised a ton of money so he can go out and buy his own full-sized version. Okay. Interesting. Who would ever want to kill such a harmless geek?"

Judith led the way upstairs to see what else would shed light on the tragically short life of Herbert Holland. His bedroom was perfectly kept. Even the bed had been made, which baffled Judith. Who wakes up in the morning and their first thought was to waste time tidying the sheets? Surely one's day held more promise than merely the lure to go back to bed. To her, that behaviour was reminiscent of an obsessive-compulsive. There was a compact bathroom, a small spare room, which had been converted into an office filled with paperwork, box folders, opened mail, a computer that was off, and shelves groaning with literature about railways from all around the world. A pair of printed invoices from a web-hosting company called *Go* Daddy, were pinned to the wall awaiting further attention that would never come. There was the obligatory train-themed calendar, with the sad sight of future dates filled in for appointments and dreams that would no longer be fulfilled. Judith tried to shake away the melancholy. Something about Herbert's death had touched her.

A pinboard held the scheduled maintenance for different parts of the locomotive, which included a mosaic of photographs depicting beaming team members taken from the early days of the line opening. Judith couldn't help but notice every member looked joyfully happy, as if they were living the best moment of their lives. A far cry from the pale faces she had met just an hour earlier.

Judith wasn't surprised to find a second bedroom had also been converted into a giant train diorama, although this one still had stretches of track stacked up, ready to be laid down so the service could be put into action.

"This was so useful," Sarah said sarcastically. "I can't imagine why Raymond didn't want to be here."

"There may be things of interest back here," said Judith, re-entering the office space, and mindful of the financial irregularities that Augusta had mentioned. She had said the Society was run from their official office on the edge of town, at the old Little Pickton Station they'd renovated. She scanned the box files and mountains of paperwork, knowing somebody would have to work their way through the evidence but she was loathed to do it herself and equally unhappy to rely on a police officer who might not have the nous to know what they're looking for. Not that Judith knew either, but she was certain that she'd know something was important when she stumbled across it. "Perhaps we should take a look in the Society's office?"

"That's out of bounds for now. Once SOCO has finished with the engine, that's where they're heading." Sarah caught Judith's quizzical glance. *"It means Scene of Crime Officers."*

Judith issued a sharp *tut*. "I know that. I suppose we just sit and wait then." Judith caught DC Eastly's odd look. "Is something wrong, dear?"

"It was your deft use of the word *'we'* in that sentence. I invited you along because of your unconventional mind, and I mean that in a much more complimentary way than when the Guv says it."

"Thank you."

"And the fact you turned up uninvited to the meeting made me feel a little coerced in bringing you along here."

"Never wise to coerce a police detective."

"Is there something you're not telling me?"

"Of course," Judith said brightly. Her eyebrows provocatively rose with each hesitant motion of Eastly's lips, but the direct question never came. Some questions were best left unasked because the resulting headache wasn't worth the pain.

"Right," Eastly said, somewhat deflated as she glanced at her phone. "That's that then. Oh, forensics has finished up at the train, and they're moving it tomorrow morning. It looks as if we may have some answers when they tackle this then."

"Good. Any help I can be..."

"I'll be sure to pass that on to the DS. Although I can save time by passing on his feedback now, which will be: *'stay away, oh, God, oh, God, please don't poke your nose in and let me play with my train on my own.'*"

"Duly noted," Judith said as she calculated what time she needed to wake up in order to reach the scene of the crime before it chuffed away.

The frosty pre-dawn air would have frozen Judith to the core if she hadn't dressed in so many layers that she could do a credible impression of the Michelin Man. Her chunky black wellies made driving a little difficult, but the double-layered socks kept her toes warm. Jeans and crinkly bubble jacket bulked her out, and she kept her beret in place, folding the cloth down over her ears.

She drove through PC Barry's whisper-thin police tape and parked her Clio behind a hedge in the empty forest car park and walked at a brisk pace to the steam engine. She knew police resources were stretched, but other than more half-hearted strands of blue police tape across the train's elevated doorway, there was no other protection. She supposed that was justification enough the police had finished with the crime scene and now it was up for grabs.

The engine was covered in a sheen of frost that caught the early golden light. She had spent the previous night on her laptop, researching the Society. They had purchased the tank engine when it was a rusting heap in North Wales. The Ivatt Class 2 engine, built by the London, Midland, and

Scottish Railway in 1947 had been a regular workhorse at the time. It had taken a generous National Lottery grant to restore it, with almost every part replaced. A task made more difficult because nobody made them anymore. Derek Rivan had overseen the larger structural restoration of the carriage, while James Wani had sought craftsmen for the finer details and precision parts for the engine.

Judith clambered up the ladder into the cab. It was exactly how she imagined, with pipes and levers bolted to the boilerplate and three large dials bolted to the wall. An enterprising spider had already woven a web amongst some of the levers and gauges. The gate to the furnace was open, and the body had been thankfully removed. Behind her, the small hopper was filled with coal, which was accessed by a small hatch from the cab. Some of the coal had spilled out onto the floor. She experimentally toyed with a few levers. They were well greased and moved with ease. The floor space would struggle to give three people much room to manoeuvre, so she imagined a fight between two people would be a limited affair.

"It doesn't have an on/off button." DS Raymond Collins' voice made her jump. Judith had been so engrossed in her thoughts she hadn't heard the detective arrive, accompanied by a man wearing a thick donkey jacket and a scarf wrapped so tightly around his face that only his eyes and long grey beard were visible. He used a shovel as a walking stick. Collins led the way up to join her in the cab. "I would say I hadn't expected to see you here, except I'm not a terribly good liar. This is still an active police crime scene."

Judith feigned innocence. "Really? How was I to know?"

Collins indicated the police tape. "It says so right here."

"Actually, all that says is *police*, over and over again. And is the crime scene just this?" Judith gestured to the train. "Or the entire forest?"

It was too early for Collins to argue, especially with Judith. It was easier to accept her as a temporary addition to the team. Judith shuffled into the corner as the bearded engineer climbed onboard.

"This is Howard. He knows how to start up this beauty. I take it if I ask you to leave, you will start talking and not stop until I cave in."

"Indeed."

Collins puffed his cheeks, then turned to Howard. "She's all yours. The engine, I mean, not this busybody."

Howard spoke in a thick West Country accent as he used the shovel to gesture that Collins and Judith should stand back. "I need a bit o' room on the footplate. Gets a bit crowded." He kneeled to examine inside the furnace, using a torch to pierce the gloom. "Fire is clean."

"Everything was taken to the lab," said Collins.

Howard nodded. "That helps. Need a good clean fire to get underway. No clinkers in there." He tapped a pipe to check the tank's water levels and seemed satisfied. That done, Howard dug his shovel into the coal and carefully laid it in the furnace.

"Taking notes?" Collins muttered quietly to Judith.

They watched as Howard laid four wooden logs on the coal bed. He then placed a rag on the shovel, squirted it with a small container of paraffin, and tossed it into the furnace. Striking a large kitchen match on the boilerplate, he tossed it onto the pile. It caught immediately. He closed the door, firmly sealing the latch.

"Right then. That'll warm up nicely. I'm gonna check the

smoke box." Humming to himself, he clambered down the ladder and made his way to the front of the engine.

"Thrilling," said Judith, rubbing her thin woollen gloved hands for warmth.

"I'm excited. We'll be under way by the end of the day!"

Judith shot him a look. "The end of the day?"

"He's just the fireman. His job is to prepare the engine. It needs to warm up for this evening, when the driver comes." There was no disguising the delight in his voice as he reacted to Judith's crestfallen expression. "Yes, you could have had a lie-in, instead of skulking around at the crack of dawn. They can't just turn it on and go. This is an art."

"You're enjoying this, aren't you?"

DS Collins rubbed his hands together. "Very much, Judith. Very much indeed."

Chapter Six

If there was one thing Judith Spears prided herself on, it was her canniness in understanding people by getting under their skin, rationalising their behaviour, and deducing their motives - no matter how reprehensible they were. In Little Pickton village hall, she had silently observed how the members of the Railway Society behaved to one another. From the outside, they projected the image of a sad group of colleagues trying to cope with a dreadful murder. She was certain that is what DC Eastly saw.

However, Judith was watching an altogether different performance. A tension hung over the group, fuelled by passive-aggression, resentment, bitterness, and outright deceit. They were all emotions from people who knew one another well enough to supersede mere *colleague* status. Ex-friends? Lovers? It was apparent with every glance – or rather, the non-glances when people refused to make eye contact; the purse of a lip, the tension in one's neck, and even in the way they had entered the hall. Who sat next to whom, and how they exited, all spoke volumes. Non-verbal communication was, ironically, at the heart of everything we said. Or more accurately, everything we meant.

If she was able to help Augusta, then she needed to know more about the inner workings of the Society members. She could ask Augusta directly, but the narrative would be heavily biased, and if she didn't know who the guilty party was, it would also be unhelpful. Herbert had been close to Lloyd Groves as the two men had formed the Society, but from his arrogance, he would be a tough nut to crack.

She went for the soft targets first. That would be the most emotionally wonky of the group, Barbara Dixon. Observing DC Eastly's interview, Judith had been intrigued by Barbara Dixon's behaviour. She was a woman who was clearly out of her depth, and the death of Herbert Holland had deeply upset her. She'd sat through the entire interview process with her hands thrust tightly between her legs, which were clamped shut around them in a defensive posture that put Judith in mind of a squirrel trying to play dead. Up close, Barbara's curly, long, almost-silver hair didn't seem to age her; if anything it added an intriguingly youthful, fey-like aura around her. A feature somewhat enhanced by her round tortoise shell-rimmed spectacles.

Barbara wasn't difficult to track down in the village. From a half-description, the man in the post office immediately knew who Judith was talking about. The notion of customer discretion clearly hadn't yet reached Little Pickton as he told Judith of the battered packages Barbara regularly received from around the world. She resided in a cottage similar to Judith's, but on the southern side of the village. Judith wasn't a fan of gardening, preferring to watch it on television rather than practise it herself, but she took great pains to at least give an air of civility about her property. Barbara had veered in the opposite direction. Her garden was overgrown and feral, which drew attention to it. Even if that attention screamed *'keep out!'*

Driving to visit Barbara, Judith mulled over what excuse she could give for an impromptu interview. She was so engrossed in her thoughts that she almost didn't notice a woman heading in the opposite direction on an old Pashley bicycle with rusty blue paintwork and a brown basket mounted on the front. Only a quick glance at her profile as she passed by confirmed that it was Barbara.

Judith made a hasty U-turn at the next farmer's gate, which involved backing her Clio into the hedge. Branches scraped the rear window before she wangled the gear stick into first and quickly pursued the cyclist. She caught up with her as she pulled onto the High Street and saw the Pashley outside John Rooney's hardware store.

The shop sat mid-terrace and had broad bay windows that gave it an old-fashioned appearance, especially compared to the estate agent's next door. The dark green paint looked freshly applied, as it always did. A neat trick the owner had pulled off since day one. A white sign claimed it was *John Rooney & Sons*, although Judith knew John's sons despised the business and one was taking *media studies* in New York. Although small on the outside, the shop was deceptively larger on the inside, with narrow aisles of tools, DIY supplies, and odd bric-a-brac that simply didn't belong in any other store.

When first moving to Little Pickton, Judith had marvelled at how such an archaic place could survive in a modern world, but soon learnt where to buy an emergency ball of string, Sellotape, a battery-powered jar opener, or a cheese board for that last-minute Christmas present. *John*

Rooney & Sons store had it all. And if it didn't, John could get it.

She nodded at the storekeeper, sat as usual behind the counter reading a battered erotic fiction novel loaned from the library.

"Afternoon," she said quietly. John's eyes never left the page, but his eyebrows wiggled in greeting.

Judith flitted between the aisles until she spotted Barbara with a basket filled with half a dozen candles, a ball of waxy twine, and a large box of matches. She was browsing the shelves for objects unknown. A sixth sense made her sharply turn and look directly at Judith who thought she had been silent.

"Hello, Barbara," peeped Judith. "Fancy bumping into you here."

Barbara didn't smile. She simply nodded. "Yes, quite a coincidence. Judith Spears, isn't it?"

"Yes. Barbara *Dixon*, isn't it?"

Barbara sniffed and turned back to the shelf, focusing her attention on a set of door bolts. As she reached to inspect them, Judith noticed several faded red scars on her wrists and hoped she didn't practise self-harm.

"Still helping the police with their enquiries?" Barbara said nonchalantly.

"Not that they need help," said Judith. "From what I hear, it's a pretty open and shut case." She saw Barbara's shoulders tighten imperceptibly. "I'm just along for the ride. Maybe I'll write a book about it one day." She let the silence stretch as she prodded a box of several different sized bath plugs. "Didn't sink drains all used to be the same size? What's the world coming to?" When Barbara didn't react, she continued. "I wonder what Herbert's death spells for the Rail Society."

"Publicity is Dawn's job." Barbara gave another sniff. "She'll make everything sound fine. That's her way. She can talk the hind legs off a...." She hesitated, unable to think of an animal with detachable back legs.

"Ah, Dawn." Judith slowly drew closer to Barbara, fearful of startling her like some wild animal. "Her and Derek..." She shook her head knowingly.

"What about them?"

"Well, you're a tightly knit group. These things happen when people are in close proximity," Judith said bluntly. "But that's their business." Barbara did a passable impression of somebody who didn't care. It was only the occasional micro-movement in the corners of her eyes that told Judith the words affected her. "What about you? Are you going to stay in the Society now that..." she let this sentence drift into the realm of speculation. Again, she saw Barbara's shoulders tighten.

"I'd love to walk away, but it's not that straightforward, is it? It's a charitable concern."

"Created to bring joy to people, to resurrect a fragment of the past, and create an icon for the future," Judith said brightly, remembering some of the buzzwords on the Society's website.

Barbara sank under the weight of her basket. She turned to Judith and used an index finger to slide her glasses back up the bridge of her nose.

"That's the spiel that drew us all in. A magical opportunity to get involved in something different. Very appealing to the sort of folks who are looking beyond the mundane. But dreams don't often turn out the way you wish, do they?"

Judith managed a warm smile. "Unfortunately, terrible things happen to us all. But I'm curious, what exactly was your role? Augusta did the books. James and Derek are engineers. Dawn does PR. And, no offence, you don't look like the most technical of people."

"No. That's Derek's realm. And woe-betide anybody who crosses that line." Judith saw a weak smile tug the corner of Barbara's mouth.

"Ah, Derek is a true techie geek. If you break it, he will come." That triggered a memory in Judith's mind. Derek was a local handyman. She'd recycled enough of his unsolicited flyers shoved through her letterbox over the years.

"I like organisation. Helping people see a wider world. I adore making things work on a social level."

"Social engineering."

Barbara gave a gentle nod. "If you like, yes. After all, the boys have their head in the clouds, playing with their giant train sets. When we started, nobody realised how serious the project would be. We were talking millions of pounds for a train, a building, restoring the line, publicity, licenses..." She gave an involuntary shiver, as though remembering a hard-earned lesson from the past. "It's a beast to run. Events need organising."

"From everything I have seen, you've done a wonderful job."

Barbara nodded. "Single-handedly."

"That must have caused friction. No wonder you want to leave."

Barbara raised the basket, forming a defensive shield. "I don't see what business that is of yours, or the police, or anybody's. My business is my business."

"Of course it is," said Judith gently. "I can see the trauma has affected you quite deeply." She hesitated before continuing. "And of course, as you say, it was a lot of money. When there's a lot of money, passions grow."

Barbara looked sharply away and stared at the shelf. "You said the police think it's an open and shut case?"

"Yes, it seems so."

Barbara lifted one of the candles from her basket and examined it with unwavering intensity. "Things all come out when the spotlight is cast on them."

"Inevitably." Judith could see Barbara would give nothing away just yet, but it was obvious there were many unspoken layers within the Society that needed airing. "The only problem," Judith said as she turned away, ready to leave, "is how people perceive facts. Because facts aren't real. They're fragments of time created by people's complex emotions. Every fact can have a different meaning, depending on how it's perceived."

She caught Barbara's frown and didn't blame her. She'd cribbed the sentence from half a dozen crime shows and mashed it together in a sentence that, on the surface sounded sophisticated, but she suspected it was complete bollocks. Nevertheless, she pressed on.

"And the important thing for all innocent parties is to make sure that their version of the facts is portrayed correctly. Anyway, my condolences on the loss of your friend. Hopefully, it will all be over quickly."

Judith felt a tad guilty as she left the hardware store with a spring in her step. Barbara was clearly a frightened woman hiding under many layers. Layers of what? Fear? Guilt? Oppression? That she didn't know. But the surge of joy came from her realisation that the Rail Society really had something worth getting her teeth into.

It had been an unsatisfactory first encounter with the one member of the group she thought would easily spill her guts. Her reticent mood hinted that there was somebody she was afraid of. But the encounter wasn't a loss. She had teased a few threads of information that could take time to unravel.

Judith glanced at her watch, a small gold Cartier that she had bought when she had oodles of money and was at a loss of what to spend it on. It was still a pretty little thing, but that's not why she kept it. The battery seemed to last for several years without losing a second, although the memories attached to the watch were something she'd rather forget. She still had time to kill before the locomotive would be fully heated and chuffing its way back to the depot.

And now she had a plan on how to idle away that time.

Chapter Seven

"This is not going to be an open and shut case," whined DS Raymond Collins, throwing his hand in the air, as he watched the forensic team comb through the Rail Society's office.

The office had once been Little Pickton's train station before the main line had been relocated in the early seventies to the town of Denzel Green some eleven miles away. Now the station represented the start of the steam train line, stretching to Denzel Green on rails that had needed the occasional repair. Beyond the next town, the rails and sleepers had become so decrepit they could no longer hold the weight of a train, which had prevented expansion of the service to the larger town of Fulton, eighteen miles away.

The station itself had been left to slowly decay before the Society had purchased it. The plan had been to restore it to its former glory, but they had soon run out of cash. Instead, the main office was patched up into something usable as the Society's head office. The cold and draughts were tolerated because of the large engine shed on the track behind. It was an ideal size to house the LMS Ivatt tank engine and their sixty-foot-long passenger carriage. It boasted a large coal bunker, and was crammed with every conceivable tool the engineers needed.

It hadn't taken long for a handful of uniformed police officers, and a couple of forensic technicians, to discover letters from creditors that showed the Society was so deeply in the red, that it was at risk of inventing an entire new shade.

Collins had received a summary report of the interviews from Eastly that hinted the Society was a breeding ground for salacious gossip. Most people outside the group who had given statements all held the same opinion that they were a bunch of elitist arseholes. The detective had hoped for a nice simple murder, a ride on a steam train, and a case he could quickly solve to earn some brownie points so that he could eventually move on to a police force with real opportunities for career advancement. Now that felt tenuous at best, now he was stuck with half a body and an ensemble of trainspotters.

"Even the coroner is complaining there's little he can do with half a body!" he complained to Eastly as they looked around the office.

"I suppose that was the murderer's intention. Destroy the evidence."

"Then why did they make such a ham-fisted attempt at it? He clearly wouldn't fit in the furnace. It's far too small."

"But it is enough to slow the investigation down. Dragging a dead body through the woods would have left an obvious trail of evidence." Eastly had been giving the matter a lot of thought. Burying the body in the woods would have been the obvious solution, or at least, it would have been if the murder was premeditated.

"Did you unearth anything useful with your interviews?"

"No one reacted to any subtle accusations. Nobody really talked about anybody else. It was like getting blood from a stone."

"Were they all in shock?"

Eastly chewed her tongue as she thought about that. "Maybe Barbara and James, but the others were, I don't know, nonplussed."

"You know that word has the complete opposite meaning in America?" Eastly frowned – sparking DS Collins to point at her brow. "And *frown* means something different, too!"

"What's that got to do with anything?"

Collins rubbed his eyes. "Absolutely nothing, other than it has been a long two days and I haven't slept very well."

The truth was Collins had been feeling anxious of late. His love life was non-existent. His career, while fine, lacked any ambition. He was starting to feel life wasn't delivering the opportunities it once had. Worse, he suspected that he was at the onset of a midlife crisis. While he got on well with Sarah Eastly, he felt admitting his weakness was something shouldn't share. That just added a few more ounces of loneliness on his shoulders.

Eastly continued without noticing his inner angst. "Their comments were generic. Nothing jumped out, and I felt that was overtly contradictory."

"Almost as if they'd rehearsed it?" Collins wagged his finger around the room as if conducting the investigation.

"I wouldn't say you're grasping at straws, sir. But... there are certainly... pieces of grass... floating in the air that you're... reaching for." Eastly sighed as her analogy ran out of steam. "I doubt they had talked. At least, not all together."

"Do you know Judith turned up at the train this morning?"

"Locomotive," Eastly said automatically. She had spent the evening reading trainspotting terminology and watching clips of railways around the country on YouTube, rather than having a normal evening at home like any other young woman does. Whatever *normal* was.

"She does that. It happened to me."

"I wish I had imagined it. But, no, she was there."

"She has a knack for sniffing out trouble."

"She was useful last time." Raymond's voice lowered as his gaze flicked between the officers searching the room. They both knew that without Judith they wouldn't have solved their last case, at least not so quickly. "But it doesn't look great for us if it seems we're reliant on her. It's not as if we're incompetent," he added after a moment, as if to convince himself.

"Of course not, sir. Just poorly staffed and massively under-resourced."

"Indeed..."

"And, as you pointed out, if things aren't so open and shut as we'd hoped, then what harm is there to have an extra pair of eyes scrutinising things? Especially with Judith's background."

"That's just it," said Raymond. "What *is* her background? Perhaps we shouldn't have decided that it wasn't an avenue worth exploring too deeply..." He trailed off, realising Judith was proving to be a distraction even when she wasn't present. He rapped his knuckles on the desk he was leaning against. "Right, we need to get on top of this case. Enough pleasantries. I want *formal* statements from each of the Society members and anybody who last saw Herbert

Holland alive. And we shouldn't have Judith involved in any of that. Understood?"

"Sir." Sarah Eastly said reluctantly. She pulled a notebook from her pocket and flicked through the last few pages of illegible notes. "I've already been asking around. So far, Herbert was last seen in the Lion's Arms at lunchtime, the day of his death."

The Lion's Arms was a couple of miles out of town. Not the most convenient place to stagger to, but it had once been an old inn and situated at a busy crossroads. That was before the bypass. It now survived through good food and a posh atmosphere that was lacking from Little Pickton's central drinking hole.

"How did you find that out?"

"James Wani said he wanted to talk to Herbert about the planned line extension. Herbert told him he couldn't make it because had something to do down the pub. I popped down there during my lunch break and spoke to the barmaid. She knew him as a semi-regular and remembers he was having half a bitter and a heated discussion with an unknown male. She didn't get a clear look at him, and there are no cameras to get an ID. I gave her a description of James, Derek and Lloyd, but they didn't match."

"What extension?"

"Dawn Sanders deals with publicity and fundraising. She told me their latest venture was to extend the line all the way to Fulton. That means repairing a lot of the rails, and that's not cheap."

DS Collins' eyes strayed across a long section of map pinned to the wall that showed the length of the track from Little Pickton to Denzel Green at the other end of the line. A dotted line meandered through the forest all the way to the urban sprawl of his hometown, Fulton.

"Lunchtime, eh? So, the engine must have been warming up if he took it out later that night."

"Yes, the previous day, it had been *off-shed*," Sarah said in a posh voice, pleased with the rail vernacular she'd picked up. "They'd run it up and down the track on Saturday, with passengers for Denzel Green."

"Who was driving?"

Eastly consulted her notes again. "Lloyd Groves and Derek Rivan. Other than Herbert, they were the only ones qualified to operate it."

"And the train wasn't scheduled to run Sunday?"

"Herbert wanted to perform some extra maintenance and nobody else wanted to work on Sunday. Evidently, he took it out at some point that night and was walloped, then found in the early hours of Monday morning."

Raymond sucked in a breath. With limited resources, it was difficult for him to do anything other than follow the most basic clues. Which was annoying, because it proved that there was some value in having Judith Spears around.

"We need to find out who he was speaking to in the pub and establish why he took the train out so late. That doesn't sound like the ideal time of day for a spot of maintenance."

"Locomotive, sir," Easily said, absently.

"I suggest we digest whatever information we get from here." He circled his finger around the room. "And then arrange those interviews over the next few days. Formal ones, this time. Make sure they bring their solicitors."

Chapter Eight

Judith spent her afternoon at home conducting a little sabotage. With little else to distract her when it came to real-world problems, she immersed herself in examining the background of the LPRS members. She was more than familiar with the amount of digital breadcrumbs people left, even those who didn't use the internet. The chances were if you'd scribbled something on a form, ticked an acceptance box, or even licked a stamp and signed up for some postal spam, your information was currently doing a tour-of-duty around the internet and available to those who were desperate to see it. Even a cursory glance revealed that Lloyd Groves had a previous career in the City for a notable finance company. Judith had spent some time in that environment and knew the type of people who flourished there. Wani still worked for Denzel Green council, and Dawn was gregarious on Facebook, mainly posting pictures of food and dreaming of foreign travel. She seldom linked her personal posts to the Society's fundraising activities. The others generally had no interesting online presence other than mentions regarding the Society itself, but she didn't have time to dig deep. There was only time for a cheese toastie, made with extra mature cheddar and a liberal sprinkling of Worcester sauce, a coffee from her Nespresso machine, and a cheeky Mr Kipling's apple pie before she had to leave for her train ride.

She heard the locomotive before she saw it. Billowing plumes of white steam rose above the treeline, and the engine panted like a mighty dragon, echoing from the trees. She was delighted to see Howard the fireman was on board stoking the flames, while a second man, with thin glasses and greased back hair was doing his rounds, checking the engine was ready to leave.

DS Collins was eagerly observing from the cab. Judith chuckled when she caught the flutter of disappointment on the detective's face when she climbed aboard.

"I didn't expect you to make it," he said, offering his hand to help her up the last few steps.

"I'm not surprised. You appeared to give me the wrong time."

"How on earth did that happen?"

"Fortunately, the British railways never fail to be late! And I double-checked how long it would take to get the engine up to speed. I have no intention on missing a fun ride with my favourite detective!"

"Sadly for me, you're not." Collins nodded towards the new man who was now inspecting the wheels. "Mr Peele is our driver."

"He looks like a chartered accountant."

"Funnily enough, he is. He drives trains on the side. We had to bring him down from Birmingham. It turns out there are not a lot of steam train drivers readily available."

Fifteen minutes later, Judith and Raymond Collins were crammed into the corner of the cab as the fireman declared the engine was up to steam. Mr Peele gave a satisfactory nod and allowed Raymond to unleash a childhood ambition and toot the whistle. The piercing screech echoed across the blood red sunset, startling birds from the trees. They fluttered away with angry caws. Levers were pulled, gauges checked, tapped, and checked again. The locomotive gave a sudden lurch backward, and they were underway. Judith spun around, remembering they were returning to the shed in Little Pickton. It took a second or two for Raymond to cotton on to that fact.

The journey started off pleasantly enough. Travelling backward meant they didn't have plumes of steam drifting into the cab. Both Judith and Raymond leaned out either side, clutching onto the metal guardrail and feeling the refreshing blast of the wind as they trundled back down the track. But it only took a matter of minutes for that novelty to wear off. Judith's cheeks swiftly became numb from the frigid air, and her hands cramped from clutching the metal rail for dear life.

She hauled herself back into the cab, experiencing the full blast of heat from the furnace singe her face. With cherry-red cheeks, Raymond Collins decided to do the same moments later. The roar of the flames, the huff of the engine, and the grating of metal-on-metal drowned out the opportunity for any delicate conversation. They watched how both the driver and fireman worked in tandem, vigilantly monitoring gauges and the track ahead - or was that behind - as they effortlessly moved down the line.

The ride was surprisingly rocky as they passed over the

joints on the uneven rails. Judith shot a questioning look at Mr Peele just after a particularly sharp lurch.

"It's normal," he yelled over the mechanical symphony, his dense Black Country accent cut through the din. "All those vibrations up here are what makes her feel so alive." He laughed and patted the metalwork affectionately. "And this line is old. The rails aren't quite level no matter how much restoration they claim to have done. You're used to sitting in the carriage where it's a smoother ride. And we're a bit limited by speed. Something's not too fresh with her, by the sounds of it."

"How fast are we going?" Collins asked, his eyes searching for a speedometer.

"Probably about twenty-five miles per hour."

"Probably?" Judith yelled.

"There are no speedos on these things, so it's pretty much guesswork. When there are telegraph poles at the side of the road, it's easier to calculate because you know how far apart they are. But we just have trees and it's getting dark, so I'll just have to guess. As I say, we're doing twenty-five, no more than thirty miles per hour. And on this stretch of line, I think that's plenty."

Judith gave an involuntary shriek as the engine lurched alarmingly.

"Ah, wheelspin!" Mr Peele said with a cheery grin.

"Wheelspin? Like in a car?" Collins shouted in surprise.

"Aye. Y'know when you always get those rail delays, leaves on the line, that sort of faff? Well, it's not just a naff excuse. It really hampers performance. Leaves build up a mulch that's very slick. And then on top of that, having a good freeze can cause a bit of wheelspin. But at least we're anchored to the tracks, so won't be spinning off the side." He laughed.

"That's something," said Judith, who was starting to think that riding a train was not quite as romantic as she had assumed. "You said something sounded off?"

Mr Peele tapped the boilerplate with a gloved hand. "They've done a fine job bringing her back to life. But I think there's something amiss with the gearing. It happens over age. These things need to be maintained even after just a couple of years. They're made from steel, but they're delicate babies, really."

Another five minutes passed, and the sky grew darker. The heat from the furnace, the gentle sway, and the rhythmic sounds of movement had a soporific effect. Judith's eyelids fluttered as she struggled to stay focused. After several minutes, they saw lights flickering between the trees as Little Pickton came into view.

Mr Peele gently eased the engine and applied the brakes. As he'd never driven this engine before, he explained that he'd rather be safe than sorry when it came to testing just how good the brake system was. More streetlights appeared and the headlights from the occasional passing car as they entered the outskirts of the village. A minute later, they'd slowed to a brisk walking pace, and Judith heard clunks and clangs as the locomotive switched onto a side line. Ahead, she could see the lights of the old station and the shed where the engine was stowed. Next to it, she could see police vehicles filling the station's small car park as the forensic team continued their investigation.

With expert precision, Mr Peele brought the engine to a halt a foot in the shed, two inches in front of the buffers. The locomotive hissed and crackled with satisfaction.

"Well, that was something," Judith said, clapping her gloved hands together and forcing a smile at Raymond as she climbed down the ladder to the track below. She had noticed his coos of admiration at the start of the journey had quickly waned as his discomfort built. First from the blast of cold and then from the tropical furnace heat, with little transition between the two. She suspected the reality of the train ride didn't quite match his childhood expectations. She extended a hand to help him down the last high step down.

"Yes, quite a ride," he said tartly. He waited for Mr Peele and Howard to step down before nodding. "Thank you for that. It was fun. Do you know exactly what is wrong with the engine?"

The two engineers exchanged a shrug. "Not without stripping her down," Howard said. "I suppose the lads here had already done that so you should find everything in their maintenance logs. I doubt it's anything too nasty."

Judith and Raymond said their goodbyes and made their way towards the exit.

Judith clapped her hands together, then vigorously rubbed them, but they remained quite numb.

"Well, perhaps you and I can find somewhere for a good old hot chocolate and a chinwag?" she suggested.

Raymond's eyebrow slowly cranked up, in part due to the fact his forehead was beyond freezing. "That sounds awfully like you want to pick my brain clean of any facts pertaining to the case."

Judith feigned indignation. "How awfully sceptical of you, my young fellow m'lad."

"I'm not that much younger than you," he scowled, irritated with himself.

"And you assume that you know more than I do."

"I am the lead *police* detective—"

Judith cut him off. "Nevertheless, a sharing of minds is always a benefit." Her eyes scanned his face. "Especially since you now know this is going to be a slightly less straightforward case than you hoped."

This time both of Raymond Collins' eyebrows inched up. "What on earth makes you say that?"

Judith wanted to admit that it was a guess, but it was more fun toying with him. She looked enigmatic. "That's because I'm an excellent judge of character and situation, as you well know."

Raymond sighed and nodded. They set out to find DC Sarah Eastly who was still in the office, with the SOCO team carefully going through volumes of paperwork. Judith kept to the corner, out of the way of the busy team. They'd already searched that half of the room, so she curiously poked around the shelves. She found the Wi-Fi password pinned to the wall, and then bumped into a stack of papers that annoyed a couple of forensic officers who made a point of stacking it back in place. DS Collins suggested that she didn't touch anything and that it was time to find sanctuary in the tearoom.

Chapter Nine

Time For Tea was an oasis of warmth and comfort. Timothy had lit the real wood fire, and the heady scent sowed the air with drowsy vibes. A few of the locals had stayed late to enjoy a meal, seeing as it was the only place to dine out, if you didn't count the only pub in the middle of the village, the *Miller's Arms*, which was 'experimenting' with food.

Over a trio of rich chocolate drinks, served in tall glasses and topped with a spiral of cholesterol-infused whipped cream, Judith, Sarah, and Raymond sank into the corner of a snug to conspire.

Raymond folded his arms before quickly unfolding them because he thought it made him look truculent. He'd mentally prepared himself not to give anything away to Judith, not that he knew much, so he'd let her do all the talking. The latter wasn't easy, as it was Sarah who caved in first and hadn't stopped talking since they'd been seated.

"It appears the Rail Society is in a shocking state financially. They received money from the Lottery to get started, buy the engine, repair it, and renovate the station platform and the track. It came in under budget, and on top of that they conducted very profitable donation drives and even a Kickstarter." She leaned towards Raymond and slowed her pace, as if explaining something to her grandfather. "That's a website that helps you raise money."

"I know what it is," he growled, but Eastly ploughed on.

"Now, we haven't done any deep dives, but it seems the first year or so, everything was well on track. If you pardon the pun," she giggled and slurped the chocolate, oblivious to the blob of cream that attached itself to the end of her nose. Judith's gaze didn't veer away. She didn't want to interrupt. "When it opened, it attracted a flow of people who wanted to ride the line. More than they'd forecast. And..." she puffed her cheeks and blew loudly out, "suddenly, they were in the red. Like that." She snapped her fingers. "There is a massive paper trail to go through. We'll need a forensic accountant to really investigate that side of things."

DS Collins nodded sagely, although he could already see the cost of the investigation ballooning with the requirement of specialists. "Before we do that," he cautioned. "Which is a splendid idea, by the way. We should take a big step back and look at exactly what went on here."

"Isn't that obvious?" said Judith, receiving curious looks from the detectives. "Herbert went out on the train with somebody he knew–"

"Locomotive..." Eastly corrected with another dunk into her chocolate.

"I'd say midway through the journey an argument broke out and he was murdered. The killer panicked and tossed the body into the furnace and then fled into the night."

"That's it?" Raymond said. "That's all you've got? Judith, that is a case of the bleeding obvious."

"A title you can use for your memoirs," Judith quipped. "Obvious. Too obvious. We know it takes two people to drive the train. That's two sets of very specific skills. No doubt Herbert possessed both, but who else in the group could do so? Not that it's impossible for him to drive it alone. Not at all. It's merely not good practice."

"That narrows the suspect list down," said Eastly, suddenly aware of the cream on her nose. Embarrassed, she rubbed it off.

"I wager he'd suffered a terrible bash to the head with a shovel. In such a small cab, that would probably have come from behind."

Raymond looked puzzled. "What makes you say that? In case you hadn't noticed, all that remains of the poor bloke is from the waist down."

"The fireman chappie, Howard. He had to bring his own shovel, I noticed. So the original is missing."

After a brief embarrassed silence, Raymond squirmed in his seat. "Well, yes, that is precisely the avenue I was pursuing. Obviously, Herbert knew his killer, and off they went together to test the train..." He stumbled over the last words, as he didn't quite believe them. "An altercation took place for reasons yet unknown, and the killer fled with the murder weapon."

Judith stirred her drink. She caught Raymond gazing at it as the cream spiralled hypnotically. After the freezing cold train ride, they didn't want to leave the warmth of the tea house.

"Have any of the forensic bods reported back yet?"

Judith asked, eager for as much information as she could gather.

Raymond wrapped his hands around his cup to soak in the warmth. Even close to a roaring fireplace, he was still feeling chilled to the bone and either his clothes smelled of burning coal, or his nostrils were filled with it.

"Other than to complain about half a body not being much use, no. It's all very macabre. The torso bones didn't burn, so they have been recovered from the furnace. Other than that, not a scrap of cloth or skin north of the belt. They're running toxicology on the legs." He shuddered at the thought. "And there were signs of bruising on the shins and knees. And on the... bottom."

"So, firm signs of a scuffle," said Judith, instantly regretting the use of the word 'firm' in the context of 'bottom'. Raymond nodded. "Now, we should assume that it would take a strong person to haul the body into those flames. And if the victim was conscious and struggling, I think it would be close to impossible. It's more likely Herbert was knocked out beforehand. As you mentioned," he added reluctantly.

Sarah flicked through the pages of her notepad, deciphering her own shaky handwriting. "An email from SOCO said they found traces of blood on the steel, just above the rear coal hopper."

Judith pictured the interior of the cab where the coal was fed in from the bunker back through gruelling manual labour.

Raymond clapped his hands together in demonstration. "He was whacked with a shovel on the back of the head. Bleeding, he fell backwards against the wall, out for the count. Then he was thrown headfirst, Hansel and Gretel style, into the oven. For motives that need to be established. For a killer who needs to be identified."

The three of them lapsed into silence as they contemplated.

"Of course," Judith said, catching Raymond's drooping eyelids. "We are overlooking the elephant in the room."

"Obviously." Raymond exchanged a quizzical look at Sarah, who shrugged and finished her drink in one long satisfying gulp.

"Are we certain it was Herbert who died?"

After a moment of surprise, Sarah Eastly giggled. "He was identified from his wallet."

"Of course. The wallet. An indefatigable proof of identification and the enemy of bouncers around the world! But let us take a wild leap and pretend such things could be faked. Has his identity been confirmed through more archaic means? Such as fingerprints? Not that he has those. Does one possess toe-prints?"

That woke Collins up, and he sharply nodded. "Of course, we'll double-check that with dental records and blood and whatnot from the rest of the body."

"Wonderful. Which brings me to another elephant in the room."

Raymond gave out a long sigh. "Why is it every case with you turns into a circus?" He was pleased with Sarah Eastly's little chuckle. If policing didn't work out, there was always stand-up comedy. If you couldn't have some morbid fun during a murder investigation, when could you have it?

"The aforementioned heffalump is the manner of death. On the surface, it seems as if the killer was trying to do away with evidence. But we've seen the firebox. It's remarkably small. I always imagined it was much bigger, as I'm sure somebody not familiar with a locomotive would think too. There's no way a body could be crammed in there and incinerated. Not if you knew what you were doing."

"An accident?" Collins queried. "That sounds a tad extreme."

Judith shrugged. "It's more likely than something premeditated. It all feels... rushed. Half-destroyed evidence in a very prominent murder scene, which, let's face it, would be found incredibly quickly. I mean, if I didn't know better, it looked almost staged."

"Staged for what?" said Collins.

"Staged to draw attention," said Judith, taking a long sip and enjoying a little warmth on the back of her throat.

"Why would anyone want to draw attention to something so sickening? Or is that yet another elephant in the room?"

"Oh, my dear detective," said Judith. "That is another metaphorical idiom altogether. That's the *million-dollar question*."

Chapter Ten

Judith returned home that evening, pondering how they now had fewer facts at the end of the day than when the investigation had started. It was that layer of intrigue that held her attention as she fell asleep, ready for her visitor at eight o'clock the following morning.

As it turned out, it had snowed all night, leaving a fresh white sheet across the village. And her visitor was forty minutes late when he rang the doorbell without offering a word of apology.

"Ah, Derek!" she exclaimed as she opened the door, admitting a handyman and a flurry of snow. "I was beginning to think you'd forgotten."

"Nah," said Derek Rivan as he entered, stamping his boots on her welcome mat. His small Vauxhall Combi van was blocking her drive. Its weathered and peeling paintwork made the word *handiman* barely legible. And spelt incorrectly, she noted.

When she'd nipped home the previous afternoon, Judith had spent her time sabotaging her kitchen sink as an excuse to call out the only handyman in the village. She hoped he'd turn up within the hour. It transpired that she had to heavily negotiate to get him out so early the following day.

"Where's the patient?" said Derek breezily.

"The kitchen sink is in the kitchen." Judith led the way.

Derek clomped through, leaving dark muddy footprints on the clean white tiles. Judging by his ruffled hair and the way the collar on his overalls was tucked inwards, Judith surmised that he'd hastily dressed to leave home. He put his rusting toolbox down and appraised the modern kitchen layout that looked out of place in the quaint cottage. All the while he tunelessly whistled and gave no indication that he recognised Judith from the police interviews, where he'd been upbeat, chipper, and responding to Dawn's unsubtle flirtations.

With an unfit grunt, he sat cross-legged on the floor and opened the cupboard under the sink. He leaned in for a better look. From the angle Judith was at, it looked as if the unit had consumed him up to his midriff and she had an unwelcome flash of the body poking from the locomotive's furnace. Derek took his time, *umming and ahing*. Judith was puzzled. She'd disconnected the basin bottle trap herself so that it hung from the sink above in an obvious manner. All he had to do was tighten it up again for the old dear who didn't have a clue.

"I've seen you at the Rail Society, haven't I?" Judith said. She was rewarded with silence as Derek stopped his cheerful humming.

"Yeah, I'm one of the engineers."

"Terrible shame to hear what happened to your friend."

Derek ducked his head out of the cupboard. "Yeah, I can see a bit of a problem with your pipes."

"Really?" said Judith, with Oscar-worthy levels of surprise.

"Oh yeah. Bottle trap snapped off 'cause the threads are corroded on the pipes. I'll have to replace them before they get worse. And the trap is knackered too. You're gonna need a new one. He tapped his toolbox. Luckily, I carry spares."

"Lucky indeed. Fancy that, corrosion on the pipes."

"Uh huh."

"Isn't it marvellous the things they can do with plastic these days?" Derek had already re-entered the cupboard to do whatever it was he was doing. "Do you drive the train as well? That must be terrific fun."

"Not really," said Derek, blindly reaching into his toolbox for a heavy wrench. "Always wanted to do that since I was a kid. But that Groves is a stickler for the rules. Never let me have a go."

"Did you know Lloyd and Herbert beforehand?"

"I knew Herbert around town. They needed some professional names on the Lottery application. People who knew a thing or two. I mean, neither of them had driven a train before, let alone fixed one. They needed an expert."

"And that's where you came in."

Derek popped his head out of the cupboard. He was beaming with delight at the chance of telling his life story. "As a kid, I lived in Kent, and I worked on the steam train in Hythe during the summer. It was brilliant. Always loved it. Became an engineer and ended up working for Network Rail for twenty years, straight out of school. I got to work on new locomotives, old ones. All sorts. And I was always a dab hand fixing up my car."

"I'm relieved that my sink is in safe hands."

Derek stuck his head back into the cupboard, blocking

any view Judith had of what he was doing in there. Perhaps he'd discovered another door that led to some secret Narnian world, because he was surely taking his time to reattach a pipe.

Judith sat at the counter and played the naive victim. "Oh, I didn't know what to do with that. So, I'm so happy you could come out."

"Anything can be fixed," Derek said, poking the pipe with his wrench, presumably to make it sound as if he was fixing something.

"So, it's all down to you we have the train running at all."

"Oh yeah, I mean, to be honest. That line can't function without me. Chief Engineer, I mean this," his hand came out of the cupboard to gesture around. "This is just a day job to pay the bills while I do my passion."

"Which is playing with trains."

Derek's hand shot out again, and he cocked a finger in Judith's direction. "Exacto-mungo!"

"I had always imagined that since you'd restored the engine from new, it was quite easy to maintain?" Like my kitchen, she mentally added.

"You'd think so. But I'll tell you what, there are some tight arses amongst that lot."

"Whatever do you mean?"

"They'd always complain about the budget for parts. Now, you've got to remember, these just aren't off-the-shelf bits. You can't just go down to *Rooney's* and get them. They gotta be measured and built specifically for that locomotive and engineered with very small tolerances. It was supposed to be a feat of love restoring her back to her operational pride. Instead, it was a feat of neglect in my view."

"Neglect."

"Cheap parts wear out quicker, so it's not exactly cost saving. Luckily, I was there to sort it all out and save the day."

Derek popped out from the cupboard to fish a can of WD-40 and a screwdriver from his toolbox.

"I imagine there is always a lot of repair work to be done."

"Oh, aye. Keeps me busy. I should be a shareholder." He disappeared back under the sink.

"Don't they pay you enough?"

"Of course not. As my dad said, the only way to get skin in the game is to go and carve off some for yourself. That's why I made myself invaluable."

"So, what do you think happened to Herbert?"

"I dunno." Judith had mis-timed the question because she couldn't see his face. So the only reaction she could gauge was a slight *piff* sound. She was unsure if it was an emotional sigh or a dismissive exultation. "I'd never wish anything so sick on anyone," Derek said diplomatically. "It's a real shock. He'll be greatly missed."

Judith wasn't convinced that Derek would miss him. He'd showed no real empathy in his interview, and very little today outside a stereotypical chirpy *Bob the Builder* façade

"I daresay things will continue smoothly on," he finally added.

"Of course. He wasn't that important."

"He helped set it up. But other than that, he had his own ideas of where it was all going. And honestly, I think he had his own motivations about setting it up in the first place."

"What makes you say that?"

He peeked from behind the cupboard door. "Lloyd is the trainspotter. Knows bits about engineering. His family used to be a bunch of toffs. Herbert came to it all quite a bit late.

He didn't know a turntable from a signal box. And everything he learnt he got from either Dr Hornby or Thomas the Tank Engine. But then he loved it. He became as boring as Lloyd."

The name Hornby drew Judith back to the elaborate railway sets in Herbert's house. "Then it was a new interest."

Derek pulled a face and entered the cupboard once again. "Oh, yeah. He's the obsessive type."

Judith had drifted in and out of societies, collectors, and nerdy groups, so knew there were intricate internal structures comprised of status levels earned by gaining the upper hand over. Knowledge was the basic price of admission, but it was never enough to know about the subject. The true obsessives had to stretch to a detail-obsessed level of passion that weeded out the true geeks from the weekend warriors. That is what set internal hierarchies, established responsibilities and fuelled jealousies. Despite Herbert being the co-founder, she sensed Derek looked down on his level of mechanical knowledge, but in the hallowed halls of trainspotting nerdiness, Derek clearly wasn't allowed admission. She decided to play to his ego.

"Thank goodness we've got somebody like you who clearly knows his stuff. I imagine it's quite irritating to have somebody hanging around, taking all the glory."

Derek nodded eagerly. "You understand, love. A lot of people just don't get it. Them two wouldn't let me have any real fun. His whole knowledge was based on an on-off switch for his little model railways. It drove me mad. And then, lauding it as a co-founder. He'd be taking her out to fetes and gala days, particularly if there was a way he could milk some praise out of it." He thumped his chest with his balled-up fist. "Who actually did the work?"

Judith was surprised to see the vacuous man really did have passion.

"Well, at least people now appreciate your talent, as you just said," Judith responded enthusiastically. "Like Dawn."

"Oh, Dawn's a star!" he said with genuine affection. "She gets it. She knows what's going on."

"Good for her," said Judith. "I mean, again, she's another one, isn't she?"

"Aye, another victim to somebody else's ego. She was involved before Herbert. It was her and Lloyd who started the ball rolling. But she got pushed to the side lines."

"Why would that be?"

Derek shrugged. "She is a woman. Despite that, I swear, they wouldn't have got anywhere without her. She should've walked out ages ago. That would've taught them."

After a volley of final hammering that shook the draining board, Derek extracted himself from the cupboard, stood up, and turned the mixer tap on full blast in a grand flourish. The water effortlessly swirled down the plug hole, without so much as a drop escaping from the pipework.

"Oh, you've fixed it," Judith exclaimed with as much fake delight as she could muster. "What a hero!" Once again, Derek was tone-deaf to the sarcasm.

"Easy enough, if you know what to look for. I normally charge VAT, but cash in hand will save you a wallop. That'll be fifty-quid."

Judith's mouth silently worked as she thought of an appropriate rebuttal. But she couldn't muster one that didn't use copious amounts of four-letter words. Instead, she hopped to her feet and fetched a purse from the side of the breadboard.

"Fifty-pounds to save my kitchen," she exclaimed as she

fished out two crisp twenty-pound notes and the most crinkled tenner she could find. "And no VAT. That's sticking it to those fat cat tax avoiders!" She handed the cash over. "Thank you very much. Next time I have a problem, I know exactly who I'm going to call."

Certainly not you, you sharky bastard, she thought with an outward smile.

With a whistle and a spring in his step, Derek folded the cash into his pocket. A real bonanza for what amounted to a couple of seconds tightening of a pipe collar. But Judith thought it was worth it. He'd provided a valuable insight under the Society's skin and set the record straight about exactly what sort of person Derek Rivan was.

Chapter Eleven

The next day passed with a growing sense of tedium in which interest and adventure seemed to lie out of reach over the horizon. Slate grey skies deposited further occasional flurries of snow, which refused to melt and added to the stillness of the air.

Judith considered her approaches to the rest of the Railway Society, but couldn't quite find an organic way to start conversations. Derek may not have recognised her from Eastly's interviews, but she was certain the others were not so self-absorbed.

She had passed Barbara in the village, urgently scooting away on her bicycle and veering just enough to avoid any form of social interaction. Lloyd Groves had driven out of the village in his pristine white Range Rover, passing her cottage without either a by your leave or spilling his guts to her. The nerve of some people. She hadn't heard from the detectives, either. Detective Sergeant Collins hadn't replied to any of her friendly text messages, and Eastly only had time to tell her that SOCO had finished at the office and the Society was free to move back in. A second message said they had begun a series of formal interviews with the members, all of whom had insisted on having solicitors with them because they'd seen enough TV shows to know it would be daft not to.

That left Judith freewheeling, which is something she didn't enjoy. In the past, it had landed her in plenty of trouble, and that wasn't something she wanted to experience again. Besides, what was the point in having a good old murder investigation when there was nothing to immediately investigate?

To combat boredom, she had driven to Denzel Green, which had been the Society's last public appearance. Separated by only eleven miles, Little Pickton and Denzel Green had formed a rivalry that simmered just below the Siege of Troy levels. At first glance, they were almost identical villages. Visitors often had to double-check signs to confirm where they were, but Denzel Green was twice the size, boasting the status of *town*. To the lifelong inhabitants, they were poles apart; Sodom and Gomorrah to one another, although arguments raged about who was Sodom, mainly because nobody was sure what *doing a Gomorrah* meant. Whatever it was, Judith suspected it was terrific fun. However, she was not a small-town girl, so gave the rivalry all the attention it deserved. None.

The town considered itself the true home of the Railway. It may start in Little Pickton, but its destination was Denzel Green, and surely a *destination* was what every place aspired to be. Asking around the café for details on the event, Judith had been directed to a rotund man called Fabian Heinzel, the editor of the Parish newspaper, *the Clarendon*, and the town's mayor. He was responsible for the town's events and was an advocate of the railway. He knew Lloyd Groves well, a man he respected because he wasn't from Little Pickton, merely a denizen. When it was established that Judith was from the same foreign clan he opened up. Things became more convivial when Judith suddenly remembered seeing Heinzel back in the village with Maggie last year. At the mention of Maggie's name, Heinzel blushed and looked away. That triggered Judith's memory. Maggie and Heinzel had once dated. Had it been more than that? Maggie had been too vague to be sure.

With their newfound commonality, Judith had invited him for lunch. Over a delicious homemade broth and freshly baked bread, she learned that Lloyd and Derek had been the faces in the crowd that day. Heinzel confided that they often were. Herbert shied away from the publicity. He didn't deal with the rest of the team, except on occasion Barbara or Dawn when it came to logistics. On his phone, he showed Judith the paper's nice puff piece about the railway, and how the event had raised almost one-hundred-and-eighty pounds from the local Brownies. They were pictured around the engine, smiling amid plumes of steam. The article's wording was flamboyantly drafted by Dawn, who certainly had a flair for turning a phrase. There wasn't so much as a stray vowel hinting at animosity between the two villages. Judith had quickly gathered that Fabian considered himself, not only Denzel Green's overlord but also the constricting hand of the media, as he controlled the only local newspaper that served the area. She was lunching with the county's equivalent of Rupert Murdoch.

There was no hint of the shadow that fall. Heinzel

painted the Society as fun people to work with. If anything, he thought they were not ambitious enough, but he didn't follow that up with an explanation. If it wasn't for the soup, Judith was about to write the trip off as a useless expedition. Then Fabian Heinzel mentioned there was a petition to extend the line to Fulton, a good twenty minutes away. The Society had been pushing the idea, with the folks in Denzel Green blocking the very notion in a campaign that he led.

"That would make us the place you *pass through*," Heinzel said in a growl. "Who wants to be the *bowels* of any operation?"

Judith silently pondered which end Fabian Heinzel thought they were, but could easily guess. Fulton wasn't a village. It was a *town*. It even had some old Medieval ruins it pretended was a castle (although English Heritage had long disputed that claim), a cinema, and a Nando's. The saving grace for the mayor was that the line beyond Denzel Green was in such a terrible a state of disrepair that it couldn't be used without expensive renovation. It had been a heated source of argument within the Rail Society, although Heinzel claimed that he wasn't privy to who was for or against it. He admitted that, although he liked Lloyd Groves, he didn't entirely trust him. In his opinion, he was the sort of person who could follow you through a revolving door and come out first. He ended the lunch, believing that the matter of extending the railway was now closed.

Driving home, Judith's mind was abuzz with the thought of rivalries within the Society. Instead of knocking on the Rail Society's door as she'd planned, she phoned Augusta as she left the café. She wanted to shed some more light on the group's rivalries concerning the extension. Augusta's tone was short and clipped on the phone. She'd just been interviewed by DS Collins and his brusque manner had upset her. True to form, she didn't want to meet in the tearoom and told Judith she'd meet her on Bond Lane, a long road that circumnavigated the private Beaconsfield Estate. It was a favourite path for ramblers.

They met in the lay-by. Augusta indicated a snowy track that led through the edge of the wood and the gentle hills. Further flurries had added to the picturesque landscape. With thick socks and firm wellies, a long coat, gloves, scarf, and a yellow bobble hat to replace her blue beret, Judith was prepared for all weathers as they set off on their hike.

"I must say, the cheery face of the Rail Society depicted on your website is quite a bit of false advertising," said Judith. "Nobody's talkative, and when they do speak, nobody's particularly friendly."

"You can hardly blame them," Augusta said. "Between one thing and another - and the police's brusque manner... I know it's their job, but they're hardly the friendly type."

Judith felt herself instinctively leaping to the detectives' defence. She knew what sort of people they really were, but that didn't mean others had to. In this instance, it was probably an ideal case of bad cops/nice amateur sleuth. Plus, it made little sense to reveal her own feelings on the matter. Instead, she played sympathetically to Augusta.

"Gave you a hard time, did they?" Judith asked, her breath coming in billowing clouds as she scrutinised Augusta's Christmas themed woolly hat. It was far too early to be promoting the season of good will.

Augusta gave a shudder. "That's why I came to you. My fears are coming to life. The financial irregularities are there for all to see. I didn't try to hide anything. They are there in black and white. So where is the finger of suspicion going to fall?"

"What did they accuse you of?"

"Oh, nothing accusatory. It was just the direction their questions led. The solicitor I had, some kid who was barely out of his shorts and pimples. He told me to be very careful about what I said. He claimed the best course of action was to say *no comment*."

Judith nodded. Ironically, it was always the best course of action in any interview because technically, it didn't infer any blame, acceptance, or knowledge about the question at hand. But of course, as every copper worth their salt knew, it deeply depended on how the *no comment* was delivered. A simple inflection could reveal a whole host of hidden motivations.

"I can see how that would be stressful," said Judith. "And at least you came to me beforehand, so that's going to be worth something. As soon as I make any progress, that is. Then, hopefully things get a little easier for you. Did you mention that we'd spoken?"

"It never came up in questioning," said Augusta. "And if it had, I probably would have said no comment."

"That would imply a clear *yes* in that instance," Judith pointed out. "But good. It's no secret, of course. But for now, try not to let it come up in conversation."

Augusta nodded, and the following silence was broken only by the soft crunch of snow under their boots. Their path weaved out of the forest and gently up the hill, which offered a view across the town, made prettier with the dusting of snow.

"What about the others? Has anybody said anything?"

"I saw Lloyd in the office when the police let us back in. He wasn't talkative. He told me to stick to what I know because the moment I made any speculation, I'd be the one in the firing line."

Judith frowned. "Was he looking out for you?"

"It felt more like an accusation."

Augusta seemed the type who took every compliment as a veiled criticism, so Judith was unsure what to make of that. They pressed on until they reached the summit marked by a series of snow-laden boulders and three wooden benches, where sitting was currently out of the question because of the risk of frozen buttocks becoming permanently attached until the first days of spring. Judith couldn't help but smile at the serene view of Pickton looking like a gem nestled in the surrounding countryside. An illusion, of course, as the tension of murder simmered beneath the tranquil exterior, much like anywhere else in the world, from Milton Keynes to Baghdad.

"Why don't you invite me into the office?" she suggested. "That way, I can casually meet Lloyd and engage in a real conversation with him."

Augusta gave an imperceptible shrug. "Lloyd has made it clear he will not be in there much. The Herbert situation has put him on edge, so he's planning to work from home."

"Convenient," remarked Judith.

"I don't think anybody else is going in either. There won't be any jaunts anytime soon. We've had nothing but cancellations for the next few months when it should be getting busier. I suppose the only one with anything left to do is Dawn. And all she has to do is field phone calls from the press."

Judith looked pointedly at Augusta. "I suppose Dawn is

going to juggle the bad public relations in order to get you back on your feet. And you?"

"I'll have to see what I can find in order to present the facts to our solicitor."

"Whose solicitor?"

"Lloyd is assigning one to the Society. We all brought our own in during the interviews," Augusta explained. "He thinks there needs to be somebody looking out for the Society's interests."

Judith didn't like the sound of that. If Augusta was being framed as a stooge, then adding an additional legal eagle in the mix made things just that bit tougher for her.

"Surely, you've had a company lawyer before now. Especially when the money went missing?"

Augusta shook her head. "Lloyd and Herbert agreed it would be best to keep it quiet and not draw any negative publicity."

"And what will Barbara be doing?" Judith inquired.

Augusta snorted disdainfully. "Well, she hasn't got much to do, has she, with nothing going on. No fundraisers to organise, no convincing people that the Society's the best tourist attraction in the area. She gets to stay at home and keep being all weird."

"And what about Derek?" She caught a grimace flash across Augusta's face. Either that, or it was fleeting indigestion. "Doesn't the train still require maintenance? Isn't that a constant job for him?"

"He's always busy," Augusta mumbled. "Since there's no cash in the bank, I doubt he'll lift a finger. Besides, he's planning a holiday. Escape to the sun. Somewhere warm."

Judith nodded knowingly. "Somewhere like Barbados, I'd suppose." Augusta wasn't going to bite, so Judith prompted her again. "I heard Herbert met someone on the Sunday before he died."

Augusta remained composed, with her unblinking gaze fixed across the vista. "Who?"

"That's what I'd very much like to know. It may well be the last person who saw him alive before he took the engine out. And about that," Judith continued, recalling the calendar on Herbert's wall. "There was nothing scheduled for maintenance or taking the train out on a jolly. Why would he do it?"

"Some people still get excited playing with big toys like that. The novelty wears off for others. Not for Herbert. He loved it more than the people. But he always played his cards close to his chest. I think he enjoyed being an enigma. He didn't like people knowing too much about his personal life, or his plans. He was always arguing with Lloyd about expanding the line. He wanted another train, but what's the point in that if we're not travelling to a place people want to visit?"

"Well, it's something British Railways can't seem to manage. So, you're all in favour of going beyond Denzel Green?"

Augusta shot her a look. "Are you talking about the Fulton expansion?"

Judith nodded wisely, pleased that she'd unexpectedly struck a nerve.

"That caused ruptures amongst the group, let me tell you." There was a notable acid in her tone, but she offered nothing more until silently Judith prompted her with a hand gesture. "There were talks of a takeover. I tried not to get involved. It would have been a paper headache for me. I think it was all talk. We didn't have the money and I can't imagine anyone would have wanted control wrested away."

Judith pondered the information. She was still frustrated by the lack of an obvious introduction to Lloyd, so she might have to get a little devious to orchestrate it. An idea struck her, one that might require a bit of dirty manipulation to make progress.

Chapter Twelve

In police hands, the phone was a precision weapon that Detective Sergeant Raymond Collins prided himself on wielding with graceful efficiency. Unfortunately, for it to work, the person on the other end had to be, at the very least, semi-competent. As it happened, Raymond felt as if he'd spent the entire morning on the phone with a bunch of morons. He mused whether '*gaggle*' was the collective noun for morons. He spent the wasted time on hold contacting Susie Dent to confirm make it official. The hold music suddenly clicked, and he was abruptly cut off twenty-minutes into the call.

With a sigh, he slammed the phone down with so much force that DC Sarah Eastly, sitting at the desk opposite, jumped in her seat. Eastly had been so focused reading through the paperwork collected from the Society's office that she'd succumbed to a trance-like state.

"That's the third time I've been cut off!" Raymond sighed as he picked up the phone and stabbed the buttons to make another call. "At this rate, we're going to have to crack the case without leaving our desks."

Eastly was only half-listening. The paperwork was dense, but it was obvious that the Society, while publicly boasting success, had run up severe debts and was facing financial ruin. How those debts had been incurred was a question that needed answering. To make sense of it, they really needed a forensic accountant to peel back the details. The sort of person who breathed numbers, probably lived alone, wore beige knitted jumpers, and spoke with a slow, nasal intonation that risked anyone of a frail disposition from keeling over from a fatal dose of boredom. At least that was the person Sarah had built up in her mind. She felt embarrassed that it was one she currently found attractive. She had to get out more before she found herself like one of the many spinsters that populated the county.

Mindful of the police department's budget, Raymond was aware his choices were limited. He'd been volleying calls as he tried to reach his Super to plead for more money to be allocated. At the same time, he had been plumbing the police database to find somebody who was available.

Sarah licked a finger and turned over another sheet, giving the occasional pensive, "*Mmmm...*"

"Losing the will to live?" asked Raymond.

"Not at all. This is strangely fascinating. I mean, it's beyond me. I'm not that good with numbers."

Raymond didn't say a word. He knew she had an A-Level in maths, and his own educational experience didn't put him in a position to even joke about that.

Sarah continued without lifting her eyes off the page. "They received a big National Lottery grant and came in under budget, as far as I can tell. They were doing well with all their fundraisers." She tapped an entry on the page. "They even had a film crew rent them for three weeks. Everything looked healthy, until suddenly BAM! Between one month and the next, all their money had gone."

"How much are we talking about?"

"Several-hundred thousand is my guesstimate," said Sarah. "That's what appears to have vanished."

Raymond sucked between his teeth in sympathy at the painful loss. "What happened?"

"It simply vanished. There were no bill payments, no obvious outgoings, nothing I can obviously see."

"Stolen?"

Sarah's eyebrow raised quizzically, and she gave a tilt of her head in agreement. Then she tapped the page. "Augusta claimed the computer had a virus which she clicked on. That's what took the money."

"Did anybody else confirm this?"

"Lloyd told me that's what *she* told him and Herbert. They decided not to worry the others. Nothing was reported to the police, and nobody brought it up during any of the interviews. Digital forensics said that her hard drive had been wiped clean and everything reinstalled. Augusta claims Herbert did it because he was worried the virus would spread. So there is no sign of it."

"Very convenient. The only person who can corroborate her story is the victim." Raymond had misdialled while he was speaking, so the moment the voice on the other end of the line welcomed him to *Katsu Curry House*, he slammed the phone back down. "So, if it was stolen and nobody reported it. What's several-hundred thousand divided by seven?" His eyebrows danced up and down suggestively.

"Maybe they were all giving each other an annual bonus, eh?"

"That's why we need a proper whizz to look through this. It would be handy if we can see the suspects' personal financial statements."

"That's going to be impossible unless we make an arrest." Raymond rubbed his fingers on the table. "Of course, we have access to the deceased's records."

"I'll put in a request for those. I'm thinking that it's more about any payments that don't look like the usual bills." Sarah frowned and flicked back through the pages until she found something that had caught her attention. She'd marked it with a sticky note. "There are these occasional payments to *DG*. Five-hundred quid here, occasionally a grand every now and again. They're not regular, but there's enough of them to add up."

"Who's DG?"

Sarah had been wondering that, but now the obvious answer occurred to her. "Denzel Green."

"What are they paying the town for?"

"They do events together, so maybe there are costs flying back and forth for those."

"I thought the purpose of the events was to raise money for the Society, so why are they paying out?"

"That's something we should talk to Barbara Dixon about. She deals with all the organisational matters." They'd already interviewed Barbara in a formal setting, so it would be a little irregular to do it again. "A more casual approach would be needed to get her talking..."

Sarah's eyes widened, and Raymond's rolled as he understood the unspoken message.

"Judith!" they both said together.

Having somebody outside the investigation would be a useful tool for mopping up bits of information. Ordinarily, of course, Raymond wouldn't have hesitated in visiting Barbara again. Except this time, he was a little unnerved as Barbara's vague, ethereal manner gave him the creeps. He had to weigh that up against his resentment that proved Judith's participation was in any way beneficial.

"To sum things up, we now have a murder case on the back of missing money," Sarah mused. "Possible corruption, theft, or skulduggery."

Raymond couldn't stop himself from chuckling. "Skulduggery, what a word!" And to hear it from the mouth of somebody so young. He shook his head.

"Now *that's* frightening," said Sarah. "It's almost as if being around you is making me old." She rubbed her eyes. "OK, now the numbers are getting to me. I'm going to go out to take a break and give Judith a ring. Want to join me for lunch?"

Raymond shook his head. "I'm going to have to go through that phone call for the fourth time."

His stomach grumbled as he watched Sarah leave. His hand was on the phone when it rang. He quickly answered. "Detective Sergeant Collins," he said, in a tone so full of swagger that he'd practiced it several times, mimicking cops he'd seen on TV.

The voice on the other end was unfamiliar. She identified herself as a forensic officer. DS Collins listened carefully and leaned back in his chair. He absently rubbed the side of his throbbing temple as he digested the forensic team's latest findings.

. . .

"I'm telling you she was acting all weird," said Maggie, clueless to the lack of volume control she was employing while she sat with Judith at the *Miller's Arms*. It was, for want of a better word, the pub in the centre of the village.

Pru, the land lady, had turned it into a wine bar, only to discover most of the inhabitants of Little Pickton preferred their wine from the discount section of Budgens or at a push, from a box. Judith wasn't a connoisseur. She heartily believed that a drink shouldn't have the taste of leather, soil, or random rubbish from the garden shed. The wine bar had evolved into a gastropub, or rather, gastro *experience*, as Pru insisted on calling it until somebody had pointed out it sounded like the result of food poisoning. Now most people called the pub *empty*, as folks preferred to drink at the Lion's Arms for their range of exotic homebrewed ales. Still, Pru made a staunch effort to stay open while she tried new marketing strategies.

"Mags, with all due respect," said Judith as she sipped her half shandy, "We all act a little odd here. You, especially."

"Don't you use that filthy language with me. We all know *due respect* means *bugger all*. And by weird, I mean away with the fairies."

Maggie managed to combine the quirkiness of a Gambian village elder with the sparkling Grim Reaper veneer of a HMRC auditor. It was this precise conflict of personalities which meant she and Judith got along so smoothly. Whereas Judith prided herself at being a hawk when it came to judging character and motivations, backed by a superb memory, Maggie had an unerring gift for sensing something amiss. She called it a hunch, but Judith suspected it was more like a hound who had the ability to sniff out trouble. Maggie had repeatedly made it clear she didn't appreciate the dog reference.

"She had twigs in her hair." Maggie tapped her index finger on the table with enough force to make the dwindling ice cubes in her G&T clink. "And I swear in her teeth, too."

Since she had seen Barbara Dixon in the early evening, she had been desperate to deploy the gossip back to Judith.

"Perhaps she fell off her bike? It's still snowy out there. Slip on a patch of ice, and it's knickers in the air."

Maggie shook her head. "That was a woman riding with purpose. And with no lights when it's getting dark. Riding in the forest."

"A BMX bandit then?" Maggie's lack of smile deepened. Judith gave an apologetic sigh. "I would think it was too far from the crime scene for her to be cycling in the snow. Besides, the police have already cleared the area, so what would she be hoping to find?"

Maggie shrugged. "I know how you like these things. Murders and all," she added in a conspiratorial whisper that the eight other regulars could clearly hear. "And I'm not gettin' involved this time. But she was riding like the clappers and nearly knocked me down dead!"

"She hit you?"

Maggie hesitated. "Well, she would have done, if I'd been on the other side of the road. The woman is a menace."

Judith pondered that. Barbara was secretive, that was for sure. But she was harmless. Which meant if she wasn't presenting a threat, then...

"Maybe something had frightened her?" Judith shook her head. Because she was at a loose end, she was beginning to buy in to Maggie's conspiracy. "Or perhaps she was late and wanted to get home for Pointless."

"I tell you; she was a woman on a mission."

With few other details, Judith could only park the information away. It was always handy to have a mental map of where the suspects were at all times, but with no other conspirators in tow she couldn't see its relevance.

Maggie had invited her out. Ordinarily, Judith would have to be cajoled with the offer of a free drink – which Maggie was more than happy to provide to lure her out. She had also offered to buy dinner in the form of Pru's special tapas, which Judith politely declined on the grounds that baked beans were not a traditional ingredient. Nor were the diced fried mushrooms and sausage that were left over from breakfast. Even without these temptations, Judith would have accepted, as she wanted to tap into Maggie's unerring sense of conspiracy.

"I was down at Denzel Green yesterday," Judith said as nonchalantly as possible. "Talking to the mayor. Fabian." At the mention of the familiar name, Maggie gave a slight inclination of her head in acknowledgment. "I remember you two had a... *thing*." She drifted off.

Maggie's brow knitted. "It was a pair of dates," she corrected Judith. "A nice fella, I grant you. But a little too full of himself."

"Of course, of course," Judith was nothing if not diplomatic. "Are you still in touch?"

"On WhatsApp. But it's been a while since I've ventured so far." Since Maggie had settled in Little Pickton, she had seldom left the boundaries of the village.

"Perish the thought. It's funny, as he mentioned the railway line extension."

"I heard about that." Maggie nodded again, but offered nothing further.

"I was wondering if you could ask him about Lloyd Groves. I'm looking for a friendly introduction to him." She decided a dab of honesty wouldn't do her case any harm.

"Oh, I see. You're trying to drag me into your sordid adventure, are you?"

Judith shook her head. "Not at all. I was just thinking, who's the most connected person I can think of? And you and Fabian have history. Nobody really *knows* me..." She gave a little shrug. "Not to worry. I can easily sort it out without you."

Everybody has a trigger point. A little comment or suggestion that overrides common sense allowing people to be talked into something they'd refused to do moments earlier. Judith was aware that Maggie's trigger point was *not* being asked to do something. It invoked FOMO – the Fear of Missing Out. Implemented correctly, it would have Maggie scrambling at the bit.

"Well, I can talk to him. Maybe a text." She shrugged dismissively.

"If it's no bother, that would be wonderful. I don't want to rock the boat between you two."

"We're not in a boat!" Maggie said so sharply that it suggested Fabian had already been on her mind. Despite her enforced isolation in the village, Judith had always suspected Maggie was the sort of person who thrived on company. She hoped that her friend might find companionship as her winter years rolled into view. Not that Judith needed such things. She was quite content with her own company. Or so she kidded herself.

The little black dog of facing life alone raised its tufty-eared head, and Judith experienced a little shudder. While she was no fan of reminiscing about the past, the future was one thing Judith actively avoided thinking about.

She was saved when her mobile phone vibrated. The screen lit up with a message - somebody had triggered her front doorbell motion camera. Judith frowned and opened the app as Maggie continued her flow of consciousness. The video from the camera appeared on screen and Judith felt herself shake with a fresh wave of intrigue.

Suddenly, things were taking an unexpected turn.

Chapter Thirteen

Why was it that when people intended to perform a nefarious act, they instinctively act suspiciously? Judith wondered. It was as if it were a natural instinct built into people. A primitive inclination to do some good, by outing themselves?

She very much doubted that was the case. People tried to get away with anything they could; from pinching a biscuit to getting away with bloody murder. In Judith's experience the best way to get away with something was to do it with a smile, plain view, and maintaining eye contact, to make the other person uncomfortable. She'd always considered that was a good set of rules to live by.

From the way the torchlight bobbed inside the Rail Society's office, she doubted the intruder had considered employing a disguise, let alone subtlety. The moment she received the video alert from her doorbell camera, Judith started texting DS Collins, but stopped when she realized her own behaviour would raise more questions than she needed right now.

Instead, in lieu of the pub dinner, Judith had bought two packets of smoky bacon crinkle cut crisps to convince Maggie to accompany her on a quick drive to the Society's offices. If there was an intruder to face in the building, Judith didn't want to do it alone.

Now that they both sat in Judith's Clio, positioned diagonally across the street from the old railway station, they saw a torchlight bobbing inside and doing a laudable job of drawing attention. Had the thief simply turned on the lights, then nobody would have batted an eyelid.

"What are we doing here?" Maggie said, squinting through the car's side window as her breath slowly fogged it up. Occasional flecks of snow danced in the air outside. On their short walk across the pub car park, they had felt the temperature plummeting again, complete with the sharp smell of more snow to come.

"Trying to see who is idiotic enough to snoop around in there," said Judith, without taking her eyes from the phone screen.

"How did you know somebody had broken in?"

Judith held up her phone so Maggie could see the video stream from the doorbell camera. The image was not one of Judith's pond and driveway, but instead was the inside of the Society's office, taken at an angle from a corner shelf. It showed the thief riffling through files stacked on Augusta's desk.

"Why, you sneaky little moo-cow," snarked Maggie. "How did you do that?"

Judith pulled her finest innocent expression, which was wasted in the dark car. She had taken the camera and placed it during her brief visit there with DS Collins. Connecting it to the Society's Wi-Fi and lodging it in a shelf had been a simple case of misdirection. She wanted to get a better understanding of what was going on inside there. Like an angelic cop on her shoulder, she could hear DC Collins muttering phrases such as *'illegal surveillance'*, and other such boring legal jargon that Judith didn't think applied to her.

"So do we just sit here or go and kick the door down to arrest him?" said Maggie, crunching through her second bag of crisps. Maggie's full comprehension of modern law enforcement came solely from repeats of *Starsky & Hutch*.

"I'm not entirely certain we can do that."

Judith's eyes flickered between the phone screen and the building. She had yet to get a good look at the face. The figure suddenly became rigid and paused their search. They snatched a paper from the file for closer inspection, then stuffed it inside the open zip of their jacket. Task accomplished, they hurriedly put everything back where it belonged and, within seconds, the thief was making their way out of the office with one last sweep of light.

Judith was frustrated that she still didn't have an ID but hoped at some point on the recording she'd have a clear image of their face. She turned her phone screen off, so as not to draw attention to them in the car, just as the door to the office opened. The figure stepped out with a furtive glance around as they locked the door behind them.

"What sort of thief has a key?" Maggie asked.

"The guilty sort."

Now, under the weak light from the lamp post in the car park, she was certain it was a man who turned to face her – just as he pulled the hoodie top over his head before she got a clearer look. He didn't spot the Clio in the shadows as he jogged further up the street to a little lay-by at the side of the road and vanished from view. A moment later, car headlights switched on and a Volkswagen Beetle did a sharp U-turn, drawing an unnecessary squeal of tyres across the road as it shot past Judith and Maggie who didn't have the time nor the reactions to duck down.

Judith still hadn't had a clear view of who was inside... but she recognised the car. It was the very one she'd seen Dawn get into the night she left DC Eastly's Civic Hall meeting.

It was a delicate problem Judith now faced. People often got into trouble with the occasional mistruths and porky pies, but lately Judith felt she'd landed herself in hot water simply by not saying anything. Sometimes she pined for the good old days when a boldly told lie was worth its weight in brass, and one could get away with it accompanied by a wink and a smile.

"Did you just wink at me?" DS Raymond Collins asked uncertainly.

"I have something in my eye." Judith blinked again to justify the fib. "What is it you wanted?"

The detective lifted his mug from the kitchen table and gave a jaunty *cheers*. "One of your finest coffees."

"It's a Nespresso capsule. You could buy your own."

"You got this for free. And it would mean missing out chatting with you."

"When you knock on my door at nine in the morning, I expect it to be something urgent. I didn't know who it was. I was worried."

Collins sipped his drink and tried not to wince. He wasn't a fan of the tiny Euro-style espresso shots. He preferred a big mug of milky Nescafe instant. "Knowing you, I doubt very much you'd be worried. It's usually the person on the *other* side of the door who worries when they call here."

"No offense taken," said Judith stonily.

"And I noticed your doorbell was missing. Was it nicked?"

Judith slowly swirled her own cup without drinking it. "You must be a credit to the force. Pre-empting my doorbell theft before I can report it. Wonderful. More important than that old murder thing. How's that going?"

Raymond had been enjoying bantering with Judith. It came naturally, as if they were long-time *frenemies*. The fun was extinguished the moment she drilled down to the serious nature for his visit.

"Slowly, to be honest." He thoughtfully tapped the side of his cup as he picked his words. "There are some unusual entries in the Society's accounting ledgers." He waited for Judith to comment. When she didn't, he continued. "Payments out. Marked '*DG*'."

"And who is that?"

Collins shrugged. "I'm sure Augusta Calman would know. After all, she's the one who recorded them. And right now, she is a key suspect."

"Then ask her."

"In an investigation, one needs to tread delicately."

"You don't want to spook the pigeons."

"I was going to say *sheep*."

"That's your psychological issue I have no wish to explore."

"The other person who may know is Barbara Dixon. She

arranged events, so will be aware of what payments were needed to be made."

"I see. And what is stopping you from asking her?"

"It would require another formal interview and it may be nothing."

"Or it may throw the sheep amongst the pigeons if you have financial irregularities."

"Oh, we have those, too. Several-hundred grand is missing."

That got a reaction from Judith. "That's a little vague."

"Two hundred on the surface, but it could be more. It's not clear yet. Either way, it's not chump change. Augusta claims it was a virus. A scam. But nobody else seems sure. I was hoping you could have a word with Barbara Dixon about how they deal with billing for events so we can construct a picture of how they financially operate."

"And you want me to do it quietly."

Raymond nodded. "On the ball, as usual." He sipped his coffee, which tasted worse the more it cooled down.

"Of course. You could have asked me that on the phone. So, there is something else. Something you're not sure you should tell me."

Collins' mug hit the table with an overly loud thud. "What makes you say that?" He followed Judith's gaze to his own hand. His finger was tapping the side of the cup.

"You don't so much have a *tell*, as a *shout*. We really must play a few hands of poker one day."

"Then you operate under the mistaken belief detectives get paid well." He sighed and rearranged himself in the chair, placing his elbows on the table as he rested his chin on his hands. He'd been up most of the night fretting since he'd received the call from forensics. "The deceased... isn't the deceased. He's very much the opposite."

"The pair of legs poking from the furnace are alive?"

"You were right. They don't belong to Herbert Holland."

"Well, somebody hasn't misplaced them! Who do they belong to?"

"That we can't tell yet. There is nothing on the bloodwork, and the dental records we fished from the grate don't match anybody so far."

Judith's brow furrowed. "A lot of people get dental work done abroad these days. Then where is Herbert?"

"That's the magic question. Is *he* the killer? Money vanishes. We all think he's dead. And around and round the investigation goes."

"To make things clear. You want me to ask about a few obscure references in the accounting, while you get to hunt down a missing person?"

"Well, I am the lead detective. And don't forget, they finally put Al Capone behind bars for tax evasion." He drummed his fingers on the table – then stopped when he saw Judith glancing at them. "Of course, this adds a different dimension to the case. Whether he's lying low or has already fled the country, we still have an unidentified body."

"Are you planning on telling the others?" DS Collins' hesitation was all Judith needed. She gave a knowing nod. "Of course not, in case one of them is in on it."

She looked thoughtfully out of the kitchen window. Once again, fine flakes of snow were falling. Collins didn't want to interrupt her locomotive of thought. "The man Herbert was with at the pub, the afternoon *somebody* was killed. That could be the victim."

"A strong possibility. Only we don't have a clue who he

is. There's no CCTV. No record of the car he was driving. As of now, we must work on the assumption that Herbert Holland could be the killer." He rubbed his eyes. The lack of sleep was catching up, and he worried how he was going to make it past lunch. "Have you found out anything useful?"

Judith pursed her lips, then gave a single shrug.

"Nothing as shocking as this. I will get onto Barbara and let you know."

That was the point she knew she should have told him everything she'd unearthed, but that seemed more of a faff. She already knew exactly who she needed to talk to next.

Chapter Fourteen

To get results, you just often had to flush out your prey. Judith pulled up outside Dawn Sanders's house and took in the modest semi-detached. For Little Pickton, it would have been considered a new build, having been erected in the fifties. Somewhere along the way, the owner jumped onto the trend of stylishly pebble dashing the front, and subsequent occupants had never had the courage to remove it. Dawn's dented Volkswagen Beetle was parked in the inclined driveway. The gentle powdering of snow hadn't yet covered the wheel tracks from the night before. Judith smiled inwardly; some tracks were almost impossible to erase.

It was about ten fifteen by the time she'd ushered DC Collins from her bungalow, which had been more difficult than she'd expected. He wasn't looking forward to the graft work the new revelations necessitated and was dragging his heels, even if he was struggling to make small talk.

Judith climbed from her car, blowing into her cupped hands for warmth as she slammed the door shut with a sharp swipe of her bottom. She walked up the driveway slowly enough that she could peek through the car windows without bending, but she was hampered by a fine layer of ice that turned them opaque. She rang the doorbell. A traditional bell chimed inside and a few moments later Dawn opened the door with a broad smile. She was wrapped in a fluffy dressing gown, with cartoon birds and teddy bears printed across it. Her smile vanished when she saw it was Judith. Dawn sharply tugged the gown closed and knotted belt the as she squinted inquisitively at her unwelcome guest.

"Ms Spears, isn't it?"

"Well remembered, Dawn." Judith flashed a jaunty smile. "I do hope I'm not disturbing you. I was just passing by, and I had a few questions I wanted to float past you regarding this dreadful business." Dawn's hesitation indicated that refusal was imminent. Judith's face transformed to one of desperation. "It's just that you're the only one who can help me. You're the important one, after all."

Dawn's lips twisted as she fought her natural urge to embrace the flattery. She looked up and down the street, as if reassuring herself Judith hadn't rolled up in a police car.

"Well, um..."

"Oh, it'll be no bother, I assure you. As I said, I need somebody smart to help me." Judith gave a helpless shrug, designed to fluff Dawn's ego. Anybody who dressed like Dawn wasn't sending signals that she was an introvert; it was shouting that she was an attention seeker who thrived off being noticed. Flattery was her trigger point. "It's a bit chilly this morning. I think we're in for more snow," Judith said as she glanced up at the hazy grey sky and gave an overly exaggerated shiver.

"You better come in then. Although I don't have too

long." Dawn opened the door wider and gave a last look up and down the street as Judith entered.

The inside of the house was pretty much as Judith had imagined. There was a fluffy red throw over the sofa that looked as if a shaggy bear had turned punk moments before it died. The sideboards were adorned with cheesy porcelain animal miniatures. The few pictures on the wall were mostly of Dawn posing with friends and family. In one, she was travelling through a wilderness and gesticulating to a distant peak. In another she was standing in a river, soaked to the bone and loving every moment of it. Another showed her with three other women crammed together in front of a Gordian knot of a roller coaster. On the desk was a stack of Tui holiday brochures, with more upmarket vendors who provided tailored travel experiences, tucked underneath.

Dawn flopped into an armchair, which Judith noted was one of those super-comfy leather jobs that reclined back and was positioned perfectly in front of the television, confirming that Dawn lived alone.

"What is it you wanted to ask me?"

"It's regarding some of the intricacies about how the Society was put together. I'm just trying to get a better picture of how it ran. I mean, I've always been a fan of our village having its own railway, and I remember it being quite a stir when you announced the Lottery money."

Dawn relaxed a little, folding her hands over her lap. "Oh, it was fantastic. You know, nobody thought we'd get it, but Lloyd was quite adamant. And it was muggins here," she indicated herself with her thumb, "that created the formula for a successful bid. But still, it did seem like a dream come true, and no mistake."

Judith nodded in agreement and leaned forward a little

in her seat. "A dream for a while, then some elements of a nightmare, I hear." Dawn rolled her eyes but didn't comment. "Lloyd and Herbert took all the credit for setting it up."

"Credit they talked up. Nobody else ever said they did it; it was something they'd mention in press releases. How *they* did it all." Leading the interviews was a technique most politicians employed. Don't answer the question, answer the question with the subject *you* want to promote. Dawn tensed. "Before all of this, I had a proper job with real skills. I did a bit of computer work for big companies around London. That landed me at a boring helpdesk. At least I got to travel a bit, but I hated the nine-to-five grind. When the opportunity for the Society came along, I jumped on it."

"What did you used to do?"

"I used to work in IT support. Nothing exciting. Mostly customer service. Trust me, life in a call centre is purgatory, but you're forced to learn people skills. I was glad to see the back of it. But I like talking to people and fancied trying my hand at PR, so I made sure that was the role I took before we brought on the others." She waved her hand dismissively. "Public relations are easy. There are very few people who turn down the opportunity to ride on a steam train. Although it's tougher when you start hittin' them up for more money."

"I suppose there is no such thing as bad press."

"There is when somebody corks it on the very thing you're promoting to kiddies and families. The events for the rest of the year have all been cancelled. The lead up to Christmas should be as busy as the summer. We used to set up a German market around the train in Denzel Green. Now, nobody wants to be strollin' around a festive do and be reminded that somebody was killed."

"You have a point."

"Of course I do. The period between New Year and Easter is traditionally quiet and tough. It'll be a struggle for us to survive." She looked disheartened by the prospect.

"I assume if it's expected, then you have cash reserves to pay the wages and bills between now and then. So that's a saving grace."

Dawn didn't meet Judith's eyes, but instead stared at a fixed point over the TV screen bolted to the wall.

"I don't think there is anything left." Dawn's voice was monotonous. "Sometimes, you've got to let things go. Or maybe, move on to new things. Better things. Not a flippin' help desk"

"You sound like a woman with a plan."

"Oh, I've got several of those." Dawn's mouth twitched in a mischievous smile before she remembered herself. "Always thinkin' ahead even in the direst of circumstances. Poor Herbert." She added the last almost as an afterthought. She glanced at her watch.

"Excuse me a mo. Got to attend the lavvy" She leapt from her seat and hurried into the kitchen, closing the door behind her. She was gone for a couple of minutes, and sadly didn't return with a cuppa as Judith hoped.

"Are you okay?"

"Stomach's a bit off," Dawn mumbled, sitting back down. Her cheeks were flushed. Judith thought it best not to be the next person into the bathroom.

"I would love to know how you set things up. That's what I'm interested in. I can't remember who it was who sang your praises about being the brains behind the Society..."

Dawn's cheery visage broke her concern. "I bet that was Derek!" She stared back at a point above the television before continuing. "It was *my* idea to go for the grant. Lloyd is an ex-City trader so used to cavorting with investors, but he didn't understand how people might not have the same enthusiasm he has for renovatin' a railway line that goes nowhere."

"Renovating it?"

"As a museum. That was his original idea. It was Herbert who pressed for buying the train to tun. A more attractive idea, and much more expensive."

"Without money, dreams can't come true. That's a harsh fact of life that Disney films don't teach you. But they secured the money."

"*I* secured the money. We wouldn't have had the Lottery grant if I hadn't filled out the application, done all the research, made sure we ticked every box, and used some PR magic in drafting the proposal. Without me, it just simply wouldn't have happened. They wouldn't have then got their investors."

"I'm sure they were very grateful."

Dawn's face clouded. "I–" Her revelation was interrupted by the doorbell chime. Dawn shot to her feet. "Oh, you have to go!"

As the bell impatiently rang again, Judith was marshalled from the living room to the front door. Dawn opened it and was greeted by Derek wearing a lewd smirk.

"Here's the big D–" he began before spotting Judith. He suddenly clamped his mouth shut.

Judith gave a nod of acknowledgement. "Oh, have you got a problem with your pipes, love?" She asked Dawn innocently. Derek uttered a series of noises without offering a real answer. "This one's very handy. He'll sort out any wet patches you have." Judith experienced mischievous glee in seeing Dawn's cheeks burn bright red. "Well, have a fantastic morning."

She strolled towards her car. She hadn't even walked past the Volkswagen before the front door slammed behind her, with Derek safely ensconced inside. The handyman's van was parked a hundred yards further up the street, despite the ample parking spaces directly outside the house. Now the question forming in Judith's mind was whether Derek was the man she'd seen in the Society's office?

For her next unscheduled appointment, Judith drove from Dawn's house towards Barbara's cottage. Although a short journey, the snow and icy conditions of Little Pickton's untreated roads forced her to drive with extreme caution. She thought of herself as a competent driver. She'd even completed an advanced driving test, and a friend had once given her a day's stunt driving lesson as a gift day out. All fun but not of great use when dealing with genuine icy roads. The one rule she always abided by was believing that *every other driver* on the road was a pillock, which forced her to keep alert.

The slow pace gave her time to mull over what she'd learnt from Dawn. She and Derek were having an affair. Dawn's admiration for the man was blatantly on display since fawning over him in the village hall. She didn't doubt the rest of the Society members knew about their liaison. It was whether they cared that was important. Who knew? Did Herbert...?

She had to force herself to automatically kept thinking of him as the *victim*. Now he was the suspect, which was quite an inconvenient thing to mix up in a murder inquiry.

However, there was doubt in her mind that was the case. After walking around his home, she couldn't picture Herbert as a killer. Naturally, even the most twisted, devious mind could hide behind the mask of a man who played with toy trains. But combined with pictures and videos she'd seen of him on YouTube, she doubted he possessed the raw physicality needed for murder. He was a slight man, more naturally positioned as a victim.

Perhaps he had taken the money, the victim found out, and Herbert had been forced to kill to cover his tracks. Or if he'd taken the money, then perhaps Herbert had planned to share it with the killer who had then grown greedy and decided to do him over.

Judith bobbed her head as she mused over that. The theory had a trace of authenticity, but it relied on the utterly bonkers notion that the arguing thieves had made their escape on a slow steam train along a track that went nowhere.

There were too many questions begging for answers. What were Dawn and Derek searching for in the office? What had the police had overlooked in the Society records? Maybe the Society wasn't fully aware of Derek and Dawn's liaison, and they'd been trying to hide evidence of their infidelity? Judith filed that away. And mentally lined up the rest of the suspects.

It was Augusta who had brought her into this with the spectre of financial irregularity and the miscarriage of justice. She had told Lloyd, who hadn't apparently done anything with that information other than keep it quiet from the others. That had resulted in her pleading for Judith's help. The only issue Judith had with that, was DS Collins had just told her there was possibly more money missing than

Augusta had revealed. Was that an oversight on Augusta's part? After all, she was under a lot of pressure. But she was a competent accountant, with no apparent reason to lie, so that didn't ring true.

Judith once again swapped her line-up of suspects around. Barbara liked to play the enigma and cloak herself behind a wall of mystery. But Judith had her pegged as a good old-fashioned eccentric. Capable of murder? Possibly. Capable of large financial fraud? Very unlikely.

The gears in Judith's car gave a grinding phellem-like noise as she changed down to tackle a hill. The engine whined a series of almost comprehensible abuse as she sped up. And with it her thoughts galloped through the rest of the Society suspects.

Aside from Herbert, Lloyd Groves was in the position of being the one with the least to gain by stealing from his own company. As far as she could tell, the company had been doing well, so what motivation would he have for sabotaging that? Who had it in for him? Perhaps James Wani. Wani projected the image of somebody thoughtful, meek even. But she recalled his impulsive behaviour in the village hall.

Further pondering would have to wait as she crested the hill and tackled the curving slope that offered a lovely view of the rolling hills surrounding Little Pickton. The landscape was of little interest to Judith as her foot tapped the braked pedal.

What was of more immediate interest was why her brakes were not working.

The little red Clio picked up speed as it careened down the icy road. With a drop to one side, and the untreated icy bend ahead, Judith was suddenly running out of options regarding how to stay alive.

Chapter Fifteen

Judith Spears had once been on a date with a young chap who took her on the waltzer at Blackpool Pleasure Beach. She'd been so violently ill, that the ride had to be shut down and, as far as she was aware, industrially cleaned.

The car crash she was experiencing brought that moment to mind, but without the added humility of being escorted home by her lovely date, who then subsequently lost her phone number and never again stepped foot into the pub where they'd met. Apparently, *eau de vomit* wasn't a fragrance anybody was clamouring for.

As the back of the Clio fishtailed around, Judith tried to counter it by twisting the steering wheel in the opposite direction, just as she'd been taught. It did absolutely nothing. The gradient of the hill increased, and the car inevitably slid towards the raised embankment on the right-hand side. Which was preferable than the steep drop to the left.

The car struck the embankment with a deep crunch of metal accompanied by a stereophonic crack of breaking glass.

Her little Clio was now facing in the wrong direction and rolling backward. To her surprise, she'd remembered to stop pumping her foot on the brakes, and instead managed to shift into first gear to help her slow down. Still, the ice swept the car towards the edge. Fortunately, Judith could only see this through her rear-view mirror, which limited the terror. Seconds later, the impact with the flimsy crash barrier caused the mirror to fall from its mount. Her tummy lurched as the vehicle bounced off the road and careened, backwards, down a sharp gully.

That was the last she recalled.

When she woke up, the car had come to a stop against a tree. She'd missed the fun part of the entire experience and was left with a view back up to the steep gully to the road she had just departed.

Judith took a deep breath and slowly flexed her arms, legs, and neck, relieved to feel nothing more than a dull throbbing pain. Nothing appeared broken. The car's engine had stalled, and the silence was broken only by the plink of rapidly cooling metal. She was somewhat irritated that the airbag hadn't deployed, not that she had needed it, but it would have been nice to know it worked when it counted.

The next half hour comprised her rattling the car door until it finally opened, and she scrambled up the slick incline on her hands and knees as she waded through knee-deep snow. Reaching the road, she finally looked down to see a trail of car parts leading to her old workhorse, which was nothing more than a red scar in the snow. The exhaust pipe lay in two sections, and she was sure that the chassis shouldn't be bent in the middle.

At least standing back on the road, she had a decent signal on her phone to call for help. She thought of asking Maggie, but what could she do. Then she considered the RAC, but suspected they'd charge her for the privilege. Instead, she made a quick call to DC Eastly. She spent another twenty minutes shivering and marching up and down the road to keep warm, before an unmarked Peugeot police car skidded to a halt with a blue light on the dashboard and the siren yodelling. It was rather dramatic, and unnecessary, but she appreciated the effort as DS Collins leapt out, leaving the engine running.

He took in the situation with wide eyes.

"Are you hurt?" he barked, checking Judith up and down, with a surprising amount of concern.

"No, just freezing." She was shaking from the cold as she looked wistfully at her car. All the windows were broken. The back and one side were completely bashed in, with the paintwork stripped to the metal where it had scraped against the embankment. "I don't think the garage will be able to buff that out."

DC Eastly joined them, having the sense to turn the car engine off and retrieving a medical kit from the boot. Judith was thankful for the silver foil blanket that she draped over her, with constant murmurings that everything was going to be alright.

"Stop fretting, dear," Judith assured her. "I'm just a little shaken, and cold," she added with a meaningful look towards the warm police car.

"On the plus side, your menacing streak on the roads is finally over," Raymond said flippantly as Eastly carefully waded down the snowy incline towards the wreck.

"I don't think the exhaust pipe is supposed to be there... or there. That's a write off."

Judith sniffed indignantly. "It had nothing to do with my

driving, good or bad. And the facts suggest that I am rather good, as I survived without killing anybody."

"Because there was thankfully nobody to hit."

"I must have hit a patch of black ice on the hill and flew off. All I require is a nice, warm alcoholic drink."

Raymond nodded. "We'll have to wait for the tow truck, clear this mess up, before we get going."

He led her back to the car and opened the rear door for her, before climbing in the driver's seat and turning on the engine and cranking the heating up to full blast. Just as the chill was being vanquished, they heard the faint sounds of Sarah Eastly calling for him.

Raymond huffed as he opened the door. "Wait here. She probably can't get back up."

Judith watched him descended the slope, then closed her eyes. She felt drowsy now the rush of excitement was wearing off. When she opened her eyes, Eastly and Collins were climbing back into the car, shivering and rubbing their hands for warmth. They both looked grim.

"Maybe ice wasn't the problem." Raymond finally said.

"Are you attacking my driving again?"

He hesitated for so long, Sarah chipped in. "Your brake cables have been slashed."

If she was expecting Judith to give an explosion of astonishment, then she was bang out of luck. Instead, Judith nodded.

"Are you sure?"

"Pretty certain. There's brake fluid sprayed underneath your car. You see on TV, people cutting a pipe, so the brakes don't work. In reality, that means you're not going to get very far before noticing. The way to do it is by slitting a hole in the pipe to allow the fluid to gradually drain under pressure. Then, when it's gone, you're in severe trouble."

Despite the thermal blanket she had wrapped tightly around her shoulders, Judith felt a chill. "You're certain it was sabotage and not a mechanical fault?"

The detectives swapped a look, and Raymond nodded.

"It looks like a sharp knife was used to run through an inch or so of pipe on all four wheels." He extended his thumb and forefinger to illustrate the size of the scar. "We're going to have to investigate it properly, but on the surface, I would say that was a deliberate act. Which makes this attempted murder. Who would do such a thing?" A smile crossed his face, and he opened his mouth to add a morbid punchline, then quickly thought better not to. "Being the detective I am, I reckon you've found out something ahead of us regarding this case."

Judith sat silently, probably for too long, as she digested this latest information. She hadn't intended to tell them just yet about the previous night's antics, but now things had stepped up a notch, it was no longer the time for a game of one-upmanship. She told them everything she had seen at the railway office, and her encounter with Dawn and Derek. As her tale started from the stakeout across the street from the Society's office, she craftily edited out any indication of misusing her home doorbell camera. Luckily, the two detectives were so focused on the broader picture they didn't probe into what had led her there.

"Blimey," said Sarah Eastly, expelling a long blast of air. "So, Derek Rivan is our killer."

Judith's eyebrows rose quizzically as she stared at the ravine, prompting Eastly to speak again.

"You don't look convinced by the obvious? If he'd just

turned up when you were inside, then he had the opportunity and motive. And he's an engineer. He'd know exactly what to do. Was there anyone else around?"

Judith shook her head. She was only half-listening. Sarah couldn't resist a little smile. "So, I think you've just helped us make this an open and shut case. Derek breaks into the office to find something that may incriminate him. You turn up at Dawn's the next morning. He sees you parked outside. Panics. Knackers your brakes and off the road you go. A failed assassination!" She couldn't hold back the glee in her voice.

"Well, I suppose all we need now is some actual *evidence* that it was Derek," Raymond said, warming to the subject. "But well done, Judith. That's a heck of a breakthrough."

Again, her uncharacteristic silence caused the detectives to swap another concerned look.

"We should get you to the hospital," said Sarah, squeezing Judith's hand.

Judith smiled. "Honestly, I'm fine. Just a little shaken. It's not every day that you're a target for a hit!"

She was saved from any further mollycoddling when the tow truck arrived. It was almost two hours after the incident when Judith was able to return home. She whiled away the rest of the afternoon in a bubble bath, with Radio Four playing quietly in the background for company.

On the drive back, DS Collins was increasingly excited by the prospect of exposing an assassin. But Judith was increasingly unconvinced. She asked about progress on the victim's identity. Amazingly, it was still a mystery. She tried to be delicate when she politely pointed out that they had a murder case with an unknown victim and an unknown killer. Her near-death experience was hardly a breakthrough.

She turned the bath taps off and relaxed in the warm cocoon of suds that teased out the bruises blossoming across her body. She closed her eyes and fell into a deep slumber, only waking up when the water became tepid, and it was dark once again outside.

And as she lay in bed, she then began to ponder what exactly it was the mystery killer thought she knew. What had she stumbled across, and overlooked, that had rattled them so much, they were willing to kill again?

Chapter Sixteen

The following morning, after a surprisingly easy round of phone calls to her insurance company, Judith felt her crash-induced fatigue ebbing away. Maggie became her knight in shining armour, or rather her taxi driver in a yellowing Ford Focus that had certainly seen better days and absolutely better colour schemes.

Judith took the opportunity to join Maggie who was driving to Denzel Green, where she had arranged to meet up with Fabian Heinzel. Obviously, her WhatsApp messages spiralled into something more, but Judith thought it wasn't the time to pry. She hoped Maggie would be able to squeeze some information out of him, while Maggie could relive whatever drama she felt had befallen their previous liaisons. Judith decided it best not to mention that some fiend had cut her brake cables and instead blamed the crash on icy conditions.

Judith armed Maggie with a list of questions about the Rail Society, with a particular bent on the business pact between them and the town. Judith had suggested joining them, but Maggie issued a sonorous grumble that was so foreboding, she quickly backtracked on the suggestion.

They parked in the Denzel Green station car park, with Maggie performing an elaborate five-point turn to reverse into the space, all the while darkly muttering that cars should never go backwards. A sentiment Judith agreed with. As Judith hunted down the pay and display ticket machine, Maggie sat in the vehicle preening her hair with a diligence that Judith had never seen before. It hinted at how she expected the lunch with Fabian to end, which would mean Judith may well have to get the bus back home.

Denzel Green was almost twice the size of Little Pickton and came with the arrogant swagger of a town lording over its village sibling. It had a picturesque large square outside the town hall, with the surrounding buildings clad in meticulously cleaned Cotswold stone and sporting colourful roofs of reds and light greys. It was a frosty afternoon, and teams were already putting up bunting and decorations for the upcoming Winter Market. The train station was perfectly positioned two hundred yards from the square, with only a single level crossing disturbing the traffic flow. The Society's tank engine had been scheduled to attend, decorated like a character from *Thomas the Tank Engine* for photo opportunities, but the booking had been the first one cancelled.

Judith decided to slowly circulate the town and take in the atmosphere. She was distracted by unwelcome thoughts of her crash that she almost didn't notice Lloyd Groves briskly overtaking her. He didn't give any sign of recognition. He kept his head down and his hands shoved in his tweed shooting jacket pockets. Sensing opportunity, Judith furtively fell in step behind him as he entered the library.

She pretended to read the noticeboard as he headed

straight for the reading desks. The excuse she was formulating to use for bumping into him fizzled when she saw that he headed for James Wani. The engineer was still wearing a large bubble jacket, zipped up despite the tropical heat inside the building. He sat hunched over the table, not wishing to be recognised, but in doing so had made himself the most obvious person in the building. His right leg nervously pumped ten to the dozen, and it increased in pace as Lloyd sat opposite. Lloyd's hands were folded over one another on the desk, and his manner remained cool and aloof.

Judith hurried down an aisle of self-help books so she could move within hearing range. By the time she drew close, both men were leaning across the desk face-to-face in a heated whispered exchange. She could make out nothing more than irascible hissed syllables. Whatever was being said, James Wani was becoming increasingly angry, whereas Lloyd remained unreadable.

Eventually, James shoved a bag for life across the table. Judith couldn't see what was in it, but it prompted the first genuine reaction from Lloyd, whose brow furrowed as he quickly took it from the table and placed the bag on the floor between his feet.

The rendezvous lasted less than five minutes, and James was the first to leave. He sharply stood and threateningly shook a finger in Lloyd's face before marching from the library, pulling his hood over his head.

Judith hesitated. Should she follow him? After all, she hadn't yet spoken to him. Or should she stick with the more enigmatic Lloyd to see what he was up to? In the end, Judith went for the third option that was more in keeping with her spontaneous, boisterous instinct.

"Lloyd! *Cooee!*" she cried loudly. She waved with both hands, drawing every eye in the library towards them. "Fancy bumping into you here. What are the chances?"

Lloyd looked briefly surprised, before he relaxed back to its unreadable state. "Ms Spears. Indeed, how peculiar."

Judith sat in James' vacated seat and laid both palms on the table as if getting ready to spring for him. He had instantly recognised her, and the use of *Ms* was already triggering alarm bells. They hadn't been introduced in the village hall, indicating he had done some swotting up on who she was. Reading character was an art Judith had finessed and used regularly, if not entirely inappropriately. Behind the façade, Lloyd Groves was an easy read. Confidence bordering on arrogance, wrapped in calculating pleasantness. Judith felt a thrill that had long been dormant. An equal battle of wits.

She acted the giddy goat. "Oh, Ms, Mrs, Miss is all such nonsense, isn't it? People these days!" She rolled her eyes. "So of course you see why I'm so happy to bump into the man behind the Society. I tried calling your office, but nobody seems to be answering." Her trademark smile didn't flicker as she laid on the bubble-brain and ego-praising double-combo.

"Everybody is working from home, not that there is much any of us can do. It's a public relations nightmare."

"I feel so sorry for you. I've always been such a fan of what you achieved, although for the life of me I can't imagine what Herbert was doing taking the train out so late in the first place."

"Checking for mechanical issues, no doubt."

"In the dark?"

Lloyd's shoulders bobbed with the slightest of shrugs.

"Who knows what was on his mind?" He leaned in a little, sharing his inner thoughts. "You think you know somebody, and then something like this happens and you realise there was much more going on than you imagined."

"Oh! Intrigue!"

Lloyd's lips twisted into a thin smile. "Just the sort of grist an amateur sleuth like you thrives on."

Judith nodded eagerly. "Do you mean he was up to no good?"

Lloyd raised both palms to deflect the question. "I do not know what he was up to. It was something he never shared with me. He was always secretive, and lately doubly so. It made me so terribly anxious."

"But to move an entire train. Surely that would take several people?"

"Two. Yes. It is possible to do it alone, of course. He's done it many times before. I've had words with him before about it. It's not safe, and it's against our insurance policy."

"Why would he do such a thing?"

Lloyd weighed his words before speaking. "He had an obsessive personality. He often saw the entire Society as his plaything rather than a team effort with people's livelihoods at stake."

"When of course, it was yours and his. And Dawn's, I believe." At the mention of Dawn's name, Lloyd's shoulders tensed, and he clasped his fingers together. Judith was pleased to have finally extracted a genuine reaction from him. "I mean, after talking to her, I can't see how anybody would believe it was all her idea," Judith hastily added. "But she likes the glory, I suppose."

"Of course it wasn't. It was *my* idea. She has a habit of

always claiming success and denying responsibility when things go wrong."

Judith nodded in agreement. "That was my assessment, too."

Lloyd smiled. It never quite reached his eyes. Judith couldn't shake a caricature of the Big Bad Wolf from the children's story.

"Do you think she or James would know why he would take the train out alone?"

Lloyd shrugged and pushed back his chair as he made ready to leave. "You should ask them. And don't forget Derek. They all had their issues with Herbert, but he and Herbert..." He gave a sad shake of the head. "I tried not to get involved in personal bickering. I was burnt by that before. It was interesting bumping into you, Ms Spears, but I must go." He slipped his hand inside his jacket and produced his wallet that was swollen with ten- and twenty-pound notes. He produced a business card and used one finger to slide it across the table. Judith picked it up and examined the stylish steam train depicted on the face. "Please keep in touch. If there is anything you wish to talk to me about, please call me directly."

Lloyd scooped the bag from between his legs and deliberately held it so that it hung out of view behind his bottom. Even so close, Judith couldn't guess at the contents. With a sharp nod of the head, Lloyd Groves made a quick exit from the library.

Keep your friends close and enemies closer, Judith thought as she toyed with the business card. Lloyd certainly knew what he was doing, and that was deflecting attention away from himself with the use of charm and passive accusations. Had he played along with the deceased being Herbert Holland, or did he genuinely not know?

She drummed her fingers as she worked on that idea. If he was working on the assumption Herbert had died, then that meant he'd inherit the entire business. A strong motivation for murder... except at this point, only the killer knew the identity of the victim. That indicated Groves was innocent. Of the murder at least.

He had planted enough breadcrumbs to have both Eastly and Collins scrambling all the way to the bakery, but he had made a subtle mistake by leaving a gap in his trail, and at the same time highlighting a gap that the investigation had overlooked. That was something Judith fully intended to address today. But as she drew her phone from her pocket and saw the waiting messages, that would not be as straightforward as she liked.

Chapter Seventeen

Maggie's message briefly told her that the lunch non-date with Fabian Heinzel had gone spectacularly well. She hadn't responded to the three messages Judith had sent in reply, which meant she was stranded in Denzel Green. If only there was a train that she could get back home. Instead, she sought the bus timetables on the library noticeboard. Next to them was a poster campaigning for the rail link between Denzel Green and Fulton to be renovated. She made a note of the email and phone number, then made her way to the bus stop to wait forty minutes for the bus. She resorted to checking the time on her phone because her trusty little Cartier watch had finally given up the ghost after the crash. She was surprised by how sad she felt at losing her valiant companion; it upset her more than the loss of her car.

Since the crash, she couldn't quell the anxiety of calling for a taxi. The journey with Maggie had been bearable as they talked the entire way, but the underlying tension of who sabotaged her brakes refused to ease.

DS Collins had made it clear that he thought Derek Rivan was his man, but Judith doubted the engineer had the gumption for such an audacious act. But then who did? She had her suspicions.

After a thankfully slow bus journey along treacherous slushy roads that set Judith's nerves on edge, she finally alighted in Little Pickton's High Street. With a glance at the time on her phone, she briskly marched towards the church for her pre-determined rendezvous. She heard the mass baying before she turned the corner and spotted Charlie Walker being pulled in half a dozen directions by the dogs he was walking. Or more accurately, being dragged along by.

"Judith! They were just beginning to get restless. Do you want to take a couple?" He offered a hand stuffed with three leads.

Judith remained just at the edge of their range as the dogs strained for her, tails wagging and tongues lolling. "Hello boys and girls!" She offered the back of her gloved hands and was immediately soaked with friendly slobber by two of them. The third sniffed, but kept her jaws clamped firmly on a toy. "I think it best you keep them, Charlie."

Charlie made a decent living as the village dog walker and, when needed, sitter. He also conducted a profitable side-line in tending pets at home, from fish to cats, which was an in-demand service. And on one occasion, a horse. That meant he knew a huge portion of the residents and had become a well-respected figure. She'd even heard whispers of people suggesting he deserved an MBE for his services to people's holidays. Judith thought that may be going a tad too far.

Charlie had agreed to meet Judith at the start of his afternoon round from the church to the duck pond, circling around the cricket ground, the spinneys, and back into the village. The animals led the way, enforcing a brisk trot.

"I wanted to pick your brain about the morning you discovered the murder," Judith said between gasps. Charlie was a hardened soul after spending time in the military. It was the RAF admittedly, and as a member of the ground crew he was safely away from conflict, but he *came across* as an unshockable figure. However, the mention of murder made him blanch.

"It was awful. I don't mind saying. I used to enjoy taking the dogs along the track. There's never anybody around and it's a beautiful walk. I'm not in a rush to do that again any time soon."

"I can see it must have been an awful shock. What happened exactly?"

Charlie walked in silence for a few yards as he recalled the morning. Just as Judith was about to prompt him, he began from the moment he'd picked Reeta up. An old black Labrador he'd had a several-year relationship with because her owner was no longer mobile enough to walk her.

"That's her." He indicated to the Labrador that had greeted Judith with her mouth still firmly around her toy. Flecks of white hair around the muzzle and her barrel-like body betrayed her waning years.

In measured tones, he painted a vivid picture of the frosty morning and the silence of the woods as he'd stumbled across the train. Judith listened without interruption as he recounted calling the police and hurrying back to the car park to meet the responding officer.

He shivered at the recollection. "It was the smell that was most horrible." Then, after a thoughtful pause, he amended that to: "No. It actually smelled alright. Until I knew what it was. I've been a vegetarian ever since," he added as a sinful admission.

"Very healthy for you, too. Well done. You may outlive us all."

"It's turned my poo all weird. Like giant cow pats."

They reached the cricket pitch where some local children had made commendable snowmen to represent the batter and bowler. It was snowing again, and two of the smaller dogs were excitedly snapping at the flakes. Judith had no desire to explore the scatological effects of a veggie diet, so thought it was time to ask some questions that had been bothering her.

"Is that how you described it to the police?"

"To that Detective Sergeant fella. He asked a few questions about whether I'd seen anybody in the car park, which I hadn't. Or if there were signs of other cars recently. Of which I have no idea. He's the detective. He should be telling me."

"I don't think that's his job. Do you recall anything out of the ordinary at the crime scene?"

"Other than a steam train and half-cremated body, you mean? I wouldn't call that normal."

"I meant signs of a killer dramatically fleeing into the woods?"

Charlie shook his head. They walked a little further, with Charlie shouting at the occasional misbehaving dog, or stopping to pick up Reeta's toy and throw it ahead. The dog never attempted to run after it but enjoyed waddling to retrieve it at her own pace. The rest of the pack slowed as Charlie scooped up the inevitable dog-created poop, which stood out like a blight against the pristine snow. They were now halfway through the walk, and Charlie had many plastic bags dangling from his belt like a bandito with a bandolier of crap.

"Why do you think the train stopped there? Was there something blocking the track?"

"Not that I could see. There's a bit of a bend, then a straight run for a mile that ends in the tunnel. I don't often go that far. After that is another run straight to town."

"A tunnel?"

"Just a short thing that goes under the A-road and through a hill."

"If you were trying to commit a murder on the train, then surely that would be a better spot? Hidden from view. It would take longer to find it."

"Once the train had been reported missing, I wouldn't take a genius to track it down. Our end of the track ends in the rail shed. A side line connects a portion of it to the main line. But that's just a mile section and used for freight." It had always annoyed Judith that the nearest station was so far away. "And the other end only goes about two miles past Denzel Green before the track gets ropy. So that goes nowhere, too."

"A sensible point well made." She was sure that the flamboyant nature of the murder was designed to attract attention, at least once it was discovered. It would waste time before the inevitable discovery that the victim wasn't who they thought it was.

Judith replayed Charlie's events in her mind's eye, occasionally asking for clarification here and there. Only on her third loop of events did she pick up on something.

"You said Reeta was sniffing at the track, leading you in that direction?"

"She may be old, but she's still got a keen sense of smell.

She's a truffle hunter. You so-much as fart and she'll give you the evil eye. It was that barbecue smell she would have picked up."

"But you described her as sniffing the *sleepers*. Wouldn't she be sniffing the air if that's what got her attention? Were you up or downwind of the train?"

"Now you're asking! I'm not a big game hunter. I have no idea."

"Let's assume up-wind, or she would have picked the scent up sooner."

"Fair enough."

"So, what scent had she picked up?"

"Reeta likes to find a good stick on our walks." He rattled the back of his mind, and something popped. "That's right. She picked that bunch of twigs up." He indicated the toy in her mouth. "She doesn't normally keep the crap she finds, but I suppose as we were hanging around waiting for the coppers to arrive, she wanted something to fend the boredom off. She must be keen on it to still have it."

Judith knelt and rubbed the top of Reeta's head. The dog dropped the toy in favour of flailing her tongue and insisting Judith didn't stop scratching. Judith obliged with one hand and picked up the damp toy with the other. At first sight it was a snarl of twigs or maybe a root structure. Then she realised it was a clump of thin, dry willow branches woven together. Only when she rotated it in her hand, did she suddenly give a gasp of recognition.

"Are you sure she found this that morning?"

"Yeah. I must have thrown it for her hundreds of times."

"And how far from the train did she find it?"

Charlie looked puzzled. "I can't really say. A minute or so." After a thoughtful pause, he added: "Maybe four hundred yards as the track bent around, just before I spotted the train. Why? I don't see what the big deal is."

Judith held the bundle up so he could see it. Then she slowly rotated it. Charlie blinked in surprise as he suddenly made the connection.

"Blimey! That's a coincidence."

The twigs had been intentionally twisted into the basic form of a human figure with a square head and stubby arms and legs like a poor-man's gingerbread man. Judith was certain that it wasn't a coincidence at all.

Chapter Eighteen

Detective Sergeant Raymond Collins turned the item one way, then the other, the lines on his brow deepening with every rotation.

"I don't particularly see it myself," he said, holding Reeta's twig sculpture under the light of his desk lamp. "If you were to ask me, I would suggest maybe it's a starfish?"

DC Eastly plucked it from his fingers. "Or a really naff snowflake. Or an old star from a Christmas tree that's been gnawed at by rats."

Raymond Collins sat back in his desk chair and clasped his hands over his stomach. "You know, Eastly, there are protocols regarding how to handle evidence."

Judith sipped scalding tea from the paper cup Eastly had provided and winced as it burnt her lips. "I think Reeta may have removed the need for any such protocols, detective. I think if you ran that through any form of fancy DNA testing, you'd find a collection of slobber, past meals, and remnants of other dogs' bottoms."

Ordinarily, Judith always preferred to push ahead with

her own tangential investigations without the cumbersome need to let others know what she was up to. She would normally restrain herself from revealing everything she had discovered as the thought of gazumping the police at their own game was ingrained in her DNA. But when she'd come across Reeta's little treasure, she understood that it was her reluctant duty to hand in the evidence. After all, it might pertain to an *actual* murder. That said, when she called Detective Sergeant Collins to reveal her find, he didn't sound too enthusiastic and told her to drop it off at the station whenever she could.

As she was now a potentially failed victim in the plot, Judith was feeling closer to the case than she ought to be. After returning from the dog walk with Charlie Walker, she had sent several more text messages to Maggie, keeping them as innocuous as possible and assuring her she had managed to get home in one piece without being mugged, kidnapped or otherwise harmed, and how lovely it would be to catch up to discover what she had learnt from Fabian. She was greeted with silence. Aside from building up a possibly wrong picture of their non-date, that left Judith completely stranded in Little Pickton. The last bus all the way out to the police station in Fulton had already departed, so with the snow still falling, she trudged back to her cottage only to discover her insurance company had delivered a miracle. Her hire car was already parked in the driveway. She was stunned at the company's efficiency, having mentally allocated several days of tedious phone calls to chase it. Efficient customer service was spoiling her fun. It wasn't exactly a like-for-like model to her humble Clio. The replacement was a monster. An enormous dark blue Mitsubishi 4x4 that barely fit in the drive. It had seen better days, with scars still visible despite diligent buffing and polishing to mask them. However, it was built like a tank and perfect for the snowy conditions.

By the time she arrived at the police station, the cloak of early evening darkness had accelerated behind grey snow clouds, adding a little more treachery to the slick roads. The 4x4's diesel growl assured her that she was probably the most dangerous thing on the road right now, both to other traffic and the environment, so her anxiety softened.

She found DS Collins and DC Eastly at their desks in the open plan office, separated from the handful of CID officers by flimsy green cubical walls, one of which was covered in pictures of the Rail Society incident. After a rapid summary about how she'd found the object, Sarah had finally fetched her a cup of coffee to allow Judith to catch her breath.

"To get this straight," DS Raymond Collins said with a heartfelt sigh as he stared at the *evidence*, "the hunt for the murderer and your would-be assassin, and indeed the identity of the victim himself, you think all hinges on this bunch of twigs?" He shook it close to Judith's face for emphasis.

Judith could see that Raymond had little sleep, which also wade him irritable. And from the stack of papers on his desk and the way he astutely avoided eye contact with anyone who passed, she assumed the stress of the case was wearing him thin, so she ignored his less than passive-aggression.

"The dog fetched it off the tracks a few hundred yards from the locomotive. She caught scent of something on the rails and led Charlie to the crime scene. I think it was the same scent as that." She pointed at the bundle.

Raymond shrugged. "So, she could smell the unpleasantness." He pulled a face as he recalled the atmosphere when he'd arrived.

"Charlie was very explicit that she was following a scent on the ground, not sniffing the air. Which means a trail left by a person carrying that. And it was likely they were upwind of the crime scene."

Raymond's eyebrows bobbed in a sign he wasn't buying her logic. Eastly picked up Judith's thread.

"Are you suggesting that somebody dropped that as they walked along the track?"

Judith looked up at the scuffed ceiling tiles. "Hallelujah! The penny drops!"

It also dropped for Collins, who leaned forward in his seat. "Your saying that somebody was going to or from the crime scene carrying this?" He looked sceptical as he placed the twigs onto the table.

Judith nodded. "Until now, we have been assuming the killer was on the locomotive when it left the station. Helping Herbert drive. But when I spoke to Lloyd Groves, he suggested one person could take the engine out. As a matter of fact, Herbert had done it before."

The detectives exchanged a thoughtful look. Judith felt obliged to fill in the silence.

"Perhaps Herbert had been taking it out on its own and stopped in the middle of nowhere for the killer, sorry, victim, to join him? Then the altercation had taken place and Herbert fled back along the tracks carrying this, and maybe other possessions that would identify the victim. Did you find any evidence of somebody fleeing the crime scene?"

Eastly shook her head. "The ground was frosty. There were only footprints from the dog walker but nothing else."

"The frost may not have formed by then." Judith

pictured the night of the crime in her mind's eye. "It's a heck of a big steam train, so even idle it would have stayed hot for many hours, radiating all that heat so the area around the train wouldn't have had any frost for most of the night. I don't recall terribly much about physics from school, but I assume having travelled over the rails they too would have been warm enough to fend off frost for an hour or so. Meaning that the best way to flee the crime scene and not leave a trail would be to head back towards the village, along the line."

As she spoke, she scanned the pictures on the wall behind DS Collins' head. Images of all the Society members taken from the website, were pinned in a row, with their ages and addresses printed underneath. A map of the crime scene had the location of the engine circled, and a few photographs of the train and the victim encircled it. Sarah had grandiosely called it their murder board, but to Judith, it looked more like the scrapbook of a sick teenager.

"That would be fleeing towards the car park," Collins mused. "We found nothing there that raised suspicions. Other than Charlie Walker's vehicle, we're certain nothing had been parked there for at least twelve hours." He shook his head. "This is getting off track. I don't see what a piece of junk has got to do with anything. Dogs find dead bodies and junk. That's what they do."

"If they were upwind, Reeta wouldn't be able to pick up the scent from the locomotive. The track goes *both ways*, but she found that and seemed quite adamant about going towards the crime scene with it in her mouth. She's been using it as her chew toy ever since."

"Are you suggesting I interview her?"

"Show her your bark is worse than your bite?"

Raymond scowled. "Judith, when you said you had news,

I was hoping you'd come in here with information about the account discrepancies. Or some killer lead on a big money laundering scandal! Not waving a piece of wood in my face."

"I assure you I'm working on that," she said, putting her cup down as it was scalding her fingers, and she tapped the twigs. "What if this belonged to the killer?"

Raymond gave the bundle another cursory glance. "You pointed out the likelihood of any usable forensic evidence was almost nil. So, you're asking if somebody had fled from an early Christmas workshop carrying a bunch of decorations to a train in the middle of nowhere, then they were bludgeoned to death by Herbert Holland? And he ran away, scattering ornaments every which way?"

"That was perhaps a more embellished description of what I'm getting at, but the principle is the same."

Raymond cocked an eyebrow. "I will put out an *all-ports warning* for an elf."

"At least you'd be doing something constructive towards finding who cut my brakes," Judith replied tartly.

An embarrassed silence descended. Nobody had seen Judith cross before and she revelled in their discomfort, which had the desired effect of making DS Collins feel guilty. She treated them both to a look from the *Stern Headmistress's Handbook* and crossed her arms.

"Consider this. What if Herbert had taken the train out on his own for reasons unknown?" She waved her hand, unable to find the words to express her sentiment. "He picked up a passenger, a co-conspirator in the theft of the money, perhaps. Or maybe he was flagged down by someone attempting to stop him." Images from the classic *The Railway Children* flitted through her mind's eye. "A violent altercation ensued. Herbert is furious that his plans have been thwarted.

He kills the owner of this," she tapped the twigs. "And flees the scene of the crime carrying a few incriminating possessions to throw on a fire, far from the train."

Raymond Collins leaned back in his chair, his hands once again thoughtfully clasped across his chest and in a position that Judith was beginning to associate with his reset mode.

She scanned the murder board again. "Or perhaps he had taken something of value. Then headed back towards Little Pickton to meet his co-conspirator."

Sarah spoke up. "Co-conspirator?"

"Wherever he was going with the train, he'd need a ride on the other side. His plans took a deadly turn, so his fellow schemer had to come and pick him up." Her eyes fell back on the faces on the board. There was a picture of the Lion's Arms pub. Somebody had drawn a question mark in the corner of the page with a thick red sharpie.

Seeing everything laid out in front of her, she sensed there was a black hole sucking in the truth and deflecting the investigation through a series of misleading facts and passive accusations. "Who had Herbert met the afternoon of his death?" she mused aloud. "The victim or the accomplice?"

DS Collins sighed, drawing her back to the moment, his head tilted back with his eyes closed, and for a moment, she thought he'd fallen asleep. "This case is getting to be a real mess. The more theories you have, the more things unravel." He leaned forward and propped his elbows on the desk, resting his head in his hands. "Do you know how many homicide cases go unsolved? A good thirty-per-cent. Every detective has at least one story of that case that eluded them. Something they couldn't close. That haunts them their entire career. I don't want mine to be about a bloody steam train and a nameless victim." He suddenly caught his second wind. "This is clearly a financial crime. A sizeable sum of money has vanished. Somebody found out. Somebody was killed. And although Herbert Holland is at the centre of it all, all the evidence, and a strong detective hunch, points to Derek Rivan at the villain of the piece."

Judith's whimsical *mmm* deflated the detective's confidence. "Derek is an egotistical twerp. A man who thinks he's a Casanova, but in reality, is a poor man's Noel Fielding. He may well be a smart engineer, but he's a selfish, conniving fraud who'd happily take advantage of an old, um, middle-aged woman he deems helpless. I think he's just about as capable of conducting an elaborate financial scam as he is of correctly spelling the word *scam*."

Eastly pursed her lips. "And Dawn Sanders?"

"Dawn is a little brighter than she acts. The more I think about it, the more I wonder if *they're* the ones being set up to take the fall for a crime that they don't have the intelligence to commit."

"Oh, Judith," Raymond Collins' tone came out as a whine, bordering on pleading. "You can't take away my only lead. I'm in the process of getting a warrant to check everybody's bank accounts. The money went *somewhere*. The moment we find even a shred of it leading in their direction, we have them! Everybody makes mistakes," he added, indicating the twigs on the table. "Maybe we'll keep hold of it and put it on the office Christmas tree at the end of the year. If we ever crack this case!"

As Judith made her way to the car parked on the street outside, the plunging temperature caught her breath. She pulled the collar of her jacket a little tighter. The snow was falling with greater determination, and she judged she had little time to leave, even in a 4x4. The last thing she wanted was to be snowed out of her village when there was a nice warm bed waiting for her.

She had hoped Reeta's little piece of evidence might have triggered something meaningful, but Raymond clearly thought it was a dead end. However, the trip wasn't a complete waste. She'd had a chance to see the murder board and assess exactly where the detectives were up to in their investigation.

Not very far.

It also yielded a little nugget of information. James Wani wasn't a resident of Little Pickton, unlike the rest of the society. He was the only one who lived in Denzel Green, so Lloyd Groves had been meeting him on his home turf.

She got in the car and started the engine. Cold air blasted from the vents, but quickly turned warm as she adjusted the heating to maximum. She pulled away, pondering what Wani had passed to Lloyd Groves wrapped in a bag for life. It was something Lloyd Groves clearly felt was important enough for a clandestine meet. Blackmail documents? Or money?

The drive back home was theoretically straightforward, but with the deteriorating weather, she only passed two other cars heading in the opposite direction with their window wipers vigorously batting the increasingly heavy snow. She slowed her pace, giving careful attention to the road ahead and pumping the brakes with trepidation to ensure they were still in working order.

Approaching Denzel Green's ring road, her sixth sense tapped her brain for attention. She glanced in the rear-view mirror. There was a set of headlights, discreetly far behind. They had been following her since leaving Fulton police station. She decided to take a little detour and took a slightly longer route through the centre of Denzel Green. The car behind her followed suit, confirming what her uncanny sense had been trying to warn her.

Somebody was following Judith Spears.

Chapter Nineteen

Judith kept just below the speed limit as she passed through Denzel Green's town centre. The snowstorm was keeping everybody inside. She circled the town hall, watching in the rear-view as her pursuer circumspectly followed.

She couldn't help but wonder who would want to follow her. Had somebody been watching her talk to Lloyd Groves and was now worried she knew something incriminating? If so, that would suggest it was the brake-cutter behind her. And that didn't bode well. Judith's past had taught her to be quite artful when it came to following people, but *avoiding* surveillance wasn't something she was familiar with. Which now made improvisation the order of the day.

She casually took the exit leading back onto the ring road towards Little Pickton. Out in the countryside, there were no streetlights illuminating the way, and the snow dulled her headlights, forcing her to concentrate hard. As she hoped, the A-roads had been gritted and were still snow free. It wouldn't be a courtesy that applied to the B-roads leading home, but it was enough for her to pick up speed, briefly increasing the gap with her determined pursuer. She needed to build up enough of a lead before the series of tight curves ahead. Breaking the speed limit in dreadful weather was risky, but she goaded another ten-miles-per-hour from the engine and took the sharp bend far too quickly. Luckily, the Mitsubishi adhered to the road like glue. As soon as she was around the curve, she hit the brakes and turned sharply into a branching B-road to the left. At the same time, she turned the lights off, plunging the road ahead into darkness and making her car disappear into the shadows.

Only it didn't.

A hellish red glow lit up the road behind her. The brake lights were still on. Of course, they were not linked to the rest of the lights. She quickly turned the engine off – plunging the lane into utter darkness as, seconds later, her pursuer shot past.

Judith took a moment before restarting the engine. The lane was too narrow to turn the massive car around, so she followed it. She had no idea where it led to, but most of the roads in the area criss-crossed farmland, so, after several minutes of blindly pushing through increasingly deepening snowy tracks, she found herself on a familiar main road that led home.

By the next morning, the storm had moved on and Little Pickton found itself cut off from civilization with all roads out blocked by snow. Between flooding and blizzards, she was beginning to suspect the Four Horsemen had moved in. She'd have to talk to Father Largy about that. Not that it changed the rhythm of life in any noticeable way, but at least Judith surmised that it would keep her would-be pursuer/assassin out of her hair for the day. She had far more pressing matters in replying to Maggie's texts that had come in that morning and led them to breakfast in *Time for Tea*.

At first glance, Maggie was her usual irascible self as Judith joined her for breakfast. At second glance, she noticed the crumbs of a fruit tart on the plate to her left, while she absently stirred the tea in front of her.

"Something sweet for breakfast?" Judith said innocently.

Maggie looked everywhere except at Judith. "Always in need of a little sugar rush to perk me up in the morning. Don't do any harm."

"Especially after such a long, involved dinner," Judith said with treacle thick innocence. "I'm sure it went exhaustingly well."

"Fabian and I had a lot to catch up on, as it turns out." Maggie paid more attention to the bubbles swirling in the convection currents of her tea than was warranted. "It had been a while."

"I'm sure you've made up," Judith smiled.

This time Maggie met her gaze, and there was a flicker of mischief in her eyes. "More than that. I forgot what a hunk of fine man he was."

Judith smiled. She didn't want to tease her friend too much. If somebody was to gain a little happiness later in life, she was delighted that it was Maggie.

"He's doing well."

"Well, he's the mayor and Editor-in-Chief of the paper," Maggie said solemnly, although it was a status Fabian had insisted that he be called, rather than the more mundane sounding *chairman of the council*. It never harmed to have a little glamour in one's life, and he had bought himself a gold chain of office from eBay.

"And he acts like a king." From the look Maggie gave her, Judith could already sense that if she had dug up any dirt, it was going to be cloaked by whatever fling they'd had the previous night. "When did you get back home?"

"Oh, late last night," Maggie mumbled, once again studying the composition of her cup of tea. "Lucky, otherwise, I would've been spending all day in Denzel Green. Snowed out," she said with a sigh that couldn't disguise her bad luck.

"Lucky you."

"Mmm."

"Will you be seeing more of him? That is, if there were any bits you hadn't seen."

Maggie blushed, but then quickly recovered. She frowned and tried to make herself look as stern as possible. "I think we still have a few things to straighten out, so that's a distinct possibility."

Judith raised her cup. "Cheers," she said, and sipped. "Did he shed any light on the old railway?"

Maggie paused for a long moment. "He's sad it's stopped running for now. I mean, he made it no secret that he always thought the train should be based in Denzel Green, not here. His bid for tourism, I suppose. And there's that campaign about fixing the rest of the track on to Fulton."

Judith nodded. "Yes, I've been meaning looking into that," she said, remembering the details on the poster she had seen in the library. "The problem there is, of course, the train running from Little Pickton straight through to Fulton would have no real reason to stop at Denzel Green."

"I suppose so. And, of course, he was heartbroken to hear about the murder. It doesn't look good for no one."

"Especially not the victim. I suppose with bad news befalling us, he may well get his chance to run the train *from* Denzel Green. That would be a real coup for him."

"Maybe. He said he'd been helping them with fundraising."

Judith looked nonchalantly away. The questions she had prepped Maggie to ask were very indirect. So indirect she didn't want Maggie to know what the point of them was. For example, she hadn't told her about the money designated *DG* going from the society accounts. And while Eastly and Collins strongly suspected intrigue on the Denzel Green side, Judith would be shocked if it was something so obvious, but still a lead was a lead that needed to be eliminated from their enquiries.

"Did he say how he'd been helping?" she asked.

"He helped generate more events like this Winter one. That cost a few bob, and it's not as though the town's coffers are overflowing with gold. So, they came to a deal."

"Let me guess, the society gave them money to get underway?"

Maggie nodded, her eyes lighting up as Timothy delivered two English breakfasts for the ladies. Judith hadn't been hungry, but the heady smell from the combination of bacon, eggs, fried tomatoes, and beans made her stomach rumble in the most appreciative way.

"The second-best British cuisine," Maggie said, scooping up the knife and fork from a metal pot on the table. This was a woman who considered chocolate lime sweets the pinnacle of culinary perfection. Chewing quickly, she jabbed her fork in Judith's direction. "You're right. They set these events up. Once the Society's costs are reimbursed, they share the profits. Pretty sensible, because Fabian heavily promotes it all in his newspaper. That's about the thick of it, I think. He said it was Augusta who dealt with the money, Barbara with the organisation, and Dawn with the publicity." After rounding up more breakfast onto her fork and eating it with one gulp, she finally added: "Now Augusta's a shifty one."

"That's quite a thing to say," said Judith. "I thought you didn't know the woman?"

"I'm just telling you what Fabian told me. It was her that got Lloyd Groves divorced in the first place."

"Well, that sounds like scandal. If that's the case, but I assume nothing was ever proven?"

"Oh, it never is! And folks always get the wrong end of the stick," Maggie added. "I mean, I'd blamed Fabian for...." She tailed off as she scooped up a fork-load of beans and egg and slipped them into her mouth. Maggie had always been coy about the details of her previous rendezvous with the mayor.

"Oh, you thought Fabian had been up to no good. I hope that's resolved."

Maggie almost choked as she gave a sharp laugh. She quickly swallowed. "No, he accused *me* of having intentions... elsewhere," she said haughtily.

That surprised Judith. Maggie was a woman of solid morals. Perhaps not strictly the most *moralistic* of morals, but she had firm standards and beliefs, and Judith would never question her loyalty or allegiance. Which made it even more intriguing as to what Fabian had thought she'd done. But she drew her thoughts back to the subject at hand. Maggie's personal life could be explored at a later date. There was the more pressing matter of tracking down the killer who was still on the loose.

The rest of the conversation meandered between Maggie describing what she'd eaten for lunch the previous day, to Judith's pleasant surprise, at receiving her hire car ahead of schedule. They discussed the shifting weather patterns that seemed to centre around Little Pickton. Maggie suggested the village should be twinned with *Greta Thunberg*. The irony was lost on them that they were circling around a story of a steam train, a beast that ran on fossil fuels. It was a splendid breakfast and Judith considered they could have gone for another one, each.

Maggie's date had inadvertently pulled up a few facts that rang alarm bells. As they parted, Judith left a message for DC Eastly asking to shed any light on Lloyd Groves' personal views, and if she had heard of any relationship palaver between Lloyd and other Society members. Eastly usually responded quickly, but after a couple of hours of silence, she assumed the detectives had entered some sort of deep state surveillance on their prime suspect. Of course, with everybody snowed in Little Pickton, it also meant the detectives were snowed out. She was sure they would be asking for her help very soon.

As she left the tearoom, Judith mulled over what to do next as she sat in her car, thoughtfully browsing the internet on her phone. She recalled the poster in the library campaigning about the railway extension. She navigated to it and was surprised to find it was a group actively *opposed* to renovating the line. There were no names, but from the several thousand page views, it seemed a popular website, and the address was vaguely familiar. The thrust of the argument appeared to be the line between Denzel Green and

Fulton passed through a beautiful forested area, which baffled Judith because the line between Denzel Green and Little Pickton also passed through extraordinarily picturesque landscape but had blended itself in without harming the environment. Another two pages were under construction, and merely holding pages on the *Go Daddy* web-hosting site. That suggested the campaign hadn't been running for too long and had bigger plans. But what those plans were, she couldn't say. Something told her this was a cover for the real motivations the group had in stopping the line. After giving that several moments thought, something sparked in her mind, but it was too ill-defined to latch onto and teased her like a fading memory.

Judith locked her phone and was about to drive away when she caught sight of Father Largy shovelling the snow from the deathtrap of a pathway leading between his church and the gate. She hurried across the empty streets to join him. "Good morning father," she said chirpily.

"Ah, Judith, how nice of you to offer a hand."

Judith looked between his shovel and the deep snow and nodded heartily. "I am happy to cheer you on and give you all the spiritual encouragement you need. Although I wish my poor back could shovel like you do. You're a professional, Father. You could almost be an Olympian. I can see you now, winning gold for shovelling."

Father Largy harrumphed and continued hacking at the snow, pushing it aside with great effort as the blade scraped across the flagstones beneath. "Well, they've had many peculiar subjects in the Olympics in the past, I must say. Did you know they had professional painting? Tug-of-war. They even had equestrian jumping. *You* jump over the horse," he clarified.

"Who wouldn't watch that!" exclaimed Judith with genuine delight. She mentally changed gear and adjusted her tone. As a pillar of the community, the good Father was a hub for gossip. "Anyhow, I was curious if you'd heard any more about this sad Herbert Holland business?"

Father Largy gave an unamused snort. "Ah! Yes, I'd heard you have been snooping around. Why is it you always seem to be chasing the macabre?"

"I'm not the one with a model of a semi-naked man nailed to a cross, inside." Judith nodded toward the vestry.

"*Touché.*" Father Largy took the comment with good grace. He was a closet *Hammer Horror* film fan, a pastime some thought wasn't conducive to the Christian faith. He always delighted in pointing out the number of beautiful churches used in the films.

"And for your information, I was asked by our dear police friends to keep my eyes and ears open and see what's what and who's who."

Father Largy gave a sharp look. "Who is who? And what is what?"

Judith shrugged. "Nobody seems to know. At least not the police. Hence me being curious about how well you knew any of the Society members?"

"Not very well, I'm afraid. None of them really attended church." He gave a little snigger. "Particularly... well, you know who." Judith did not know who he was referring to. "Although I was keen to find common ground with them. Do some fundraising together, but they were a tight bunch." He lowered his voice. "And by tight, I mean quite *mean*. They told me that every penny must go to the railway rather than to the church."

"How awful."

Largy nodded. "Can you imagine? It was probably for the best. They were a gossipy bunch."

"I know. That whole Lloyd Grove situation..." Judith shook her head. She felt slightly bad for leading Father Largy astray. He was a good man who absorbed rumours and gossip with superb discretion. However, he was human after all, and with nobody to open up to, Judith found she could eke out fragments of salacious information.

"Oh well, that was a scandal. Although they did a good job of keeping a lid on it."

"Did they now?"

"Well, if Lloyd and Augusta had an affair which was provable, then Jennifer would have got half of *everything*. And the way I hear it, at that time, the Society still hadn't been turned into a charitable trust. It was still in his name."

Judith assumed Jennifer was Lloyd's wife, or ex-wife, by the sounds of it. "But nothing was proven, of course," she said, almost as if she was trying to defend Augusta.

"Not at all. I mean, Augusta may be as quiet as a mouse, but she does have *that* reputation. I mean, after all, there was that whole thing with the dentist."

"Hmm," said Judith. "Um, I think that one escaped me. Dentist?"

"Oh, yeah, again, it was a bit messy. But, you know, Augusta's name came up. Nothing was proven. Old Harry managed to retain his dental practice. The status quo resumed. But at least she makes the effort with the community, so I'd forgive her for anything. Especially because every Christmas her craft group raises an extraordinary amount of money for us. They start in September, all hunched up in the cricket pavilion. It's become quite the social gathering."

Judith thoughtfully circled back to another comment

he'd made. "You said *you know who* when talking about the Society. Do you mean Derek and Dawn?"

The priest shook his head sternly. "Not those two. I meant..." He looked up sharply, his eyes widened as he looked over Judith's shoulder. "That one."

Judith turned to see Barbara trudging up the road, pushing her Pashley through the deep snow. She was wrapped up in a thick winter coat, her nose firmly pointed to the floor as she walked determinedly past the church without so much as a second glance.

Largy's voice dropped to a hiss. "She's a rum one, mark my words. The things you hear..."

Judith watched as Barbara disappeared around the bend towards the cricket grounds. "What do you hear?"

The lack of an answer from Father Largy caused her to look back at him. He'd heard the comment because his face had become clouded, but his attention was firmly on his snow-clearing duties. Judith didn't press the matter; after all, the man clearly had his limits of rumour-mongering.

Chapter Twenty

The cricket field was smothered in calf-high snow and the snowman team had expanded to six, all positioned for a game. Judith couldn't decide if it was the village children or the adults who created the diorama, but she was impressed that they'd included the wickets and a bat.

The lights were on inside the cricket pavilion, although there was no sign of any vehicles, but plenty of footprints. As Judith drew closer, she could hear jaunty Christmas tunes playing inside. She let herself in. The room was only fractionally warmer inside than it was outside, but the club's tea urn was spewing steam. Augusta was there, joined by four other women in florid Christmas jumpers, all hunched over a table covered with glitter, baubles, glue, tinsel, and paper.

"Judith! Come to join us!" Augusta exclaimed, gesturing expansively as Judith entered.

Judith unwound the scarf from her neck and plucked off her yellow bobble hat. "These are exquisite!" she remarked as she examined the ornaments. "You all made them all?"

"You've stumbled onto my secret." Augusta winked. "Welcome to my *own* little society," she slowly turned around to drink it all in. "I've been running it for a couple of years now. You know, our Christmas starts in September, and it powers us all through the rest of the year."

Judith gave an involuntary shudder. She didn't consider herself a holiday hater, but she was firmly of the belief that Christmas had its time and place, and that it shouldn't extend beyond twelve days.

Augusta read her mind. "Ah, you're one of those," she said, circling an accusing finger. "You don't believe in the holiday spirit. I don't mean the religious sort. I mean the kind of spirit that gives hope. Well, for us, hope is a lifejacket. Something that has kept us afloat during relationship breakdowns, heartaches, lies," Augusta continued in a lower voice. "Maybe the odd drinky-poo. We've bonded over this. Half the year it gives us something to look forward to, something to plan and plot. Then the other half the year it brings us together. And right at the end we get to see the joy on everybody else's face. And raise a bit of money, too."

Judith looked around the room with renewed interest. "You've created a self-help group."

"We all need one, one way or another, right?" Judith softened and nodded. "May I offer you a coffee?" Augusta pointed to the urn.

"That would be splendid."

Augusta spooned some Nescafe Instant into a cup and let the hot water flow.

"Have you come with any news?" she asked in a slightly quieter voice.

"Sadly, not yet. These things take time, and the police don't exactly tell me everything." Judith nodded when

Augusta indicated the carton of semi-skimmed milk. "But I hope to have some promising news soon. It was my inner Grinch that drew me here," Judith gestured around. "When I heard you did this sort of thing, I was intrigued."

"Oh. How so?" Augusta inquired.

"I've been to and from Denzel Green a little bit more in the course of events—" Judith explained.

"Ah, the enemy," Augusta smiled. "I'm joking. They put in one heck of an order for Christmas decorations. More so than our little Whoville here."

"I was toying with the idea of putting an event on to bridge the sense of kinship between our villages, considering what happened. Something that speaks of renewal, and nature..." Judith improvised like crazy. "And I was hoping that you had some surplus left over from last year or, I don't know, if the funds could be raised for you to create some more trinkets. I was thinking more like twigs and vines and that kind of thing. Maybe a heart or tree woven from branches." She held up a beautifully painted bauble. "Not something so Christmassy. More about Nature and rejuvenation."

"We don't have anything like that, I'm afraid, as you can see. Our stock seems to be more commercial Christmas than artisan."

"So, you have never made anything in that range?" Augusta shook her head. "Oh, that's a shame," said Judith. "Do you know anybody who makes such a thing?"

Augusta looked thoughtful, then shook her head. "Nobody in our group. Maybe you need a weaver. Care to join us?"

Judith was adamant not to, but found herself agreeing and unfastening her coat as she joined in with the ladies around the worktable. After twenty minutes or so of amiable banter, she had created a decoration that looked more like a kindergarten project than belonging to a luxury Christmas ornament collection.

"This is more challenging than I'd thought," said Judith appreciatively. "I must say, it's rather fun, too."

Augusta gave her a fresh, unadorned bauble. "Try again. You can only get better. Judging from your last effort, you can't get worse," she chuckled.

"It is rather therapeutic," said Judith. "What was it that made you turn to this?"

"Me? Well, a rather messy relationship situation, I'm afraid."

"Oh, I am sorry. I don't mean to pry," said Judith, prying. "But we've all been there. I've got an ex-Mr Spears," she wagged her eyebrows. "Although it wasn't terribly traumatic. For me at least."

Augusta focused on applying sparkling beads to the bauble in front of her. "You were lucky then. We've all been through the wringer one way or another. My fella was cheating on me. There was a lot of nonsense when he tried to deflect it off himself. He accused me of cheating on *him*, and he got a little bit physical about it."

Judith felt her shoulders bunch. Augusta may be on her suspect list, but that didn't forgive any violence towards her.

Augusta hesitated. "A few black eyes. I even broke my arm," she managed a small smile. "But I learned there's only so much you can take, and that you must stand up for yourself. So that I did. People don't like it when the weak fight back." Augusta's smile faded as her eyes never left the intricate pattern she created on the bauble in front of her.

"You found some comfort, at least. Especially as you

were accused of infidelity. I'm sorry to ask, but is this connected to you and Lloyd?"

Augusta's lips pressed together tightly, and there was a drawn-out silence before she answered.

"We never had a relationship. We were... flirting, I suppose is the phrase. But nothing ever happened. His wife found out as did my other half and, well, matters eventually resolved themselves." Judith remained tactfully silent as Augusta considered her words. "In retrospect I think Lloyd was using the situation to annoy his wife. I'm the one who got caught up in all of it." She expelled a long breath and forced a smile. "But that's just what I think. I can't prove that he was deliberately manipulative. Our relationship after that was purely a professional one, as if nothing had ever happened." She lifted her bauble up so Judith could see. "See? This one doesn't look as nightmarish as yours."

Judith examined the curving abstract light. "No, it doesn't," she conceded. Sometimes nightmares were best left forgotten.

Time flew in the pavilion. It was an hour and a half before Judith left after a very companionable time with the women. And although Augusta hadn't revealed any more, Judith had the chance to watch her interact with the others and was able to build a picture of a vulnerable woman who, against the odds, had built a strong presence to the world. But despite that strength, the fragile girl inside was always terrified it would shatter and reveal her weakness. Judith couldn't help but relate to that. However, she never took people at face value. Augusta obviously had a strong motivation to extract some sort of revenge against Lloyd. After all, he had destroyed her life – or arguably, rescued her from a violent partner. Either way, there was some salt to their relationship, which meant Judith couldn't entirely put Augusta on the innocent list. However, it was also a stretch to believe the mangled twig bundle Reeta had recovered would come from Augusta's workgroup.

When she left, she called DC Eastly to concede that her phantom Christmas decoration smuggler theory was probably nonsense after all. The last thing she wanted to do was feed more red herrings into the muddy investigation. She reached Eastly's voicemail and left a quick message as she examined the snow around her car. It was unblemished, so nobody had been inspecting her brakes while she'd been making decorations. She fished the key fob from her pocket to unlock the doors, when something caught her attention.

A furrow cut across the cricket field leading from the entrance gate to the far fence. It hadn't been there when she arrived. In the monochrome light, Judith could just make out a gap in the fence, accessing the forest beyond. To get a better look, she snapped her bobble hat on, wound her scarf tightly around her neck, and crunched through the snow, which almost reached to the top of her wellies. Closer to the track she could see it was a trail of single footprints. They could be anybody's, but what had caught her curiosity was the smooth line carved through the snow parallel to the prints.

It was the unmistakable indent of a bicycle.

Chapter Twenty-One

The thump of the racket followed by the soft swish of the shuttlecock arcing through the air was therapeutic to Sarah Eastly's ears, despite breaking into a sweat and panting hard as she lunged her whole body to return her opponent's shot. She was eager to keep the rally going, which she now counted at twenty-six shots.

With some satisfaction, she reminded herself this was not a date. Her opponent, Kevin Fenton, was the young PC she had bumped into at Little Pickton village Hall, and subsequently repeatedly at Fulton police station. She didn't know if she was just noticing a now-familiar face more often or if he was actively turning up at convenient moments. Either way, in the staff canteen, she had bumped into him when he was holding a badminton racket. After an awkward apology, she had pointed at it and declared, *"tennis!"* She had to admit that it was not the most scintillating conversation starter, and it had resulted in several minutes of awkward *umming and ahing* before Kevin revealed he'd just taken up badminton for exercise, but his regular partner had just quit. It wasn't one of those sports where he could knock the shuttlecock off a wall on his own, so had found himself at a loose end. Eastly found herself stepping in, with fuzzy notions of building a social life and perhaps getting some exercise to boot, although the idea of a social life with a copper wasn't exactly what she'd had in mind.

Sarah powered from one side of the court to the other, building up a veneer of sweat that indicated she was far more in need of exercise than she'd thought. The final rally came crashing down after a satisfying forty-seven returns. She tried to ignore the fact that Kevin hadn't broken a sweat, and if he was out of breath, he hid it well.

The court was little more than a net strung between two tarnished metal poles, in the leisure centre's only hall. It had an odd smell from the absorbed sweat of thousands of people who'd visited before, combined with a rather relaxed cleaning schedule. She sat on a peeling wooden bench to the side and retrieved her red-metal water flask from her bag. In a series of long gulps, she finished the cold drink before noticing a message on her phone from DS Collins:

WHERE ARE YOU? FINANCIALS HAVE COME BACK.

Her eyes didn't leave the screen as she typed her reply, and she was only vaguely aware Kevin was talking in his usual hesitant tone. Something about catching a drink. She hurriedly shoved her racket into a small sports bag. The handle was still poking out as she zipped it up. She tossed her tracksuit top over one shoulder as she hurried to the door.

"Yeah, great," she said absently. "Got to go."

She darted out, only catching Kevin's bewildered look as the hall door swung closed behind her. She wondered what he'd said. After a quick shower, Raymond Collins picked her up outside the leisure centre. She flopped into the passenger seat, her legs shaky from all the exertion. She was thankful for not having to trudge back through the snow to the station.

"Wow, what is that smell?" DS Collins barked as she closed the door.

"Passion fruit exotica," she replied.

Collins' nose wrinkled. "You smell like a holiday."

"Are we going to Little Pickton to see Derek?"

Raymond started the engine and shook his head. "The village is snowed in. Some of the banks have replied, and our financial fellows have identified a few intriguing bits 'n' bobs. Now we know how much cash is really missing."

The two detectives sat at Fabian Heinzel's desk for five minutes before the mayor bustled in.

"Sorry I'm late. I've been run off my feet between the local paper and this place."

"Oh, I know that feeling," Raymond said, standing to shake hands.

"You run a paper too?"

"Well... no. But it's all multi-tasking, isn't it?"

After a quick round of introductions and a pause to order a pot of tea, Fabian leaned back in his seat and clasped his hands together under his chin.

"So, how can I help you?"

"We're investigating the Rail Society murder," Raymond explained.

"I thought as much."

"What makes you say that?" Sarah asked.

"Two detectives surrounded by a bunch of small towns like this with nothing much happening. You don't have to be a detective to put two-and-two together, and it was front page news on my paper. Although I'm not sure how I can assist."

"We need details regarding the business relationships between the council here and the Rail Society."

Fabian leaned back in his chair. "It was all straightforward. We both wanted to benefit from one another. Even if it was based in Little Pickton, I was always looking how to make the idea of coming to Denzel Green as a great place to go!"

"Difficult," Eastly said automatically. She received a dark look from the mayor.

"We discussed quite a few plans, such as a restaurant service, as you enjoy your ride between stops."

"Would that be long enough to actually eat anything?" Sarah inquired doubtfully. She was sure polishing off a grab-bag sized packet of crisps would be a challenge.

"I see why you're a detective, young lady. You have struck at the very nub of the problem. You'd have to go back and forth four or five times to have a decent meal and dessert and time to digest it all. But still, these issues are all about thinking outside the box."

"How did you pay for the events?" Sarah asked.

"We're a typical town council, so we're strapped for cash," Fabian explained. "But the Society had some money, so they'd pay for advertising and anything we needed. But on the understanding that it would be recouped first. The town puts on as much as possible for free, such as facilities. Then once we made the money back, we'd split the profits equally."

"Advertising in your newspaper?" DS Collins interjected.

"The best way to advertise!"

"I see. You gained from both pots?"

"I'm not a charity. And the fact is we didn't lose any money and they pretty much broke even each time. But whether they made a profit is another question. I suspect they were paddling water to stay afloat. The issue we all have is how do you entice people from further out to come here."

"Hence the talk about extending the line to Fulton," Raymond said.

Fabian waved his hand dismissively. "That place is nothing but a bunch of shops and a bigger place to do nothing."

"We have a Nando's," Sarah chimed in before regretting opening her mouth when Fabian scowled at her. "And it might be just long enough for the train to run a meal service from Little Pickton to Fulton."

"But who would want to go to Fulton?" Fabian questioned. "Or more to the point, who would want to go to Little Pickton? That *doesn't* have a Nando's. And its slogan should really be: *'A great place to leave!'*". He moved his hands as if framing the words in an overhead banner.

Raymond smiled. "And it would leave your town off the map if it didn't stop here."

"But it's all moot because it will not happen."

His surly attitude was beginning to grate at Sarah's patience. "There were many payments made between the society and an account marked DG, which has been traced to belonging to the Town Hall."

"That's right. Their money paid for advertising, which we got at a discount by using authorised Council suppliers."

"Meaning your paper," said Raymond.

Fabian shifted uncomfortably in his seat. "What are you suggesting?"

"Who authorises those payments?"

"We're only a small team, so that would be me. And the Treasurer, but she's been off sick for months now. The Land Registry Clerk has been subbing it. We all have to take on multiple roles when we can."

Sarah made a note of that in her notebook. "And who is that?"

"James Wani."

Raymond and Sarah exchanged a surprised glance. "That same Wani from the Society?" said Sarah. Fabian nodded. "Isn't that another conflict of interests?"

"He's a local!" The mayor sounded almost offended. "He's been working as the Land Registry Clerk for the last eight or nine years. Reliable fellow."

"And the two of you were the only ones with access to the accounts?" Sarah clarified.

"As I already told you, Margaret has been off for a while. Why, what's drawing your attention there?"

Sarah used her index fingers to bounce an imaginary exchange from one to the other. "It's all very unregulated, isn't it? All this money flying back and forth between private hands, filtered through the council."

"There is little choice in small towns."

Raymond spoke up. "And for such small towns, a large amount of money was drawn from the Society's accounts in a piecemeal fashion, and passed into your accounts, before being moved on again."

Fabian was suddenly finding his seat uncomfortable. "I'm sure there's a perfectly reasonable explanation for it. How much?"

Raymond studied the mayor's face carefully. "Four-hundred grand."

"Okay, that's no small feat. What was that for?"

"I was hoping you could enlighten us. Somebody here transferred some of that money onwards, to an offshore account, which we're trying to trace now." Raymond didn't do a terrific job of keeping accusation out of his tone. "Is that regular practice for Denzel Green council?"

"Obviously not." Fabian propped both elbows on the desk as he looked between the two police detectives. "Are you accusing somebody on my staff of money fraud?"

"Technically money laundering, I suppose," Sarah's head bobbed uncertainly. "I mean, we're investigating further to find out where it's gone."

"That is a serious accusation."

Raymond shrugged. "I would say the dead body is a more serious concern than the money, but I get your point."

"Of course. It's such a shame Herbert Holland died, but none of that is connected to *my* office. I didn't even have dealings with him. He kept out of things other than complaining about the rail extension."

"We require a list of everyone who works here, and who has access to financial information." Raymond firmly tapped his finger on the desk to emphasise that this was a demand, not a request.

A thought struck Sarah. "Was Wani ever involved in discussions about extending the railway line?"

"Naturally, yes," Fabian confirmed. "As the Land Registry Clerk, he was key to the proposal."

"Another conflict of interests."

"Not really. It was a public debate too. If the track to Fulton was repairable, then maybe the extension should be considered. Not that I want it to. And from the Society's point of view, money would have to be raised for that, in an economy where they were just about solvent. However, I'm pleased to say that it's all too late, anyway."

When Eastly and Collins left the town hall, it was snowing again. They had taken a detour to James Wani's office, but he wasn't in, and his assistant said he hadn't been there for the last two days. Eastly phoned his mobile and left a message on his voicemail to get in touch.

"Murkier and murkier," Raymond Collins said, wiping the fresh veil of fresh snow from his windscreen. "Forensics said that whoever was skimming the money knew what they were doing when they passed it out of the town hall accounts. It was converted to Bitcoin almost instantly."

Due to a half-day training course, Eastly had a vague notion of how cryptocurrency could be rendered untraceable. All Collins had gotten from that course was that crypto wasn't real money, it was a virtual representation of it. He was happier with a twenty-pound note in his wallet. At least he knew where he stood with cold, hard cash.

"We need look into whether the mayor is skimming cash into his newspaper. I wouldn't be surprised if the Society turns out to be their biggest advertiser."

"Unscrupulous, maybe. But I'm not sure it's illegal. What's your best guess on who stole the cash?"

"Augusta's the obvious one."

"She claims they had a computer virus. Lloyd backed that up."

"Just the two of them, though. The others were never told. And the Society accounts are wishy-washy. Two-hundred grand came through to here. But the other half seems to have gone in piecemeal over the last couple of months. But all the records were signed off by Herbert."

"He was looting his own company."

"Well, of course it's possible. These days you just need a few clicks of the mouse needed to transfer anything anywhere. But then why would Augusta invent a story about a virus? I'm not sure Derek is clever enough for that." They lapsed into silence as they thought through the possibilities.

"Although it begs the question whether Augusta was a willing participant or coerced? Could Derek have forced her to make the transfer?"

Raymond unlocked the car doors. "This is too much speculation. And don't forget that Lloyd would probably have had access to everything. I mean, it all boils down to who would kill for almost half a million pounds?"

"That one answers itself."

Raymond agreed. At this stage, he didn't trust any of the Society. Especially as they all seem to have their own agendas. He turned the engine on before Sarah Eastly could close the door as she sat in the car.

"I think it boils down to who would attempt to kill Judith? Was it to cover something up, or to mislead us in the first place."

They both sat in silence for a moment, thinking the same guilty thought. If Little Pickton was currently snowed in, did that mean Judith was currently trapped there with the killer?

Chapter Twenty-Two

Imitating particles of fairy dust, flurries of snow drifted through the canopy of towering oaks as Judith followed the bicycle track and footprints up an inclined trail that was nothing more than an indented path through the snow. Having hopped through the gap in the cricket ground fence, she walked up the gentle wooded hill for five minutes, and it was now becoming noticeably darker through a combination of thickening trees and increasingly leaden clouds.

The last thing she wanted to do was be stranded in the twilight with sub-zero temperatures. Judith wondered if she ought to have gone back to the car for her torch but remembered that she had a tiny light on her phone. She felt certain Barbara wouldn't have gone much farther pushing her bike. Why else walk through the claustrophobic forest, if not to take a shortcut? As a woman who generally kept herself to herself, she began to wonder why Barbara frequently pottered around the village, actively avoiding general contact with the other villagers.

Her foot snagged a buried root, and she caught her

balance before she face-planted into the snow. She stifled her breath. It was unnaturally quiet. The silence was broken only by the soft crunch underfoot. The winter wonderland swallowed every sound, although the silence was occasionally interrupted by the harsh caw of a crow echoing through the forest.

After another eight minutes slogging uphill, Judith's calves ached. Her mental map suggested that she was veering away from the village, which raised questions about Barbara's shortcut. With the trees shielding the brunt of the weather, it was difficult to judge, but she sensed it was snowing heavier.

"Bugger this." She stopped and panted billowing grey clouds of vapour.

There wasn't a soul around. She swivelled to retrace her steps and then stopped, cocking her head to one side. Did she hear something? She pulled her hat off so she could hear clearly.

Was it the wind chiming through the trees... or was it singing?

Having spent most of the afternoon listening to seasonal tunes, making festive decorations, and surrounded by women in large yuletide jumpers, she wondered why people were in the middle of nowhere singing Christmas carols when it wasn't even November yet. The holiday season was indeed taking over people's sanity.

She cocked her head. It was louder in the direction Barbara was headed. Curiosity got the better of her, and Judith continued to hike uphill. As she drew nearer, she realized it wasn't any festive carol she was familiar with, and there was a distinct percussion and jangle of tambourines. She frantically tried to recall if Jehovah's Witnesses had a percussion section.

She squinted. Was that a light ahead?

With a growing sense of unease, she scrambled up an incline on her hands and knees, as it became steeper. Through the trees was a flickering fire. She could barely contain a gasp of astonishment. She instinctively threw herself down into the snow, sheltering behind a fallen log. Just yards ahead was a clearing in the forest, where an enormous bonfire was ablaze. A dozen people danced around it, singing and chanting to drums and bells. That wasn't the unusual part.

They were all naked and wearing rings of woven twigs around their wrists and heads.

Judith recognised several familiar faces from the village. She swore one of them was the receptionist at her doctor's. The woman leading it was Barbara Dixon. Judith had stumbled into some sort of Little Pickton pagan Wicker Man situation. The group was fully immersed in their ceremony, some with their eyes closed and their heads tilted upwards in rapture. Judith didn't have a religious bone in her body, but nor was she judgmental. When travelling she'd always visited temples, mosques, and churches and found them equally fascinating. She was fascinated how cultures had evolved around religion, and she certainly harboured no dark preconceptions about pagans. After all, they were the bedrock of almost every other religion around the world. But still, it was more than disconcerting to bump into a group of naked people, frolicking in a snowy forest. The odds were in her favour that she wasn't about to be used as a sacrificial lamb.

She raised her head slightly, keeping behind the cover of the thicket to watch. Barbara moved near the bonfire and raised her arms. Judith had to admit, for a woman of her age, she had the enviable physique of a much younger woman, despite the hairy armpits.

"Imbue us with light to see the unseen," Barbara bellowed to the heavens. On cue, the music and chanting stopped. Was it Judith's imagination, or did a gust of wind blow the flames skyward, scattering embers to combat the snow?

Barbara continued. "Sight beyond sight." She waved her hands in mystical patterns. "Danger walks amongst us, so we seek protection from the wise."

Her voice and posture commanded attention. This was not the meek figure that Judith had spoken to. This was a woman with a powerful presence. She kept one hand in the air, reaching higher as the other extended to the warmth of the flames as if she were channelling the heat.

"We call upon the souls of the lost to find peace, and reveal the evil that walks amongst us!"

The group gave a collective sigh of agreement. Judith heard a dull thump behind her. She twisted round to see a naked man carrying a large plastic carry box under one hand. Another box had fallen from his other arm, making the noise.

"Who are you?"

"Um," said Judith, her head snapping back to the clearing as the crackle of the flames became more evident because of the cult's sudden silence.

Everybody stood stock still and stared at her. If she had expected Barbara to shriek and become her shrew-like self, then she was very much mistaken. If anything, Barbara's gaze hardened as she pointed an accusing finger at Judith.

"Spy!" she bellowed.

Embarrassed, Judith clambered to her feet, brushing the snow from her coat. "Actually, rambler," she said, giving a half-hearted wave, trying to ignore the fact none of the naked people looked particularly inhibited. "I heard your singing and thought I recognised the tune."

"You mean *Gaia's* praise to *Cernunnos*?"

"I was thinking more Des O'Connor. I didn't mean to disturb your..." She circled her finger as she searched for an appropriate adjective.

Barbara took several steps towards her, but sensibly kept close to the warmth of the fire. "It's bad luck to interrupt a High Priest's rite."

Judith filed away '*High Priest*'. In addition to the woven headbands, some had twig-like talismans hanging around their necks or arms. Around her wrists, Barbara wore bracelets made from brambles and shaped in the vague form of a person. The thorns left faint scars. Judith felt her stomach flutter; there was no hiding the similarity between the talisman found at the crime scene and those worn by this cult.

"I apologise for the interruption," said Judith, trying to keep it light-hearted as she fought a wave of panic. Perhaps the likelihood she'd be tossed onto the bonfire was not as remote as she first thought. She indicated back down the path. "I didn't mean to disturb you, so I'll be on my way. I'll let you carry on in peace."

"You can't leave," snapped Barbara.

Judith's heart began to hammer as two nude men blocked the path behind her.

"Do you believe in possession?" hissed Barbara.

"Well, it is nine-tenths of the law, or something like that." Judith shifted her weight from one foot to the other.

"I mean *spiritual* possession."

"I've never considered it."

"There is a darkness that has come here."

Judith took an involuntary step back as Barbara edged forward. "Well, other than some trapped wind, it's nothing to do with me."

She looked around. Which one of these people had helped Herbert Holland commit murder? Who had slashed her brakes? Was it the same person who had followed her home from Denzel Green?

She felt well and truly isolated.

"One has been taken from us by this darkness." The emotion caught in Barbara's throat.

Judith weighed up her options. They were not looking wonderful. She needed to stall for time.

"Exactly what dark spirit is abroad in Little Pickton?" she said as solemnly as possible.

Barbara's lips twisted into a snarl. "You know full well, Judith Spears. Spirits walk these woods and bring misfortune. The fate of Herbert Holland echoes through these boughs." She waved her hands dramatically around the darkening forest.

Once again Judith wondered how she had timed the bonfire behind her to give a whump and spray another fountain of embers. Tension was thick in the air, and she was certain she'd soon hear the dreaded words: *'Guards! Seize her!'*

Chapter Twenty-Three

After reaching Judith's voicemail for the second time, Raymond Collins drove to the outskirts of Little Pickton to see for himself how formidable the snowdrifts were. Sure enough, the three roads he attempted to use were impassable in his police pool Peugeot. Not that he was worried about Judith. She was a woman that one simply couldn't be too concerned about. Instead, he worried about the suffering of *other* people who encountered her.

Before checking on her, he and DC Eastly had tried to track James Wani down. His assistant in the office had assumed he was working from home, which was perfectly normal working practice for the team. At his house, a small, terraced property on the edge of Denzel Green, they had received no answer. Judging by the fresh fall of snow, there hadn't been any activity to or from the house overnight.

The mayor's constant use of the past tense when it came to discussing the rail extension had bothered Collins. It was an unconscious tell that he considered the matter closed.

They needed to flesh out the information about the deal, so he dropped Eastly back to the town hall to rummage through the land registry files.

He'd only been gone for fifteen minutes before she called him to reveal the housing estate had started building on a brown field site. The stretch of railway line that was being sought was on an adjoining green field site, which was an entirely different level of bureaucracy. A new estate would be very much within Fabian Heinzel's interests. New residents, new income, and a new audience for his newspaper. There was a whiff of corruption, or was it the unknown scent of a government official doing what was right for the town? Oddly, neither detective could tell the difference.

While there was correspondence correctly filed away in the town hall vault, the folder containing the official Land Registry documents was missing. DC Eastly asked the assistant to find it as a matter of urgency. Collins did a U-turn from the borders of Little Pickton to pick her Eastly, and they both drove to the building site to see it for themselves.

They were forced to take several B roads that were sheltered by the hills so had only suffered a smattering of snow before they turned onto an old A road, which had been cleared of deeper drifts, revealing cracked tarmac underneath. They passed fields and several small warehouse areas that would have been buzzing in the 70s and 80s, but keeled over and died in the 90s and had since been left abandoned.

The housing site itself was delineated from the road by a long metal mesh fence with the occasional 'security patrolled' signs tied every few hundred yards. In reality, it was only patrolled by badgers and foxes.

They pulled up at a mesh gate. A padlock and chain held the double gates closed. Beyond was flattened ground, although there was no sign of machinery. Eastly was the first to climb out and test the lock. Collins joined her, stamping his feet for warmth as he took in the rather ambitious 'Beware of the dog!' sign.

"Poor sod would have frozen to death," he mumbled. "Makes you wonder why anybody would want to buy a house way out here, let alone build one."

"I saw the plans at the town hall. It looks very posh. Upper-crust countryside living. All very cosy," she indicated vaguely towards the northwest. "With a private retirement home planned over there, it would be a gated community-type thing. And all the houses are going to be big, detached properties with large gardens." How she longed to have a garden of her own. In her flat, she barely had room for a potted plant. The idea of being able to go wild in a proper garden was a dream. Not that she was green-fingered. She'd leave that to her mythical boyfriend who would be more than capable of digging through the garden with his shirt off and sweaty muscular torso glinting in the summer sun.

"In the middle of nowhere is still the middle of nowhere," Raymond said pragmatically, bringing her fantasy crashing down.

Eastly tugged at the gate again. With a little coercion, she was able to open it wide enough to slip between the two gates. After much swearing, Collins followed her through, his extended stomach catching on the metal frame. Even breathing in didn't make it much easier. Convinced he was going to rip his coat, he lunged through and almost tripped on the other side.

"Gracefully done, sir," Eastly said with breezy sarcasm.

Walking across the levelled land, they could feel uncleared rocks just beneath the snow. Work had been abruptly abandoned. Up ahead, they saw the snowy bulge of the train track under the snow. As they drew closer, the damage that time had inflicted on the railway became apparent. At some point, the ground beneath the sleepers had sunk, and the track was buckled as far as they could see in the direction of Fulton.

"They're well and truly knackered," Eastly commented. After two hundred yards, the rails had practically sunk into the ground. "So, this is what Lloyd Groves was attempting to raise the money for."

Collins nodded and mentally tried to picture their location on a map. He pointed in the direction of the snow-covered rails. "The town centre's that way. If this was in good shape, then there really would be no reason to stop at Denzel Green, would there?"

"That's why some of the townspeople were more in favour of the housing estate. There was an online group pushing hard to stop the rail extension."

Something caught Eastly's eye. She crossed the track for a better look. On the other side, a ridge angled gracefully down to a valley. On the slope, construction of the houses had already begun. They'd been abandoned as half-finished frames, offering spectacular views across white blanketed fields. The detectives now realised they had approached the site from the back.

"Ah, now I see," said Collins. "A nice little countryside plot with a lovely view. That's a slightly better sales gimmick."

"As far as I can tell from the documentation, they started this phase when negotiations were underway for the ownership of the tract of green-belt land that includes this." She gestured back to the railway line and their car beyond.

"Everything was going tickety-boo, and then the foreign landowner pulled out of negotiations, by which time they'd already started building. So now, everything's on hold."

"Of course. Who wants a train track running through the back of their garden, even if it is an irregular novelty service." Raymond Collins rubbed his hands together and wished he'd brought along a pair of gloves. "I spoke to the financial team again, and they said the Society was just about ticking over. They weren't losing too much money, but they could hardly go to the bank or back to the Lottery to ask for more. From piecing together the email threads we have, Herbert Holland didn't want this to go ahead."

Eastly was surprised. "I thought that would have been his dream."

"It seems it was Lloyd's dream. Herbert thought it would bankrupt them. They exchanged a few testy emails on the matter."

"Lloyd Groves failed to mention that in his interviews. He used to be a city banker. A man who takes risks."

"I supposed that's why he saw the potential and he talked about purchasing the land."

"But with what?"

Collins raised a knowing eyebrow. "With what indeed? Maybe with the Society's own money, which Herbert wasn't allowing. So why not steal it?"

They both looked at each other as they mulled over that implication.

Raymond chewed his lip thoughtfully. It helped stop it from going numb. "Imagine, elements within the Society steal the rest of their own money at Lloyd's behest, so he can use it to buy the land." He hesitated, not quite sure where his next line of thought was heading.

"That would leave the Society on the edge of bankruptcy and Herbert unable to stop the extension." Eastly frowned, lost in her confused thoughts. "Only he isn't dead."

Collins held up a finger, using it to conduct his thoughts. "He steals a train and kills... somebody..."

Sarah pulled a face. "That sounds very odd."

"This whole matter is odd. In a sense, that's the nature of crime. It's either driven by very simple passions, or bizarre faulty reasoning. Either way, I think it's clear we need to talk to our Mr Wani as quickly as possible."

Sarah didn't respond. Her mind was prodding strands of the case that refused to connect. It wasn't helped by a pair of text messages in rapid succession. Both were from PC Kevin Fenton. The first was playfully request for a badminton rematch. The second casually reminded her that she'd agreed to go out for a drink later tonight.

Eastly sighed. What typically bad timing. She had no time to flirt when she was trying to find a killer.

Chapter Twenty-Four

Raw flesh hissed as it was thrust towards the flames. The intense heat charred it remorselessly. More logs had been added to the bonfire, aggravating its intensity.

Judith gave a squeal of pain.

"Don't hold it so close," said Roger, the moustachioed naked man who had been carrying the plastic boxes when he'd discovered Judith. He reached out and gently guided Judith's hand away from the flames. She was holding a sharpened stick, on the end of which was a quarter-pound beef burger.

Thankfully, the coven was now all fully dressed and gathered around the bonfire, toasting marshmallows, burgers, and hot dogs, while sipping hot chocolates. A convivial atmosphere descended when they agreed that Judith was no threat.

"It's a pleasant little social circle," said Barbara, as she squirted ketchup on her piping hot burger, which was held between two sesame seed buns in her left hand. "In normal life, we're all wallflowers. People don't understand our beliefs, and we lost interest in trying to convince them."

"And what exactly are your beliefs?" Judith asked, examining her own burger, which was now almost cremated. The smell still made her tummy rumble, and she slipped it in a bun offered by Roger, but only after she'd asked him to sanitise his hands once he had put his clothing back on.

"We're all spirits of the land," Barbara said earnestly. "Tied together by unseen forces and energies. Some people are scared by it, but it's nothing frightening. It's merely nature."

"Chanting in the woods and dancing naked around giant bonfires can be misconstrued," Judith pointed out. Barbara didn't seem to think so. "Is anyone else in the Rail Society a member of the coven?"

Barbara shook her head. "Nobody's interested. They think I'm weird. They've got their own little schemes, so why would they care? The only person who ever gave me the time of day was Herbert. Such a caring man." Judith didn't say a word. She wanted to hear Barbara's unfettered chain of thought. "He loved the Society. He saw it as something that gave the area a real cachet, and he was right. The railway has been part of this landscape for over a hundred years. The main track follows a ley line, bar a couple of curves. Once there used to be turn-offs and tracks reaching out to villages across the area, connecting people. We've lost that connectivity now. Everything is online, and digital zooming. Not so much zooming really, just staring motionless at a screen." She lapsed into silence, gazing at the flames.

With nobody else willing to chip in, Judith thought she should say something. "This is a wonderful burger."

"Totally organic," said Roger proudly.

"From me own farm, north of town. I got a little farm shop and we make everything ourselves."

"I will have to try it out," Judith said earnestly.

Roger winked. "Mention *white horse* and you get a ten per cent pagan discount."

"Fancy a sausage?" offered another man, who'd been introduced as Ben.

"I don't mind if I do." She turned back to Barbara. "You said Herbert knew about this and respected your life choices."

Barbara nodded. "He wasn't shy in asking for spiritual help. Whether or not he was a believer, he still believed in seeking a hand wherever he could. So, we asked the spirits for guidance in retaining the land to preserve what we had, rather than grab for more. He joined us at the last gathering. I think he really enjoyed it."

Herbert didn't want the line to expand. That was the nagging thought at the back of her mind. The anti-expansion poster in the library had a familiar web address. It was the same URL she'd seen on an invoice in Herbert's study. He had been behind the campaign. She reminded herself that the identity of the victim was still something the police hadn't officially divulged, so she was careful to play the party line. "Yet unfortunately, Herbert wound up dead."

Barbara's eyes narrowed. "Dead? I refuse to believe that!"

Judith's stomach fluttered, but she was careful not to give anything away. "They found his body on the train. You know this."

"They found *a* body!"

Judith studied her for several seconds. "Can you elaborate?"

Barbara gave a sharp laugh. "If the police haven't worked

that out then gods help them. I know Herbert wasn't killed. He's very much alive." She gestured around. "Maybe out here somewhere."

"If he is alive, then my guess is that he got on a plane with all that missing money and is now living it large in Costa Del Sol."

Barbara shook her head. "That's not in his nature. I feel he's still here. I can feel his presence."

Judith opened her mouth to reply, but swallowed a sarcastic comment that was about to topple out. Aside from it being impolite, she needed to keep Barbara on side.

"I'm not entirely sure what you mean." She licked her lips and tried to frame the question as delicately as possible. "But if he wasn't the one killed on the train, does that mean *he* killed somebody and then fled?"

Behind Barbara's Harry Potter glasses, her eyes became wide saucers of astonishment. "Herbert, kill somebody? What planet do you live on? He wasn't capable of that. He released spiders outside and held windows open for flies."

Judith shook her head, puzzled. "Then where is he?"

Barbara snatched out and clenched Judith's knee, squeezing it tightly.

"Herbert Holland is very much alive. He has been kidnapped! His life is on the line."

Judith's composure wobbled, and with it, her sausage fell into the snow.

Raymond Collins sat at the chip shop counter, eagerly awaiting his chips and curry sauce, as it was layered in a cardboard tray and slipped into a paper bag.

After freezing at the building site, he and Eastly had

called it a day. He was tired and found it difficult to focus his thoughts on any one line of investigation to pursue.

His plan to take his chip supper home was sidelined by hunger compelling him to eat in the shop instead. Shadowed by Eastly reluctantly discovering that she was about to have a date, the thought of returning to his empty apartment was unappealing. He refused to acknowledge his growing anxiety over the potentially dangerous mission he set Judith on, fearing it would be his fault if anything happened to her.

He sat at the raised bar stool near the window; took a wooden chip fork from the tray on the counter and began eating straight from the carton. There was one other customer in the restaurant. Raymond observed the solitary figure eating fish and chips while scrolling through his phone. He took pity on the man who cut a lonely figure. He hoped his life would never become so desperate.

Despite his hunger, Raymond resisted the urge to eat quickly. Instead, he savoured each mouthful, even as his phone chimed with a message. It was an email from Wani's assistant who had stayed late at the office, struggling to locate the land registry document. There was no sign of it in the archives or Wani's office. Even more peculiar, it had been deleted from the digital files. She felt it was an admin error and promised to keep looking. Raymond was convinced someone was deliberately stalling to keep the facts murky for as long as possible.

Finally leaving the warmth of the shop, he was dismayed to see it was snowing again, prompting him to check the weather forecast for the coming week. It would not get any better. Despite his initial plan to head home, he found himself driving past James Wani's house once more.

This time there were lights on upstairs and footprints on the snowy path.

Raymond checked his watch. It was only seven thirty, so not too late to disturb Wani. He parked outside and strode to the house. As he approached the front door, he saw the wood around the door lock was splintered and the door had been carefully moved back into place. He slowed his pace as he drew near. The signs of forced entry were unmistakable.

There was an intruder inside.

With his heart racing, Raymond prepared himself to confront the danger alone.

Chapter Twenty-Five

The warming glow of the bonfire had a soporific effect, lulling Judith into losing all track of time. Only when the flames began to die down did she start feeling the chill and realise night had fallen.

The coven dispersed into three different directions, all heading to their various cars parked on narrow country roads. None of them felt ill at ease in the darkness, and they were all armed with powerful torches.

Barbara had her trusty bike propped against a tree, and Judith joined her in retracing their tracks back towards the cricket club. Barbara, true to her character, carried an archaic-looking lantern, except it was battery-powered and vaporised the forest shadows. Judith was glad for her company as they walked, even as Barbara's fey attitude returned as she shared her Wiccan beliefs. Judith, meanwhile, kept sneaking glances at her phone, waiting to pick up a signal so she could inform the outside world of Barbara's suspicions.

"I don't understand. If you think he's alive, why on earth haven't you told anyone?"

Barbara sighed. "Because I don't know who would have done such a hideous murder. I merely know the victim couldn't be him. The only thing I lack is tangible proof."

"That would be very useful." Judith hesitated from sharing what she knew about the victim's identity. After all, Barbara was still a suspect, but her claim that Herbert was alive was too much for Judith to suspect her. What sort of murderer claims the victim is still alive? "I suspect you know a lot more than you're letting on." Barbara shrugged. "Why do you have such an affinity with him?"

"I'm very fond of Herbert."

"Does he know?"

"Of course he knows, but I'm not his type."

"A pagan warrior queen might be a bit too much for most men."

"I mean, I'm a woman."

"Ah," said Judith. "Okey-dokey."

"Herbert had fallen in love with some Spaniard. A businessman he was involved with. He was hazy about the details."

"That still doesn't explain your hunch that he's alive."

Barbara swung the lantern, gesturing to her solar plexus. "We're spiritual beings connected right here. He shared things with me."

Judith listened as Barbara continued, revealing details about Herbert's financial woes and Lloyd's bullying tactics. Lloyd was determined to buy the land to stop a housing development and allow restoration of the line, but he needed the remaining Society money to do so – and it still wouldn't be enough.

Barbara snapped her fingers. "Then it all vanished with one click of a button. An internet scam. Augusta should have known better."

"Scams come in all shapes and sizes. What did she do, exactly?"

Barbara looked vague. "She clicked on a dodgy email, I think. It's not really my area of expertise. I only heard bits through Herbert. Lloyd claimed that it was a sophisticated fishing expedition. I still don't have a clue what he meant by that."

"I think he meant *phishing*. With a '*ph*'." Barbara looked none the wiser. "It's an internet thing."

"Herbert blamed himself. I don't know why. But they lost everything."

"And they didn't report it to the police?"

"To whom exactly? They didn't tell anybody else. Herbert only told me the day before he died. He said they never told us because they were worried about the bad publicity. That was as liable to kill us and bankruptcy. He even asked me what insurance we had to cover the losses."

"And what did you have?"

"Just for the office and the train, of course. Public liability for accidents. But nothing covers financial scams."

By the time they reached the cricket ground car park, Judith was convinced by the depth of Barbara's concern and wanted to reassure her that Herbert was not the victim. But as he was also the police's prime suspect, she held back. Judith offered her a lift home, but Barbara preferred to walk in the crisp night air. As they parted ways, Judith couldn't shake the feeling that Barbara held more secrets than she let on.

The cricket pavilion was dark, so she couldn't immediately pursue Augusta for details on the scam. Sitting in her car, she finally had a phone signal and received a flurry of messages from Eastly and Collins. She sent a brief reply, thanking them for the concern but too exhausted to engage further. She'd tell them about Barabara's suspicions once she had time to digest it at home. Barbara had said several interesting facts, nothing more than mere words, that had triggered Judith. She needed peace and quiet to work out which ones mattered the most...

DS Collins clutched his phone in one hand and considered calling Eastly, but talking aloud would draw the attention of the intruder in James Wani's home. And as the superior officer, he didn't want to give the impression that he wouldn't go anywhere without his DC backing him up.

Stealing a breath, he gently shoved the front door. It silently swung open on well-maintained hinges. Remains of splintered wood were on the floor inside. He listened intently - and caught movement from upstairs. Double-checking that his phone was on silent, he brought up Eastly's number. His thumb hovered over it instead of calling it.

He crept upstairs, taking each step as delicately as he could, hoping the old floorboards wouldn't betray him with a creak, and wishing he'd gone easy on the extra-large portion of chips and curry swilling inside him. He was halfway up before a floorboard whined under his weight.

Gritting his teeth, he froze.

Drifting from the intense silence emerged a gentle tapping noise from one of the rooms above. He felt a stream of cold air, but he couldn't hear any further movement. He hesitated, unsure what to do. His training told him to shout, alerting the intruder that the police were present. However, this also had the drawback of revealing he was on his own and giving away his position.

Tracing the draught to one of the dark bedrooms, every muscle in his body tensed. It was now or never, Collins told himself.

Creeping up the remaining steps, he froze again, hoping he was lulling the intruder into a false sense of security. Now he had to decide: should he sneak into the room, or go running in with full shock-and-awe?

He surged forward, shouldering the bedroom door open and bellowing at the top of his lungs.

"Police! Police! The building is surrounded!"

He hoped his subterfuge would give him the edge. But there was no sudden flurry of activity. Nobody leapt on him to wrestle him to the floor.

His hand instinctively groped for the light switch. Flicking the naked bulb on, his attention was drawn straight away to the open window and the billowing curtains, which made a gentle tapping noise as they brushed the wall. The window was thrown wide open, providing an escape route for the intruder. Glancing down, he noticed blood on the floor leading to a single bed and the body lying on top of it.

It was a man, still wearing his outdoor coat. Lying face down, blood had dripped from a wound to the back of his head, but now it pooled in the white plastic shopping bag that had been wrapped around his head to suffocate him.

DS Collins dropped to his knees and tore the bag free. In doing so, the victim's head lolled to one side, and Collins was unable to mask his gasp of surprise.

It was Derek Rivan.

Chapter Twenty-Six

Working for the police afforded one the authority to blast the blues 'n' twos, and race through traffic faster than the speed limit. It was a perk of the job that DC Sarah Eastly seldom enjoyed. As a detective, she was never rushing to the scene of an active crime. Usually, she travelled to the aftermath of a horrible incident. But now, she was thrilled to have the blue light strobing away on her dashboard. The siren was probably overkill as there were no other vehicles on the road, but she had no intention of switching it off. She arrived outside James Wani's house, just as the paramedics were wheeling out his body on a gurney, watched by a pale-faced DS Raymond Collins. When Eastly caught his eye, she saw a glimmer of relief.

"He's alive," Collins said, licking his dry lips. "Barely. Just a minute later, and I think his attacker would have finished him off."

Eastly was the next person he'd called after the ambulance. Lucky for him, she'd returned to the police station following a text message from Judith, which scuppered her date night. They both spoke excitedly at the same time, but Collins held up his finger to interrupt her.

"We need to search the garden. The assailant jumped out of the back window."

They made their way through the house, and out of the rear kitchen door, mindful not to disturb the ground outside before the Scene of the Crime team arrived. Collins photographed the disturbed snow underneath the bedroom window where the killer had landed and traced the fleeing footprints towards the back fence. The moment the snow started thawing – or falling – this fragile evidence would be obliterated. With nothing to measure the prints, Eastly put her extended hand and arm in the shot so that they could later use it as a guide.

Behind the garden fence, a narrow access alleyway ran parallel to the house on either side. It was used by residents to take their wheelie bins down for roadside collection. Even under the harsh beam of the torch taken from his car, Collins couldn't see which way the fugitive had fled. He suspected there had been a vehicle waiting somewhere. He had been too busy trying to stem the blood from Derek's injury to listen for the sound of an engine. He hoped the killer had been clumsy enough to leave enough DNA evidence around, if they had the intention of tidying up the crime scene after committing their heinous act. The detectives returned to the house to examine the front door.

"What was Derek doing here?" Collins said almost to himself as they studied the broken lock. It would have taken a few powerful kicks to the frame to cause this damage. That would have surely raised attention in the quiet residential neighbourhood.

Eastly had already dispatched a couple of uniformed officers who'd arrived, hoping to see a little action for a change. One of them was PC Kevin Fenton who greeted Eastly with a wry smile. He'd been about to end his shift for their date. For some reason she didn't feel it was right to reciprocate with a smile, so instead sternly ordered the officers to knock door-to-door to see if anybody had heard anything or caught suspicious activity on a doorbell camera. She felt guilty for the hurt look on Kevin's face as he set about the task. She followed DS Collins into the hallway as he imagined how the scenario unfolded.

"Derek broke into Wani's house and was attacked as if he was an intruder."

"Which he was. And Wani would have a solid claim for self-defence, so why go into all-out psycho-killer mode? And what was so pressing that he had to kick the door down? It blows our suspect list apart."

"Just because Derek's a victim now, doesn't mean he didn't do-in the bloke on the train." Collins sounded like he was almost trying to convince himself.

"Juan Carlos," Eastly declared.

"Huh?"

"Juan Carlos is the name of the deceased." Eastly couldn't hold back a smug grin, driven by the astonishment on her boss's face.

"How on earth did you find that out? Well done, Eastly!"

Eastly's smile wobbled a little. "Well, it was Judith who... helped." Raymond Collins blinked in surprise. "It turns out Herbert and Juan Carlos knew each other. Juan Carlos was a Spanish entrepreneur living in Navarra. One of his ventures bought land all over the world to sell to property developers. It turns out one of the sites—"

"Included the proposed extension of the track on the greenbelt," Collins finished.

"All the land registry documents here have gone missing, and the digital files have been erased. That would presumably leave him with the only hard evidence he owned the land."

"I still don't see how Judith stumbled across this."

"Believe it or not, I did put in some detective work, too," Eastly said defensively. "Judith discovered a few little facts we'd overlooked. Herbert Holland is gay. Barbara Dixon is in love with him, and they became confidants. She very much believes that he's alive." Raymond's eyebrows shot up, but before he could speak, Eastly cut him off. "The spirits of the forest told her so. She's a pagan high priest, apparently."

"There's a turn up for the books."

"As it transpired, Herbert mentioned that he was having a bit of a tangle with a Spanish man. Judith asked me to check Interpol for anybody in Spain who was registered as missing."

"Plenty of people, I suspect."

"And she pointed out that the deceased's dental records didn't-match *British* files. So, I cross-referenced them with the Spanish authorities. Lo and behold, it turned up a match: Juan Carlos."

"If I had a hat, I would doff it. Well done. And he owns the parcels of land…"

Eastly took delight in watching her boss's face stretch through a range of emotions before finally settling on one she could only label as '*the penny has dropped*'.

"Herbert killed him for the land rights. That's why they're still missing!" He pointed towards the floor of the house. "And James Wani was in a position to steal the files and erase evidence. What if Carlos didn't have the papers on him when he was killed? Maybe Herbert came here expecting to confront Wani and instead found Derek snooping around?"

Eastly pulled a face, considering it was a viable suggestion. "Maybe. And on the plus side, if the killer was here, then at least Judith's got nothing to worry about, trapped in Little Pickton."

Chapter Twenty-Seven

After texting Sarah Eastly regarding her new suspicions and leaving the cricket ground, Judith had returned home to a toasty warm cottage. She'd luxuriated a long shower that warmed her through to the bones, and then put on a black and green onesie she had bought on impulse from the market. It had a thick artificial fur lining, a hood, and its own rubber padded boots. When she put it on, she felt like an enormous teddy bear.

She was prepared to settle in for the night, but upon receiving Eastly's excited update about Derek Rivan's assault, her mind began percolating various theories. For just how long land rights could remain undisclosed, she didn't know. But somebody was keen on finding out just how far they could push that, which now placed James Wani at the centre of the conspiracy. But she had trouble believing that. She had witnessed how much control Lloyd Groves had exerted over him when he'd traded the bag in the library. She made the guess that the missing registry files were inside and now in Groves' possession.

She still couldn't see how Derek folded into this arrangement, nor what would drive anyone to try and kill him - other than to beat the smarmy arrogance out of him. Derek was an engineer, a village handyman. He had no skin in the game when it came to ownership of the Society.

That lay with Lloyd and Herbert.

Judith replayed various people's testimonies through her mind. Criss-crossing Groves' voice with, Derek's, Dawn's, Augusta's, and Barbara's as she desperately searched for overlapping threads or any obvious omissions.

One omission was very clear on her part: she'd had no chance to speak with James Wani. Other than his outburst at the initial village hall meeting, he'd projected a shy figure. Nobody else spoke about him, either. He was the sort of person who was just always there. Unassuming yet ever-present, like somebody with beige DNA or a ghost in the machine.

That triggered Judith.

The very phrase, 'ghost in the machine,' suddenly felt pertinent. Had he been one? She was now groping around the notion that he was the lynchpin that could unlock everything.

How Juan Carlos had come to be on the train, she was still unsure, but she was certain that was who Herbert Holland met for lunch in the Lion's Arms the day he died. The barmaid recalled there had been a low-key argument. Here was the man who owned the land he'd presumably prefer to sell to the housing company, who was also in a secretive relationship with the man who didn't want the extension to go ahead. Was it a lovers' tiff? Or had Juan Carlos taken Lloyd Groves' money instead?

Judith sat on her sofa, clutching a mug of Horlicks and

staring intently at the black screen of her television as her thoughts tumbled about. The television might have been off, but the puzzle before her eyes felt like a magic eye picture; a series of random dots that, as she stared harder, began to form shapes, patterns, and connections.

How could Lloyd Groves pay for the land? He had business connections, but such a shady deal would drive off legitimate investors. No, thought Judith, you do a dirty deed with dirty money.

Stolen money.

The money from the Society's own bank accounts. Augusta had clicked on a scam email, and it had emptied the Society's account with a virus. And twice the amount of money she had thought had vanished, backed by dodgy bookkeeping. Augusta could easily be implicit in the ruse, but Judith recalled back to the moment she was asked for help. There had been a genuine concern that she was being set up. She might not know by who or why, but it looked like her hunch was correct. And Judith was pretty sure Lloyd Groves was the one setting her up.

Her heart thumped faster when she recalled being followed back home from Denzel Green. Groves knew she was in town because they'd bumped into each other in the library. And he lived right *here*, in the same village Judith did. She took a deep breath to calm herself. If Groves was the killer, then had he'd just tried to eliminate Derek back in Denzel Green? If so, it at least meant he wasn't in the village, so she was safe.

Her anxiety eased. But why Derek?

The phrase '*skin in the game*' popped back into her head. Now she remembered where she'd heard it before - that's what Derek said when he was under her sink pretending to fix the trap. *'The only way to get skin in the game is to go and carve off some for yourself,'* he'd said.

Did he stumble across Lloyd Groves' devious plan and try to blackmail him for a piece of the action? It certainly kept within Derek's mercenary character, and it would make him a loose end that Lloyd Groves could set-up if the authorities came knocking. If Derek had been killed in James Wani's home, it cast another red herring away from the truth, and set James Wani up in the firing line.

She followed her logic trail further. Lloyd Groves had stolen the money to buy the land, then he'd used Augusta as a shield to take the fall.

Still, Judith was annoyed. While she was doing an excellent job of convincing herself Lloyd Groves was at the heart of darkness, the evidence was circumstantial, bordering on pure speculation.

There was still something she was missing.

A chime from a mobile phone caught her attention, breaking her convoluted thoughts. Somebody was at the door. She wondered who would be calling at this time, and in this weather, before remembering she still hadn't had a chance to retrieve the doorbell camera from the Society office. She put her Horlicks onto the coffee table and inspected her phone. She tapped on the screen to open the doorbell app. It took several seconds for the remote camera to activate... and she saw what was happening in the Rail Society's office.

Raymond Collins couldn't get video games out of his head. He shouldn't be thinking about his younger days sitting in front of the TV, watching colour bars flicker across the screen as he waited for an hour in greedy anticipation for his Commodore 64 to load *Manic Miner* or *The Hunchback*, games that had obsessed his youth. It wasn't quite the same level of excitement sitting in a hospital, lulled by the steady rhythmic beeps from the array of medical monitors attached to Derek Rivan. However, it had been a lesson in patience which he needed now as he waited for the man to regain consciousness.

Eastly had stayed at the crime scene, helping with the door-to-door inquiries, although Collins suspected she did so to spend more time with Police Constable Kevin Fenton, who had taken a shine to her. Still, who was he to judge?

The paramedics had stemmed Derek's bleeding and applied stitches to a nasty gash on the back of his head. He was now pumped with a liquid IV drip and had an oxygen mask over his face. Collins felt a rare sense of achievement when the doctors told me that Derek probably would have died from his injuries if the detective hadn't turned up in time.

Already on his third trip to the dreadful vending machines at the end of the hospital corridor, Collins kept glancing at his phone to check the latest updates on the search for James Wani, who was now their prime suspect. That was awkward, because up until now, their prime suspect had been the man lying unconscious in the bed.

It was almost eleven o'clock and, despite the caffeine, Raymond Collins was struggling to stay awake as he fought a wave of increasingly deeper yawns. He ambled back to the private ward to see the doctor and several nurses crammed around Derek. His initial fear was that the patient's condition had deteriorated. Collins was experienced enough not to barge his way through, demanding answers. That was only something TV cops did. Instead, he hung back and was relieved to see a nurse propping Derek up and giving him a cup of water to sip. He waited until Derek had been made comfortable and the nurses retreated, leaving only the doctor. Collins slipped into the room.

"Evening, Derek."

The doctor was still scribbling notes and caught Raymond out of the corner of his eye. He jerked his head in the detective's direction. "And this is the chap who saved your life."

Feeling slightly flummoxed, all Collins could do was raise his plastic coffee cup in *cheers*. He mumbled the words, "*my pleasure*." Collins cleared his throat to take on a more authoritative tone. "Mr Rivan, how're you feeling?"

"Weak." The words were little more than a long breath and his lips quivered from the effort. His left eye was black and swollen shut. Derek had obviously fought hard for his life.

"I need to know who did this to you," Collins said, stepping closer. "Did you see your attacker?" Derek stared at him through his one good eye. "Did James Wani do this to you?"

Derek didn't respond, but Collins saw a tear form in the corner of his good eye. His cracked lips parted, and he whispered one word:

"Dawn."

"Don't worry," Collins assured him. "She's alright." He sat on the chair close to him. "Whoever did this to you, got away. I don't know if they're likely to try again. Who was it? What were you doing in James Wani's house?"

The doctor, who Collins had forgotten was still standing at the end of the bed, suddenly spoke up. "Detective, he needs time to recover and rest. I think in the morning he might be more talkative."

"In the morning, somebody else could be dead." Collins was impressed with his own dramatic grit. It was enough to silence the doctor. He replaced the patient chart at the end of the bed and quickly left the room.

Collins focused his attention back on Derek. "Derek, what happened?"

"Papers..." Derek muttered.

Collins' brow furrowed. "Papers, I'm not sure..." Then he made the connection to James Wani. "Are you talking about records James Wani stole?" Derek gave the faintest nod and gasped from the effort of doing so. Excited, Detective Collins continued as the case threads unravelled. "You wanted the land registry records from Wani?"

Derek gave a soft chuckle, which ended with him wincing in pain. "No. He already has them. I took the insurance form. He wanted to meet me there... trade it..."

Collins shook his head in confusion. "Insurance? Who wanted it?"

"Dawn..." Derek began again, his face contorting once more in pain.

"I'm sure she's fine. If it makes you feel any better, I'll send an officer around to check on her. It might be a tad difficult right now, as Little Pickton is snowed in, but I'll get somebody there, I promise. I have to ask again, was it James Wani who did this to you?"

Derek's hand slid across the plastic sheets, leaving a smear of dried blood. "I've been set up. They're trying to frame me."

"Wani is trying to frame you?"

Derek gave a whimper and his one good eye closed again,

as his head nestled back in the pillow. Despite the computer game like tweets coming from the bank of monitors, Collins' eyes strayed to Derek's chest to check he was still alive. He'd fallen asleep or unconscious once again, but to Collins couldn't shake the feeling that Derek was more alert than he was letting on, perhaps stalling for time to get his story straight.

Collins slipped into the corridor to call Eastly. She answered on the fifth ring and sounded far more awake than he was feeling. Collins gave her a quick update on Derek Rivan's condition.

"We've finished our house-to-house calls, Guv," she said. "Nobody saw anything, although there are a couple of doorbell cams we're obtaining footage from. I was going to call it a night."

Collins considered asking her to join him at the hospital, more for company than necessity. But he decided it was best one of them was able to have a decent night's sleep before tomorrow. He was about to tell Eastly to head home when he heard movement from inside Derek's ward.

"Hold on a mo," he said to Eastly, stepping back into the room. Derek still had his eyes closed. Collins spoke loudly into his phone. "Do we have any officers who can check on Dawn Sanders in Little Pickton?"

"We have no PCs there. So that only leaves Judith."

"Any chance you can ask her if she minds popping round to check on Dawn? It will sound better coming from you and it'll put Derek's mind at ease." He said the latter part of the sentence loud enough to ensure Derek had heard.

"Sure thing, Guv," Eastly said with a sigh. "I'm still not sure when the roads back into Little Pickton will open. It's not forecasting any better weather tomorrow."

Collins wasn't listening. His eyes were drawn to Derek's left hand, which was making a vague beckoning gesture. Curious, Detective Collins leaned closer.

"Is there something you want to tell me, Derek?" He was so close he could smell Derek's stale breath. He flinched as Derek suddenly sneezed straight into his face.

"Lloyd." He pointed to his face.

"Lloyd Groves?" DS Collins shot bolt upright, wiping the moisture from his face with his coat sleeve. "Did you hear that, Sarah? Lloyd Groves attacked him. Doesn't he live in Little Pickton?"

"If he's our suspect, then he must be snowed out, then," Eastly said.

Collins' fatigue was being replaced with a burning desire to find his man. "Get everyone mobilised. Find his licence plate. I want Groves arrested before sunrise."

Chapter Twenty-Eight

Judith was already at her car and scraping off the ice that had formed across the windscreen when DC Sarah Eastly called her, asking if she could check up on Dawn.

"I thought you were going home. It sounds as if you're still out and about?"

Judith's breath came in sharp gasps from the bitter cold. "It is almost the witching hour. I was on my way to the Rail Society office," she reluctantly admitted. "I think somebody's broken inside."

"Broken in? Who? Hold on, how could you know that?"

"I accidentally left my doorbell camera inside the office," Judith admitted sheepishly.

To Eastly's credit, she just gave a knowing snort. "Uh-huh. Well, it happens." Before adding, "Do you know who it is?"

"I didn't see a face. They were ransacking the place, then they found the camera and hurled it across the room. It's going to be expensive to get a new one," she added. "I'm not sure my house insurance will cover it."

"I don't think you should go there alone."

Judith hadn't intended to. The first person she'd called for backup was Maggie, but she hadn't answered. A tiny part of her thought she was already in bed and asleep. A more salacious part of her suspected she was on a call to Fabian. Then she was struck by an idea.

"I'll ask Dawn to come along with me. After all, she's a bona fide member of the society and has every right to be there."

Eastly made an indecisive noise. "I'm not sure putting you both in danger is something I can condone."

Judith chuckled and opened her car door. "That's very sweet of you, detective. As you pointed out, if Lloyd is our man, he's certainly not here. After what happened to Derek, I think you're the one who needs to watch your back. There's no telling what he's capable of."

"Point taken," Eastly said. "Let me know as soon as you arrive at the office."

Judith hung up and sat in her car. But before she could close the door, something made her listen to the thick silence of the night. There was no sight or sound of movement, yet she couldn't shake the feeling she was being watched. Had Barbara's mystical society imbued her with a magical sixth sense? Or was it just her natural paranoia?

She closed the car door, ensuring to lock it before starting the engine. Once again, she was grateful to have the monster-sized Mitsubishi as it made mincemeat of the bad weather. She felt like a tank commander as she drove to Dawn's house. Her eyes kept straying to the mirrors, searching for telltale signs of vehicle lights following her, but the village was deathly quiet.

Parking outside Dawn's home, she noticed all the lights were on. She trotted up the drive and rapidly thumbed the doorbell, expecting to shout her name before Dawn opened, but that wasn't needed. Dawn opened the door full of gusto, dressed in a thick fleece jacket and wellies. Her expression froze when she saw it was Judith.

"Judith, what are you doing here this time of night?"

"Oh, sorry. Am I disturbing you from going somewhere?"

"No, just coming back." Her eyes swept the street outside. "What's going on?"

"The police have been trying to contact you all evening." Dawn's expression didn't twitch, but she nodded for her to continue. "Derek was attacked tonight in James Wani's home."

Dawn's face remained unchanged, as if shock had paralysed her.

"Dawn, are you okay?"

"Is he alive?"

"He's in a stable condition in hospital. He kept mentioning your name and obviously we're worried you might be next. I assume they've been trying to call."

"My battery is dead. Why would he come after me?"

"I was hoping you could tell me. Why would anybody attack Derek? Why was he visiting James?"

"They're friends I suppose. And because of the weather, Derek would struggle to get back here, I mean to *his* house, here." She quickly amended. "So maybe he asked a mate for his couch? We, er, we've been arguing. We split up."

Judith digested that and resisted the urge to ask any follow-on questions. It had already been close to twenty-five minutes since her doorbell camera had alerted her of the intruder.

"I came because I need your help," she said. "Somebody has broken into the Rail Society office and the police can't get here. I'd like you to come with me so I can get inside."

Dawn mutely looked at her coat and then back at Judith before nodding. "Why would somebody break in...?"

Judith fought the urge to give her a knowing look. "Perhaps they've overlooked something incriminating? Wouldn't you like to find out?" She took some joy in seeing the indecision creasing Dawn's face. "I suspect somebody is actively setting up one of you as we speak."

"Who?"

"I can explain more on the way, but really, you'll be a smashing help."

Dawn stared into space before nodding. "It sounds like there's a lot I should know. Of course I'll come along. When will the police arrive?"

Judith gave a shrug. "Who knows? For now, it's just the two of us, so let's do our best!"

Both DS Collins and DC Eastly were on their separate ways home when they got an email update from Constable Kevin Fenton. Doorbell camera footage from James Wani's street that showed a man hurrying into a large white Range Rover and driving away at speed. Although the man's features were hidden under a hood, the description of the car matched Lloyd Groves' own vehicle, although due to the angle, it didn't catch the license plate. Fenton had quickly reviewed the footage, and saw the same vehicle pulling up, twenty minutes earlier. The occupant had casually made their way towards James Wani's apartment.

By the time Eastly arrived at the station, she found her boss asleep at his desk with his head cradled in his arms. Quietly, she circled to the kettle and made them both a strong black instant coffee, doubling up the sugar in Raymond's cup. DS Collins perked up with the first sip.

"I think it's clear now," he said.

"Now that you've slept on it?" Sarah teased.

"Funny. Groves is getting sloppy. I don't think he was expecting to find James Wani at home. Wani clearly stole the land registry documents. Let's face it, sooner or later the true ownership would have resolved itself. Especially with our Spanish player in the mix. So why try to get them."

"Perhaps he was planning to fake them."

Raymond waved a finger at her. "Good thought. If they were not questioned, then the sale would go through. So, for whatever reason, Wani steals the documents for Lloyd. But Derek said something about insurance. I think that's why he was at the house and expecting to meet Wani."

"Does any of this imply Herbert was behind the missing money?"

"Not necessarily." Sarah crossed to the mugshots pinned to the wall. She tapped on Herbert's picture. "He was very much opposed to the whole expansion idea, so wasn't motivated to steal from the Society. Unless he was going to run off with the cash and wipe his hands with the sorry state of affairs."

"If that was the motivation, Augusta, Herbert and Lloyd are the obvious suspects." She stared at the faces on the board and another thought occurred to her. "We're thinking about this as one single motivation."

"What are you getting at?"

"What if we're dealing with *two killers*? Or potential killers? Two opposing views have created this mess. Lloyd attacks Derek, trying to silence him from whatever truth he found. Meanwhile Herbert kills Juan Carlos during an argument over the land rights..." She trailed away. They both looked at each other and pulled a face. It didn't sound quite right, but there was something there.

Raymond stood up and paced between Herbert's picture and the newly added one of Juan Carlos that had been printed from his company's website. He stood in front of a yacht - a handsome, sport-perfect, stubbled middle-aged man. His white shirt was unbuttoned to his mid-chest. Eastly thought he belonged in a catalogue.

"Herbert and Juan Carlos were in a relationship of sorts. The money had already gone before he was killed, and Herbert about to lose everything." He sat back down and stared at the screensaver on his monitor that was cycling through a series of idyllic tropical beaches. For a moment he wished he could wish himself away to one.

After a thoughtful silence, Sarah explored a new thread. "If Derek found out what was going on, it's safe to assume Dawn knew too."

"Makes sense."

"So, he'll naturally be worried that Groves is going to go for her next. But luckily, she's safely snowed in." She held up her phone. "And Judith texted me to say she'd arrived at Dawn's house."

"Poor woman," Collins sputtered. "Put yourself in Groves' shoes. What would you do if you tried to silence Derek but were not sure you succeeded because the police burst in as you tried to finish the job?"

"I'd go on the run." Sarah thought about it some more as she sipped her coffee and winced as it burned her tongue. "I'd kill him there if I wanted to set Wani up for it."

A thought struck Collins. "What if Groves and Wani are in it together? After all, they'd both have to be in on the land-scam plan."

"Both Wani and Herbert are still missing."

"Assuming Groves knows this, the logical thing is the police would search for Wani as the prime suspect. I would try to clean up any loose ends that would lead to me."

"That would be..."

"Dawn. But he can't, because the roads are snowed in."

"He's got a 4x4."

Sarah pulled a face. "Still, the roads are heavily drifted up. Even in a Range Rover he'd more likely flounder and get stuck. Why take the chance?"

"I suppose it depends on how desperate you are. But those roads are the only way into Little Pickton. You remember the flooding?"

They both fell silent again, lost in thought, until Eastly spoke up.

"No. They're not the only way in."

Thirty minutes later, they were at the rear entrance of the housing construction site. The gates they had squeezed between last time had been rammed open. One lay at an angle, hanging from a single bent hinge, while the other lay flat in the slush with clear tyre marks cutting across it.

"Well, that's certainly one way of doing it," Collins muttered, impressed that his DC's hunch had pulled off.

Eastly drove the police vehicle, which wasn't suited for

off-roading. They were tossed left and right as she followed the Land Rover's trail, clearly visible under her full-beam headlights. The wheel-prints arced across the site, and onto the railway lines. Groves hadn't been attempting to balance on the rails, but the snow hadn't drifted much in the valley, and it packed out the gaps between the sleepers. If anything, it helped provide a smoother ride along the rails, back towards Little Pickton.

Chapter Twenty-Nine

"Are you sure you're fine?" Judith asked without taking her eyes off the road ahead.

It started to snow yet again, and despite the safety and comfort offered by her hire car, the experience of her last crash meant she kept her hands tightly adhered to the steering wheel.

Dawn nodded and then realised Judith couldn't see her. "I'm trying to process everything you've told me."

"I'm sure it's a lot to take in and I'm certain that we'll find it's all a misunderstanding in the office, but one must check these things."

"You're not the Police. You don't know any of us. Why are you so involved?" There was a bitter note to Dawn's voice, which made Judith glance sideways at her.

"That's a jolly good question. When somebody asks for help, I suppose I find it difficult to say no. Especially when there's a little bit of a mystery around it!" She gave a little giggle. "That's me I suppose. I'm just a sucker. Always at the wrong time, and the wrong place. As useless as a *Nigerian astronaut*."

Dawn gave a knowing chuckle, which caused Judith to look at her askance. Dawn was staring straight ahead out of the windscreen. Her expression now a little more peaceful and relaxed. "I know exactly what you mean."

"I thought you would," said Judith. "You and I are cut very much from the same cloth. Sometimes you just can't say no."

"Who was it asked you for help?"

"Who do you think?"

Dawn's eyes narrowed. Despite her outward relaxed demeanour, she wasn't in the mood to play games. Judith got the hint.

"It was Augusta. After all, she was the only one with access to the accounts. Apart from Herbert and Lloyd of course. It vanished just like that–" She tried to click her fingers, which didn't snap, through her gloves. "That makes her the obvious suspect."

Dawn nodded. "She was always complaining that she was broke. She didn't like any of us."

"You don't think she meant to kill...?"

"I wouldn't put anything past that woman," Dawn said sharply.

"Fascinating. Who do you think her partner in crime is?"

Dawn was so silent it almost amplified the growl of the engine and the wet slush passing under the car tyres. When she finally spoke, it was barely above a whisper.

"I fear you're going to tell me it's Derek. She's tried to make her way through the group. He and her had a thing way before me. And she was very jealous, about that. And Derek, there was just something not quite right about him."

"You two look very much the happy couple."

"He has a dark side, that one. Violent when he wants to be."

Judith's mind went back to Augusta's domestic violence incident. Had this been Derek? Or was it another red herring?

"I always pegged him for arrogance but violent... That's awful to hear." She reached out and gave Dawn's hand a little squeeze. "I certainly hope you weren't at the receiving end of that."

Before Dawn could give a further response, Judith turned into the Rail Society car park and stopped at the fringes of the lone streetlight. There was no sign of any recent vehicle activity from the would-be intruder and no indication a door or window had been forced.

Judith cut the engine and turned off the headlights.

"Shall we take a look inside?"

Dawn jangled the office keys in her pocket as they crunched through the snow towards the door.

"I have to admit, the one thing that's puzzling me..." said Judith. "How somebody like Augusta could have accomplished such a sophisticated and clever theft."

Dawn slid her keys into the lock. The door gave with a creak as she nudged it with her shoulder and entered. "Oh, it takes all kinds."

Judith followed her inside. Dawn reached for the light switch and immediately the chaos of the room became apparent. It looked like a tornado had torn through it. Dawn gasped in surprise. Judith, who'd seen some of the destruction on the webcam, wasn't fazed.

"It takes all kinds, but in particular, I think it takes somebody with specialist knowledge of computer programming. Somebody capable of making, oh, I don't know, a virus that Augusta was sent. Once clicked on it would drain the accounts of money and make it look as if she was a victim of a terrible phishing scam."

Dawn didn't turn around. She was still looking at the mess. Judith slowly circled her.

"I would say the type of person who was capable of such a thing would really need to know exactly what they were doing. The sort of person who would know all about the futility of *Nigerian astronauts* and know all about *spoofing*." Dawn finally looked at her. Her expression unreadable. Judith smiled. "It takes a scammer to know a scam." Dawn frowned and Judith extended her arms as if she was a performer taking a bow on stage. "Some of us may have a history in that era. I know as well as you, the *Nigerian astronaut* was quite a famous scam."

Dawn gasped. "You?"

Judith brushed her hand aside modestly. "I know. It looks like butter wouldn't melt..."

"You don't know what you're talking about."

"Oh, I'm afraid I do," said Judith. "Why did you do it? I'm sure that will all come out in a wash. But *you* took that money, and that led to murder."

Dawn raised her hands defensively. "I didn't kill anyone!"

"So you claim," said Judith. "Yet somebody is dead and somebody else was almost murdered to conceal your insidious plan."

Judith had been feeling confident, but felt a slight wobble when she saw Dawn's shoulders relax, and a smile slowly pluck her cheeks. "You're only a stupid busybody, Judith.

Snooping around, making accusations and not quite understanding what is happening right under your nose."

Judith drew in a breath to retaliate. She thought a flat denial was better than a half admission, as Dawn had a point. But before she could react, she heard a rustle of movement behind her, and something was thrust over her head, blinding her. The next second, there was a crushing pressure, around her stomach–

And then, utter darkness, as she slid unconscious.

Chapter Thirty

The smell of oil slapped Judith's nose as she woke up. It instantly put her in mind of her father's garage before she left home as a teenager. Fireworks danced in the darkness behind her eyelids, and a dull pounding emanated from where she had been struck at the base of her skull.

Her eyes half-opened, but everything remained dark. She inhaled deeply, sucking in a section of oily sacking, confirming that she had a bag over her head. Most people would panic and struggle at this point, but Judith remained calm and composed. She'd long ago learned that calmness and a smile was the best way to get the upper hand in any situation. It went hand-in-hand with knowledge. Absorb every fact regarding your situation, and a way out would often present itself.

She was sitting upright with her hands bound behind her back. She still had her gloves on, which hampered a quick prod around. Her eyes were already accustomed to the darkness and if she squinted, she could just make out dim illumination through the hessian. Giving her feet a quick tap told her she the floor was made of stone or concrete. Underscoring this was a slow, deep rumble, like an old boiler churning away, and she could feel the warm waft of air drift across her cheeks. She summarised that she hadn't gone far. From the office to the train shed was her guess.

The last few moments raced through her mind. And the image of a smirking Dawn loomed large in her mind's eye as she was struck from behind. She had registered, far too late, the shift in Dawn's eyes as she looked over Judith's shoulder to the door outside. She was irritated with herself for being so sloppy. As Dawn and Derek had broken into the office once before, she had assumed the new intruder was unconnected to Dawn and would have long fled. The bump on the head proved her wrong. However, while it confirmed that parts of her theory were inaccurate, it also had the virtue of verifying other thoughts she had been playing with must be true.

She cleared her throat loudly and sat upright, trying to ignore the ache that orbited around her skull when she moved. There must be a nasty welt on the back of her head. She heard movement from behind, the scuffing of feet on concrete and hushed whispering. Then, with a flourish the bag was plucked from her head.

Dawn stood in front, dressed in oil-stained denim dungarees, much loved by train engineers. She wasn't holding the bag, which meant her partner was standing behind Judith. As she deduced, they were in the train shed. Only a few of the lights were on, but enough to see the tank engine was belching steam as it warmed up. The carriage was attached, and the shed doors were open, beyond which the snowfall had increased.

"This is all very pleasant," said Judith. Her voice sounded a little slurred. "Are we going on a train ride?"

"Yes, we are. Although, to be honest, I think you won't enjoy it, as it will be your very last one."

"To be fair, I didn't enjoy the first one as much as I thought I would. Are we going far? Only I've had a tiring day."

Dawn's mouth worked, but she couldn't immediately find the words. "What I mean is, you won't be going on anymore, 'cause you'll be dead."

"Ah, thank you for explaining it. The plot thins," said Judith as casually as she could. "Are you going to do another *Hansel and Gretel* on me?"

"My love, I have no idea what you're wittering on about."

"Grimm Fairy Tales? Oh, never mind. They threw an old witch into her oven to kill her."

"Oh, the gingerbread house? We're not going out for dinner—"

The frustrated voice from behind caused Judith to turn around, but that resulted in a pain twinging through her neck.

"Bloody hell, Dawn. She means tossing her into the fire! No, that was bloody hard work last time."

"You needn't hide behind me, Lloyd, you've been rumbled," said Judith as nonchalantly as she could. Lloyd Groves gave an exasperated gasp worthy of a teenager as he stepped into view, also dressed in engineering overalls.

"A good guess, Ms Spears, or merely a calculation?" said Lloyd.

"You are aware you're circling down the drain, resorting to committing crime after crime to patch things up. Sometimes it's best to admit things have gone wrong and give yourself up. See what mercy the courts can offer you. I'm sure it will be a far more lenient sentence than it would be if you added yet another murder to your repertoire."

"What would the point of that be? I'm not the prison type. This could have all gone so much easier if people were not so stubborn and arrogant." His eyes narrowed behind his glasses. "Or nosy and persistent. *Everything* would've been fine if Herbert had listened. We would have bought the land and extended the railway. Sure, we may have had to cut off some of the riffraff, Barbara, Derek, James. We could've stayed afloat, still run the line as we fundraised, and then finally open the new line all the way to Fulton."

"All this for a slightly longer train service? That is the definition of madness."

Lloyd smiled. "Not entirely. I happen to own a bit of land in Fulton. An old family patch which we'd clung onto but have never been able to sell. No commercial value."

"Unless a new tourist attraction ploughs through it."

"Then I could get the whole lot off my hands and hoover up a tidy sum."

"I am shocked greed is at the heart of this," said Judith, dripping with sarcasm. She was pleased to see the flicker of irritation in Groves' eyes.

"People are so selfish. Like Herbert. He has a passion for complicating things. He prefers the status quo. The small plans. Having a blasted comfort zone, when all I was trying to do was make things better for everybody."

"How has any of this made things better?" Judith snapped, struggling to keep her composure in the face of his arrogance. "You convinced this feckless woman," she nodded at Dawn, and tried to ignore the pain jolting through her neck, "into writing a computer virus to fool Augusta."

Dawn frowned. "What does feckless mean?"

"You can stop pretending to be the airhead, dear," Judith said in her most matronly tones. "It does you a great disservice. Especially for somebody who's skilled in IT and was wasted in a call centre."

Lloyd Groves pulled a face as Dawn looked blankly between them. "It's not an act. She really is like this. Whip-smart on anything technical. But general knowledge and common sense..." He seesawed his hand to indicate it was her Achilles heel.

Judith sighed as she met Dawn's eyes. "Oh, you poor thing. So easily manipulated."

Dawn was puzzled. "What?"

Lloyd draped his arm around Dawn's shoulder and diverted the conversation back to his favourite topic. Himself. "My plan had no collateral damage. It would have looked like Augusta clicked on the wrong email and we'd been scammed out of everything. A good excuse to fire the others and convince Herbert I was correct all along. Or even better, it would cause him to resign, and I get the whole thing. There was no real victim. We were stealing from *ourselves*."

"I think technically, the crime is *fraud*."

"Nonsense. I wasn't keeping the money. It was going to reappear as I miraculously raised the cash from my investment network to keep us afloat and buy the rail extension. Simple."

"Simple plans often lull you into a false sense of security because you never really explore the chances of failure."

Lloyd's eyes narrowed. "That sounds as if you're speaking from experience. My plan was beyond simple. It was eloquent. But people couldn't stop themselves interfere with it. They had to try to find a way to benefit themselves."

"You're now talking about Herbert? Because he wouldn't participate in any of this?"

"No, no, no," said Lloyd. "That fool decided to fall in love with Juan Carlos. Or claim he was. I saw it as a cheap charade to gazump the land."

"But he didn't know you were subverting everything to buy it. And it turns out they really were in love." Groves pulled a face of disgust. He obviously was not liberal leaning. "And wasn't Juan Carlos going to sell the rights to you, anyway?"

Lloyd's arm slipped off Dawn's shoulder. His hands had become fists. "He was. After all, he was a businessman and saw the upside of the deal. Except it was *that* morning he decided to grow a bloody conscience and tell Herbert *who* he was selling it to."

"Which is why they argued that lunchtime at the Red Lion's Arms."

"That pushed Herbert over the edge, so he jumped on the train and set off to a merry old sunset."

"Intending to crash it."

For once, Lloyd looked impressed. "Very good."

Judith shrugged nonchalantly. "He was going to claim on the insurance money to replace the locomotive and use the crash as the reason the line shouldn't be extended." She felt a sense of pride at the worried exchange between Lloyd and Dawn. "You're wondering how much I know and in turn how much the lovely detectives know. You should be worried. Your cunning plan left a trail of obvious clues." Judith was improvising and settled back into her calm demeanour. "That's why you came back to the office, looking for the insurance forms, wondering if police forensics team had taken them or if Herbert had." She smiled. "However, I had found them when I popped my doorbell camera in there. And it got a fantastic shot of your face," she lied. "You thought Derek had them, didn't you?" From his reaction, she was suddenly inspired. "That's why Dawn convinced Derek to break in here to find them. But he didn't, did he. Or at least you didn't believe him because he was blackmailing you."

Lloyd scowled. "Oh well, it's not like the olden days when you needed a piece of paper to prove anything. I know who our insurance company is. It'll just take longer for them to dig up the policy. Nothing will change really. I just wanted more time to get everything sorted and sold." He held up Judith's phone. "And as the camera app is on this, I can easily delete the video. You lose. I don't think anybody is rushing here to save you, and I certainly don't think you have any evidence on me." He slipped the phone into the pouch on the front of his overalls and indicated the train. "Now you are going to climb aboard, and as Dawn said, we are going for a little ride."

"I don't really wish to go to Denzel Green tonight."

"You're going to be going a little further, Judith. You're going to the end of the line." He smiled as fear crept across Judith's face. "It turns out Herbert's idea is now the one that will save me, and mean I can keep the money we purloined. Ironic, isn't it? You are going on that train for a once in a lifetime experience."

Chapter Thirty-One

Judith was frogmarched towards the train carriage, still with her hands tied behind her back. Lloyd Groves' fingers dug deep into her forearm with such force that she feared he would dislocate her shoulder. She noted that Dawn kept a wide berth when he showed any sign of violence and her expression vacillated between being besotted with him, to apprehension as his darker side was exposed.

"Crashing the train is insanity," Judith said, attempting to keep her voice level.

"Worst case, the authorities close us down and we can't open the line again. We'll just lie low, cash in the insurance and my land and buy up an estate in St Lucia."

Judith directed her comment at Dawn. "Derek was just a pawn in all this? Well, dare I say he *is* an arsehole, but I don't think he needed to be beaten within an inch of his life." She paused, considering for a few moments. "Well, perhaps a *couple* of inches."

"Oh, don't shed a tear for him," said Dawn. "He was just

as rotten as the rest of 'em. As soon as he cottoned on to the fact Augusta had lost the money, he worked out Lloyd had been wooing her."

"More manipulation." Judith gasped as Groves jerked her arm painfully upwards to silence her.

"Can you believe he tried to blackmail me?" he said with disbelief.

"The cad!" Judith exclaimed.

"Exactly. He was the one who started fishing about for the land registry deeds, not me. He roped in Wani, with promises of money. The moment Juan Carlos started being indecisive, I knew I had to take control of the situation."

The penny dropped for Judith. "He tried to blackmail you. So, you deployed your secret weapon: Dawn." Her eyes scanned Dawn's face for any trace of regret. "You pretended to be in love with him and encouraged him to break in here to find the documents Wani stole." She was pleased to see the surprise on Dawn's face. "You would be shocked by how much we know," she added with false bravado. "You should have reported him to the police."

Lloyd chuckled. "Hmm, I'm not entirely sure that would have been beneficial for me. Dawn took a bullet for the team and embedded herself in Camp Rivan."

They reached the steps leading up to the carriage and stopped. Judith would need her hands free to grip the vertical handrails to help climb the last couple of steps.

"Quite literally *embedded* herself," she said salaciously. "But Wani didn't really want to be mixed up in all of this did he? He had second thoughts and didn't give Derek the documents. Instead, you persuaded him to hand them over when you met him in the library."

"The man is a coward. He didn't want to hang around, so

he has gone to ground in some god-forsaken hole in Scotland."

"An ideal excuse for you to stitch him up by killing Derek in his home. You had the insurance form, so could pretend Wani had a change of heart and wanted in on the scam. She became thoughtful. "I sympathise with you, though. It must be difficult, as you're rapidly running out of people to frame." Her eyes met Dawn's, and she saw another glimmer of uncertainty. "Who will be next in the firing line?"

"Enough jabbering. Let's get you on board; I'll take you for a ride." He indicated for her to climb up.

"I will need my hands free to pull myself up. My dear boy, you're such an amateur when it comes to threatening people."

Lloyd glowered at her before pulling the cord free from her wrists. He evidently didn't think she was much of a physical threat. "Up you go now."

Judith obliged and entered the restored carriage. The full sixty-foot length was dim inside. The only illumination came from the rows of upholstered seats, positioned to face one another, giving an air of Victorian grandeur, complete with pale yellow, ornately lacquered tables between them.

In the centre sat Herbert Holland. He was pale and thin. A flocculant beard covered his cheeks. His hands were strapped together with a plastic zip tie; another bound his ankle to the pole supporting the table. Judith took a step towards him, then felt Lloyd's firm grip on her shoulder, propelling her quickly to the table so she could sit opposite him.

"Hello, Herbert," she said with a soft smile. "I'm here to rescue you."

Herbert's eyes searched up and down and, despite his

weakened state, grew wider. "In that case, we're both in deep trouble."

"It's nice to see you alive."

Judith was thrust into her seat. Lloyd bound her hands with a single red plastic zip tie that looped around Herbert's, attaching them together. He used another to attach her right ankle to the single stanchion under the table.

"Just in case you were thinking of having a little wander." He flinched when the train whistle suddenly gave two jolly shrieks. Dawn was growing impatient. "*Au revoir.* Enjoy the scenery." He marched out of the carriage without a glance back.

Herbert's head flopped against the seat's headrest in an acceptance of his fate.

"Have they been keeping you here all this time?"

He nodded. "In the far coal bunker. Lloyd thought the police wouldn't search here looking for me if they thought I was already dead. He was right."

"And by the time they found out it was Juan Carlo, there would be no reason to come back. They would assume you were on the run for his murder."

"They killed Juan Carlo." He drifted off with a haunted look in his eyes. "I was going to derail everything. Quite literally. When Juan Carlos admitted that he planned to sell the land to Lloyd, I saw everything was being snatched away from me. I foolishly thought if the train crashed, the insurance money would keep us afloat. It wasn't my finest idea, but I was feeling pretty wretched. Even as I left this shed, I was still debating whether I should even jump off and save my own neck."

"What made you see sense?"

"Juan Carlos intercepted me along the track. Standing

there with a lantern, waving me down like *Jenny Agutter*." A fond smile fleetingly appeared before being consumed by grief. "He agreed it would be stupid to sell to Lloyd. He was going to keep the deeds and wanted us to face the future together."

The carriage gently jerked as the locomotive edged forward. Herbert didn't seem to notice. He gave a feeble indication towards the engine. "Then they turned up, having got wind of my genius plan. And everything spiralled into hell. Lloyd was furious that Juan Carlos had changed his mind. They started to shove each other. Dawn struck Juan Carlos with the shovel. It was horrible. She never showed a single emotion." He shivered at the memory.

The lights from the shed disappeared as they pulled out, and Judith saw nothing but her own pale reflection against the inky darkness through the window. The gentle sway of the carriage could have lulled her to sleep if she wasn't about to face a sudden end. Herbert didn't react. He was lost in the trauma of his own thoughts.

"They panicked and decided to throw him in the furnace before realising that was futile. I was a wreck. In no state to fight back. I remember little as they dragged me out of the engine. It was only later I realised they were keeping me alive to pin everything on me. The last thing I remember is having my head slammed against the tender. I woke up bound and gagged in the coal bunker. At first begging for rescue, and then when I found out Juan Carlos was dead, I begged for death."

Judith felt a lump in her throat. His words were weighted with regret and sadness. His eyes searched hers, and he gave a gentle smile. "Silly, isn't it? Two grown-up men fighting to the death over a train set."

Judith reached out to clasp his hand before remembering they were tied under the table. "One man was an idiot. The other one was full of heart, trying to protect several things he loved."

Herbert pondered her words and gave a brief nod. "I think I would have liked you, Judith."

"I think you would like me too," she smiled.

The carriage suddenly gave a jerk as the train sped up. Herbert rested his head against the window. "We don't have much time to find out each other's secrets, I'm afraid. The track will disintegrate under us, and we'll end up sailing through a half-built house."

Judith tugged her hands apart, but the plastic tie was unforgiving.

"The problem with me," she said as she tried to move her bound right leg, "is that I am a relentless optimist." She could now smell the distinctive scent of hot metal, oil and steam as the wind and driving snow blew through the draughty carriage. "And if I looked at my list of ways that I thought I'd be exiting this world, tied up in the back of an old steam train wasn't even in my top hundred. I plan to do better than that!"

She smiled bravely... but couldn't think for the life of her how they could avoid their impending fate.

Chapter Thirty-Two

In any emergency, the agreed standard of behaviour optimum for survival is calm, collected thinking. Judith drew in a deep breath as she tugged the plastic zip tie around her wrists. Every time she pulled it, she moved Herbert's hands too. She yanked at the one binding her leg to the table, with no results. The sway of the carriage and the clattering of the wheels over the joints in the track increased tempo, and with it, the pace of her struggle. After several attempts, her idea of calm, collected reasoning was tossed out of the window in favour of brute force and panic. Yet the strap was not coming free. With every attempt, she could feel it digging tighter into her skin.

"Come on, you *barstool!*" she snarled as she repeatedly kicked at the table leg. She glared at Herbert, sitting calmly opposite her. "Is that it? Have you totally given up?"

Herbert gave a slow, bovine blink. It was the sign of a man who had accepted his fate.

"We spent seven months restoring this carriage," he said

dispassionately. "James and Derek slaved over every detail. We used the finest materials to get her into shape."

Judith stopped struggling and regarded the table between them with fresh eyes. "Are you telling me Derek Rivan was the craftsman on this carriage?"

Herbert gave a long sigh, and a slow, deep nod.

"Ha! In that case, I require you to apply some brute force. Kick this blasted support post as hard as possible from the top. I'm going to put all my weight against the table itself."

Herbert frowned, but Judith didn't give him the satisfaction of questioning her plan. She sharply stood and half-turned, her free knee on the seat and her bottom pressing against the table. She grunted as she piled all her weight against it.

"Now kick it as hard as you can!"

Herbert gave the table support a half-hearted kick and was surprised when the structure wobbled.

"Again! Harder!"

This time he followed Judith's instructions. Three... four kicks, and the support pole began to tilt. Under pressure from Judith's bum there was a sudden crack as the screws fixing the table to the pole tore loose and the cheap bolts attaching it to the wall sheared.

Judith tumbled into Herbert's lap. The hardwood table toppled painfully in between them. Herbert groaned as it crushed him. The support leg came free with a metal clang, and Judith was able to slip her restrained ankle over the end to free herself. Herbert followed suit. Using the sharp exposed screws, Judith made short work of slicing through the zip tie on her wrist. Herbert followed suit, rubbing life back into his red-raw wrists.

Judith worked at the plastic tie clip around her ankle with her fingernail. "That was solid teak, as installed by Derek Rivan. I bet after a few knocks this entire carriage will fall apart. Derek really is a cheap sod, through and through. I bet he pocketed the savings."

Herbert shook his head in disbelief as Judith began searching the luggage racks above the seats. "You can't trust anyone these days. What are you looking for?"

"The emergency stop cord."

"It doesn't have one. They weren't obligatory in 1915," Herbert said, somewhat apologetically.

Judith crouched on a seat opposite and cupped her hands against the window to peer outside. It was too dark to make out details other than flurries of snow splattering against the glass and the occasional dark outline of trees that swept past at an alarming rate.

"How fast do you think we're travelling?"

Herbert considered. "If we're at full steam, then forty-miles-per-hour. If they've pushed it, almost sixty. If you're thinking of jumping into a big fat snowdrift, at low speed we might break a leg or two, a few ribs, an arm, but if we're lucky, we'll be fine. But it's pitch black, so there's no way of judging what's out there. We'll literally be leaping into a void. So, goodbye, spine."

Judith weighed up their odds. "How do we stop the train?"

Herbert indicated the front passenger doors on either side.

"You open a door. You grip onto the handrail for your life and swing around to the front of the carriage." He indicated the area. "The coupler is there." He tapped the centre of the wall. "It's solid steel, so you can stand on it. Then, there's a good two-and-a-half-foot gap to the back of the tender. That's the bit storing the coal. It's going to be difficult to see anything in the dark, but if you can clamber onto the top of that and towards the engine, you can swing Zorro-like into the cabin. Then it's a straightforward act of applying the brakes and praying we haven't run out of track. Assuming they're not stupid enough to have stayed inside the cabin, in which case they'll try and stop you."

Judith nodded earnestly. "That is a well-formed plan. Are you sure *you* can carry it out?"

Herbert blinked in surprise and then burst out laughing. "Judith, even if I hadn't spent a week, half-starved in a dark bunker, thinking my life was over, with my muscles withering away – even without that, I'm not sure I'd possess the strength to be an action hero."

"And I don't know how to stop a train."

"I could teach you."

"I'm a terrible pupil." She had no intention of attempting the Errol Flynn moves he'd prescribed. In her mind, she tried to judge how close they were to Denzel Green. Her head was spinning, making it difficult to concentrate on essential points. They had been talking and tied up for at least five minutes, and the entire journey usually took just over twenty minutes at a leisurely pace. So, did they have fifteen minutes left, or ten? Or was she drastically miscalculating, as it was impossible to see anything outside to judge where they were.

Herbert had been thinking the same thoughts. "I reckon we're at full speed. If we're lucky, we've got ten minutes before we pass through Denzel Green, and then two minutes later, on to the bad section of track."

Judith nodded and stared out of the window again, reappraising their chances of jumping into the darkness. She had already decided that was more favourable than the certainty of staying aboard and not surviving a high-speed crash in a Derek Rivan-built carriage. She wouldn't be surprised if the walls were made of balsa wood and held together with Sellotape tape. Still, she had to thank Derek's frugality, otherwise they'd both still be attached to the table.

"Can we disconnect this carriage from the locomotive?"

"There is a pin that can be pulled out, just like yanking a plug out of a bath." He tapped the dead centre of the wall. "It's about here, and you're probably going to have to stand directly over it to pull it free. Same issues as before, I'm afraid."

"With fewer gymnastics."

"And..." he indicated his frail condition.

Judith rolled her eyes. "I know, I know. Bloody men can't lift a finger when it's needed." She was pleased to see a genuine smile creep across Herbert's tortured face. "And I suppose I'm dressed for the part." She patted her padded jacket and then stomped her Wellie-clad feet on the floor. "And these bad boys have got a heck of a grip. There's every chance I won't slip between the gap and be diced apart by this rather cheap carriage."

Herbert regarded her boots enthusiastically. "With those bad boys on, I would say your survival rate has already increased to twenty per cent. What are we waiting for, Judith?"

They silently stared at one another, hoping a better plan or saviour would suddenly present itself. When it didn't, Judith sheepishly nodded towards the door. "Right then, you open it. I'll hurl myself out."

Herbert crossed to the door with Judith close behind him. He gripped the catch, and looked at her for confirmation she was ready. When she nodded, he squeezed the catch and pushed the door outwards.

Instantly, the wind took it from his hand. The door opened and swung back on itself with such force the glass in the door and the window it struck shattered. At the same time, a howling gust of snow blustered in, stinging both their faces. Judith's cheeks went instantly numb, and the draught sucked the air from her lungs. She turned away, to catch her breath.

"Blimey," said Herbert, as the broken door creaked and fell off its hinges. "You weren't wrong about Derek's handiwork, were you?"

With a crunch of splintered wood, the entire door fell away into the darkness.

"I suppose it's now or never!" Judith pumped herself up. She turned around so her back was teetering over the door's edge.

The howling wind that ruffled her jacket was almost deafening. She reached to her left, groping into the darkness until she found the vertical handrail passengers used to climb aboard. She gripped it as tightly as possible and was relieved to feel Herbert clutching onto her right arm.

She sucked in a deep breath and bobbed to the side. Once, twice, and then on the third attempt, she yanked her arm free from Herbert and reached out for the handrail. Her fingers tightened around it as her upper body floundered through the doorway, almost dragging her feet out of the carriage. Luckily, the grip from her wellies was as good as she had imagined it would be, leaving her, like a slovenly comma, draped half out of the carriage.

She grunted as every muscle she possessed took her weight. She freed her left foot, flinging it around the front of the carriage. It flailed over the gap between the locomotive and the coach. It was too dark to see anything, which was quite alright because Judith decided her mission was best achieved with tightly closed eyes. Once again, she was relieved to find Herbert's arm reached back outside to grip her own. He'd lost so much weight there was no doubt that if she fell, he'd be tumbling with her. But there was some companionship to be found in a mutual suicide pact.

Her left foot searched fruitlessly for the metal frame she knew was there that linked the carriages together. In her mind's eye, she tried to picture exactly where it would be. For the first time since freeing herself from the table, a serene calmness descended. She pictured herself slung far too low out of the doorway. Her foot must be searching *beneath* the coupling mechanism. In fact, any lower and she'd probably be scraping the sleepers.

Her limbs tingled with the onset of numbness. She hauled herself higher. Somehow, her arms granted the wish, and she raised her body a couple of feet higher. No longer slumped, she was now perched upright on the corner of the carriage. Her foot tapped the solid steel coupling. Carefully, she laid the sole of her boot firmly down.

It held. At least this was one part of the carriage Derek Rivan had no part in constructing. This was solid steel workmanship, created by a true artisan. Satisfied it could take her weight, Judith used the handrail to draw herself a couple of inches higher before swinging her right leg out with her foot smartly snapping next to the other on the safety of the coupling link.

At the same time, she released her right hand and used the left one as a hinge, spinning her around to the flat front of the carriage. She was relieved to feel the wood pressing against her back. The rush of wind had vanished, confirming she was standing in the gap between the engine and the carriage. In the lee of the storm, the sound of the wind was replaced by the guttural mechanical pounding of the engine itself. The smell of hot oil, burning coal, and searing steam fumes encompassed her. She blindly reached out and could just feel the cold steel back of the engine. She leaned forward and propped herself against the tender.

Now came the difficult part.

Chapter Thirty-Three

Judith was sandwiched between a runaway locomotive and the frail carriage that had imprisoned her and Herbert Holland. Ignoring the bedlam around her, she kept her eyes closed and relied on her other senses. Except smell. The odour from the overheating train boiler was searing her nose.

Without relying on vision, the mind was remarkably adept at establishing the body's exact position. She was angled thirty-degrees between the carriage and the train, with nothing but the wagon coupling mechanism and the track whipping beneath her.

Then, in a move she hadn't tried since gym class in junior school, Judith used her arms to crab down the tender, positioning herself into a squat.

So far, so good.

Steadying her nerves with several sharp inhalations, she braced herself firmly with her left arm, and used her right hand to reach down. Her fingertips grazed the coupling mechanism beneath. As Herbert had described, she felt the dull outline of the thick chain that attached the coupling pin to the body of the carriage. She wrapped the chain twice around her hand and prepared to pull it up. Only then did she hesitate.

Her intention was to pull the pin free to detach the locomotive. It would race on ahead as the carriage slowly ground to a halt safely some distance behind. A simple plan, and like most simple plans, it had one glaring problem. The moment the pin was out, and the gap increased, she would topple headfirst to her death.

That wasn't an ideal scenario.

As an experiment, she released the chain and reached her right hand out as far as she could to the edge of the carriage. She blindly probed around, but felt nothing but the wooden wall. She was too small, and the corner was too far away for her to reach. She knew on the other side, inches away, was a handrail and the carriage door. The only problem was, in her current position, she was not acrobatically accomplished enough to reach it.

"*Bugger*," she muttered under her breath.

While she had always harboured a strong sense of self-preservation, Judith had never been selfish. She'd had a good innings and an interesting life. An interesting life was one that had been well-lived. If this act would save Herbert, she knew it was something she must do.

Judith crouched back down and once again twirled the coupling chain around her knuckles. She gave herself a mental count to three and then yanked the pin upwards. She was rewarded with movement as the well-greased rod yielded by several inches, but not enough to disconnect it. She wrapped the chain a little tighter, then pulled again. Once more, it slid a few more inches free. She gambled that the next tug would free it. There was nothing to be gained by a dramatic pause. It was now or never.

Summoning the very last of her energy, Judith heaved the rod for the third time while using her left arm to push herself away from the tender and against the carriage. The metal pin came free with a clank, and the sudden slackening of the chain reeled her backwards with a thud against the carriage wall. That unexpected consequence of Newton's laws of motion, which she hazily recalled from a question on the TV show *Pointless*, probably saved her life.

She dropped the pin and her knees cracked as she stood upright as quickly as she was able, with her arms splayed flat against the carriage. It was only then she realised her eyes were open and peering into the inky void. That is until she could make out the dark form of the locomotive slowly pulling away. She shrieked with delight as the distance increased. Then a blast of dust-filled steam struck her face, and her eyes watered as grit irritated them.

Squinting with increasing joy, the shadow of the locomotive moved onwards. The plan had worked!

Almost.

The carriage wasn't slowing down *quite as much* as she had expected. In fact, not very much at all. As she tried to process this information, she was shocked to hear the sudden whoop of a police siren and see a blue dashboard light fleetingly pass by close to her right side.

For a moment, she thought she'd imagined it. Then DS Collins' Peugeot drew alongside, its full-beam headlights revealing the track ahead. It bounced like a bronco on the snowy gravel at the side of the track. At times it seemed out of control, jerking with such wild movements that the windscreen cracked, and the bonnet unfastened itself and snapped wildly.

Judith did a double take when she saw Sarah Eastly was at the wheel, grinning like a demon. The detective was shouting, but without the shielding from the tank engine, the wind deafened her. Judith pressed herself as flat as possible against the wagon as the police car bounced onto the track in front of her with such speed, it took to the air for a second before slamming down and hopping across the sleepers. The jolt snapped the bonnet hinges, and the entire chunk of metal was caught by the wind. It slammed backwards against the windscreen before flipping end-over-end across the roof - straight towards Judith.

Driven by blind instinct, Judith crouched as the bonnet smashed through the flimsy wood a foot above her head and into the carriage behind her, marking yet another testament to Derek Rivan's engineering skills. But Judith was no longer concerned about the quality - or lack thereof - of his craftsmanship. She was toppling forwards into the yawning red abyss before her. Everything seemed to move in slow motion as her brain warned her the red abyss was not a hallucination, but was the glare of the brake lights from the car as Eastly slammed on the brakes.

The runaway carriage rear-ended the vehicle with an ear-splitting crunch. The impact was so severe, the back window imploded in a mosaic of white safety glass, which Judith toppled through. The glass was designed not to shatter and formed a plastic-like shield that embraced her as she fell into the boot of the car. Squealing metal deafened her, combined with the smell of burning rubber and hot metal. It roared for an eternity... before everything fell silent.

After several moments, Judith risked opening her eyes.

The rear car door was flung open and, remarkably, activated the interior light so she could see the harrowed face of Raymond Collins lunging towards her.

"Judith! Judith! Are you okay?" he yelled, reaching for her.

She blinked, and then nodded. "Nothing a dozen glasses of wine wouldn't wash out of my system," she said in a fragile voice she didn't recognise as her own.

Raymond gripped her hands and gently pulled her out. Judith was relieved that all her limbs appeared to be attached. Her ribs ached, but nothing as severe as she'd experienced driving her car off the road. She was irked that she had to lean on Detective Collins for support as she took in the remarkable view of the carriage, illuminated by the crumpled taillights of the Peugeot. Its rear chassis had folded under the weight of the carriage with such force, the two rear wheels had snapped flat, poking out either side from the car like a spatchcock. The destroyed vehicle had caught Judith in its glassy embrace, then formed a wedge that had brought the carriage to a swift stop.

Raymond Collins was nattering away, constructing a detailed timeline of events that had led them to the timely rescue, but Judith wasn't listening. She was watching as Sarah Eastly helped Herbert Holland down from the carriage. Sarah's teeth chattered from the cold as she'd draped her jacket around Herbert's shoulders. He met Judith's eyes with a relieved smile. Having faced the prospect of death several times in such a short space of time, he now appreciated the sanctity of life.

Judith felt a flutter of joy in her chest that they were both alive. She was about to comment on it when something else occurred to her, and she spun around to see if she could glimpse the runaway locomotive. She could only see a wall of falling flakes in the car's headlights–

Then came a distant reverberation in the darkness. A prolonged thunder and shriek of twisting metal. Then the snowfall consumed it back into a deathly silence. Only then did Raymond Collins clear his throat.

"That sounded hideously expensive."

Chapter Thirty-Four

The adage that time healed all, was not something that Judith Spears generally subscribed to. History was very clear there were some vendettas that could last a lifetime and even beyond. However, she accepted that time was a salve for fractured thinking. Sometimes, one needed to step back from situations so the subconscious could fill in the cracks and holes.

It took five days to return to the Rail Society's office, which had been left untouched since her own abduction. It was odd to be back, knowing that Dawn and Lloyd Groves were safely behind bars. Much had happened with the minimum of action.

Once Eastly and Collins had launched their brave rescue, a pair of ambulances and further police vehicles were not too far behind, making the treacherous off-road drive to Little Pickton via the rail track. They had almost been bowled from the line when the kamikaze locomotive thundered towards them, but luckily the drivers' reactions had been swift. One ambulance had become stuck in a snow drift, but the other vehicles had made it to the carriage.

Judith watched Herbert being taken away on a stretcher but had refused to go with him for her own injuries to be assessed. She had more pressing thoughts on her mind. Primarily, revenge.

She insisted on accompanying the detectives on the manhunt that was currently encircling Little Pickton to find Lloyd and Dawn. In the end, it had been a relatively simple task. So certain was the duo that their assassination plan would work. They'd leapt out of the locomotive as it left the shed. Dawn had broken her ankle, so Lloyd had taken her back to her house where they planned to stay and act shocked when the fatal crash was reported to them. Every step of the way they intended to play innocent and had enough of an alibi to cover each other.

However, the first place Judith had instructed the detectives to raid was Dawn's house where the culprits had just arrived. Lloyd was examining Dawn's swollen ankle in the kitchen as the police grandly kicked the front door down. Subsequently, the two had bickered, accusing one another of murdering Juan Carlos and attacking Derek Rivan.

During the unfolding events, DS Raymond Collins had eagerly repeated how he and Eastly had deduced Groves was the killer and rushed to save Judith and Herbert. But each time he told the story, Judith unconsciously kept zoning out as gaps in the case fought for her attention. During the fourth recital, Raymond Collins finally got the message that Judith wasn't listening. But rather than feel hurt or suffer dented pride, he knew Judith well enough to see something was bothering her.

That something had finally blossomed over the last two days.

After being forced into an overnight hospital stay so she could be monitored and bandaged, Judith received the news that Herbert Holland was recovering well in another ward and had suffered no long-term physical effects. The mental scarring was another matter.

She spent the night imagining the story unfolding from his point of view. A handy exercise, as it began dislodging some of the idiosyncrasies she had been mulling over. Given the all-clear, she had attended the police station to submit her formal statement of events to Collins and Eastly. As they walked out of the interview room, Judith was about to raise one issue that had been nagging her when the answer to that question stepped into the corridor and introduced himself.

"Detective Hamper," announced the small, balding, moustached man. He had the sort of smile that Judith associated with stand-up comedians. He presented his identity card to DS Collins and DC Eastly, and finally to Judith. She noted it was a London Metropolitan Police identity card. "I was hoping to have a word with you eventually, but seeing as I'm now tied into your official statement in a murder case, I thought it was pertinent to bring that forward."

Judith caught the detectives swapping a confused look, but she was already racing ahead with the answer. "Oh, you're the gentleman who followed me on my way home."

"I am indeed, and you're the lady who diligently managed to avoid the tail with professional expertise."

Judith gave a small smile and shook her head. "Dear Detective Hamster, I wouldn't confuse bad driving with expertise."

The detective chuckled. "I would never say that your driving was bad. And it's *Hamper*."

"I wasn't talking about *my* driving."

Detective Hamper gave an uncomfortable grin and looked sideways at DS Collins, who was unable to muffle a snigger.

"I've been investigating several financial cases. I was hoping to have an informal chat. And as I see you've done much good here." He indicated around. "I wouldn't want any of us to get off on the wrong foot."

Behind the Met Detective, Eastly and Collins swapped a concerned look.

"Excuse me, Detective Hamper," said Collins, stepping up. "Judith Spears is a material witness to a very serious murder case. Whatever you wish to talk to her about, which I *cannot fathom*," he added pointedly, "will have to wait."

Hamper pulled a face, but reluctantly acknowledged the weight of the situation. He was about to speak when Collins pushed on, and Judith swore he straightened up, increasing his stature by an extra inch.

"And while *my* investigation is open, any discussions between Ms Spears and yourself need to come through me. Understood?"

Hamper met Collins' gaze in a brief, silent, testosterone-fuelled standoff before finally nodding and mumbling his goodbyes as he left. Only when he was out of the bullpen did Collins turn sharply to Judith.

"That buys you a little bit of time. Not that I know *anything* about past misdemeanours that you may or may not have been involved with."

He stared hard at Judith, who nodded and then bit her lip to stop uttering a banal quip that would simply tick the man off. She knew that Eastly and Collins had dug into her chequered past and assembled a file of... questions. They'd even offered the file for her to read, but she had declined. At the time it had been an act of bonding between the three of them, but now she was annoyed at denying herself the opportunity of knowing exactly what they thought they had on her. That was another bridge to cross another day.

With the identity of her mysterious pursuer out of the way, other odds and ends were suddenly not too difficult to untangle. It was time to share her thoughts with the detectives and throw them a favour so they could take the credit for wrapping the case up.

That brought her to the Rail Society office the following evening. She nudged some of the detritus on the floor with her foot. The forensic team had descended on the train shed and the coal storage, but, as per the detectives' request, they had yet to tackle the office again. Judith was uneasy returning here alone, and it was fifteen minutes before Augusta arrived – late yet again - and immediately gave her an enormous hug.

"Thank you!" she said simply.

"For what?"

"For solving this mess." Augusta looked around with a sigh. "It hasn't ended the way one would hope, but they didn't get to set me up, thanks to you."

Judith chuckled. "You are far too clever for that."

Augusta nodded. "I know. Bringing you in saved my bacon. Thank you. This place," she indicated around, "really was a den of snakes, wasn't it? In some ways, I'm glad the train crashed... and nobody was hurt," she added quickly.

The runaway locomotive had taken the bend into Denzel Green at close to sixty miles-per-hour. It had teetered to the side and come off the rails as it approached the station. Fortunately, it missed five quaint railway cottages before ploughing full speed into Denzel Green's train station, demolishing the building. The train had continued through to the car park on the other side, which, due to the late hour and bad weather, had been thankfully deserted.

Augusta leaned against a desk. "I, for one, am turning my back on the whole thing. The society, this village, *everything*. It's about time I started a new life somewhere hot and sunny."

"Almost certainly," said Judith with a smile. The snow had thawed as the temperatures rose, although winter was still in the air with patches of icy dander scattered right across Little Pickton. "That was your plan all along, wasn't it?"

Augusta flashed a quizzical smile, uncertain what Judith meant.

"Taking the money and running. That's what you planned to do."

"What money?"

Judith smiled and wagged a knowing finger. "You see, Dawn thought the same as you. She thought she was far too clever for people to understand the true nature of her genius. I recognise the same in you. And I told her the same thing." Judith was about to repeat the statement she had told Dawn, but suddenly stopped herself. "And here's the thing, you're right, this whole place is a den of thieves, a hive of mistakes and mistrust. There's only really four innocent people trapped in this. There was Herbert. Well, we all know now what happened to him. And poor Juan Carlos who walked into the situation confused by love. Barbara, of course, who accepted she couldn't have what she wanted with Herbert, but still clung on to the dream. And then there was James Wani. Okay, he was semi-innocent, I suppose. He was talked into stealing the land registry records. He'll probably get away with a slap on the wrists. They found him, you know? In an Airbnb in Inverness."

"Living a life of luxury," Augusta said dryly, without taking her eyes off Judith.

"Indeed. And then we have Lloyd. Well, we all know he's a nasty piece of work. I mean, you should know more than anyone because he crossed paths with you in the City. Interestingly, it didn't occur to you to mention that to me."

"Our paths through mutual friends at a party."

"Lloyd desperately wanted to play with his train set." Judith pointed towards the engine shed. "He wanted to expand and have fun. And, of course, get rich from it all. He's a simple man. Corrupt, emotionless to the point of being a sociopath, but he's not a killer. Although he did a reasonable job on Derek. Dawn, now there is a killer. At least, I bet that's the verdict the jury will arrive at."

Judith gave a knowing smile and decided not to divulge the fact the shovel that struck and ultimately killed Juan Carlos had been found in the coal bunker, with the Spaniard's blood and Dawn's fingerprints all over it.

"And she's the one who is madly in love with Lloyd. And him with her, well, I suppose *madly* is a moot point. They conjured up this hi-tech plan to steal the money and pin it on you."

Augusta gave an audible sigh of relief. "I'm happy that's where you were going with this meandering blame game."

"I have a destination, I assure you. Derek Rivan. What can I say about him? Aside from he's just an arse who couldn't hurt a fly, because the fly would outwit him."

Augusta nodded in agreement. "An understatement."

"When he stumbled across their plan, the poor man was unable to stop himself from trying to blackmail Lloyd. That's Derek, always looking to have something for nothing."

Augusta frowned. "But you said Dawn and Lloyd were..."

"Yes, they were. But when Lloyd found himself being blackmailed, he deployed Dawn as a honeytrap. She convinced Derek they should blackmail Lloyd together. All the while he was naive enough to believe she had no interest in Lloyd. So, I suppose he was a sort of innocent as he was just being used."

"Like me."

Judith nodded. "I suppose so. You were lined up to take the blame for financial fraud, should things go wrong. As you told me, only you, Lloyd, and Herbert had access to the account. And only one of you was a trained accountant. You're the obvious patsy. However, when it turned into murder, that was something they couldn't pin on you, so they positioned Derek to take that fall."

"As I said: a den of snakes. That's why I'm washing my hands of them all. Nobody can be trusted. But Dawn," Augusta shook her head. "I didn't think she was the killing type. That's quite chilling, the number of times I've been alone with that woman."

"Did you know when I popped to her house to talk to her, she took the chance to nip outside and bodge my car's brakes?"

This was news to Augusta. Judith was surprised when the woman lunged and embraced her in another tight hug.

"I'm relieved that you're OK. And I'm so sorry for putting you in such danger."

"It takes a lot of improvisational malice to do that on the spot. She knew Derek would be arriving and it would look as if *he* was the one who tried to *do me in*. Then all the while, she and Lloyd can sail away into the sunset."

"Wicked people!"

"Indeed. But there was somebody far cleverer than all of them, wasn't there?"

Augusta's innocent expression suddenly became as stony as a gorgon.

"Augusta Calman. The real snake in the grass!"

"You flatter me." Augusta's polite tone had evaporated.

"Lloyd's desperate search for the land registry documents always bothered me. Missing deeds would certainly stall a sale for months on end, unless the ownership was forged. True ownership would reveal itself in time and he told me he only wanted it to stall for time. And then I remembered that it was you who put idea about the deeds in my head from the very beginning, before it was raised by anybody else. A clever deflection from the fact that he was really desperate to find where the *other half of the money had gone.*"

Augusta straightened up, her brow knitting into a frown.

"You see, I think all of this would have gone unnoticed if Herbert had died, as you believed. But here's the thing—he knew exactly how much was in that account. As did Lloyd. As did you. The problem was, Lloyd had orchestrated the scam, so he could hardly complain that half the *'missing'* money had gone into an offshore account of his, via the town hall. Using Wani's computer to forward it into his cryptocurrency account. But the *other half* had simply vanished. If he raised that thorny issue, then he may as well admit his own guilt."

She waited for Augusta to plead innocence. Instead, the woman glared at her with increasing loathing.

"I don't know when exactly, but you cottoned on to what was happening. You knew Dawn and Lloyd were planning this scam, so you took it upon yourself to out-scam them. In your words: you're the only other one who had full access to everything. The only one who could be blamed for stealing the money. However, that also meant you're the only one who could doctor the books to show there was *half the amount of money* in accounts. And out of the only other two people who would know you're lying, one was thought to be dead. And the other was the original criminal."

Augusta started to pace around Judith, but Judith astutely blocked her path, keeping her corralled in the office. Judith pressed on.

"You diligently erased evidence that you'd pilfered that cash long ago, and then covered yourself superbly well. You know all about shell companies, you know all about moving cash around, because you and Lloyd are forged from the same cloth as all those other crooked city traders." There was a twinkle in Judith's eye. "I know how that works." She winked, which had a disconcerting effect on Augusta.

Augusta cleared her throat, her eyes flicking between Judith and the ceiling as she thought through the situation. When she spoke, her voice was low.

"Let's be very clear, Judith. There are only your wild assertions against the evidence. I know how to hide cash. You can bring in an army of forensic accountants, but it will never reappear. You can accuse me until you're blue in the face. But all the evidence points to Lloyd stealing what was there."

"And what do you say when they find you on a luxury

beach with a two-hundred-thousand-pound hole burning in your bikini?"

"Then there'll be a lovely record of a windfall through clever investments that I happened upon. I know exactly *your* cloth, Judith Spears—hubris, you think you're far smarter than everybody else. My plan was clean and left no victims. I never thought it would result in murder! What kind of monster do you think I am? I just want to be done with this bunch of morons and live my own life away from all the soap opera bickering and nagging and," Augusta rolled her eyes, "all their boring personal melodramas. I was blamed for his divorce. They tarnished me with a reputation that got me banned from my dentists! I was a victim because of them! But still, mine was an elegant solution. Lloyd could bugger off and do whatever he wanted, but he'd be unable to frame me. Anyway, he's behind bars. Now I will be the one walking into a very literal sunset. And if you're thinking of trying to blackmail me or demand cash for your silence, I'm not that dumb."

"You're far from stupid, my dear," said Judith. "It's not as though I'm going to be able to wangle a written confession from you, am I?"

Augusta sniggered and shouldered past Judith. "So, you brought me here to gloat, in the place it all happened? To show me how smart you are? I overestimated you, Judith Spears. But that doesn't matter. I win."

Augusta reached for the door handle, but stopped when Judith gave an amused chuckle.

"I'm sorry, you overestimated me? Or do you mean underestimated? I didn't quite catch what you said. Let me think... yes, you definitely *underestimated* me. I'm not naive enough to think I'll get a written testimony from you." Judith reached up to the shelf and pulled something from it. "One thing I am surprised at is how durable these things are."

She held up her doorbell camera. It had been pointed straight at Augusta, the exact place where Judith had penned her in.

"They have good quality cameras. Easy to make out faces, even in low light like this. And the sound recording quality is top-notch. I bought it in a sale on Amazon. Amazing, really. There it was, recording away as you delivered your confession..."

Judith took great pleasure in watching Augusta's face turn ashen. Augusta flinched as the door behind her suddenly opened and DS Collins stepped inside, looking as stern as he could, despite fighting the euphoria of cracking the case.

"Augusta Calman, considering your recent admissions, I am placing you under arrest."

He held up Judith's phone and on the screen was the relayed video image from the doorbell camera in Judith's hand.

"Smile for the camera," said Judith, holding it up to capture Augusta's crestfallen expression.

Chapter Thirty-Five

Sarah Eastly was exhausted after the last couple of weeks, so much so that she was considering taking time off. She couldn't remember the last time she took any annual leave. Days from last year had already rolled over into this one. It was a sad reminder that she had no hobbies or friends beyond work – and even there, the pickings were slim. However, she couldn't deny that, since Judith Spears had appeared in her life, work had become far more interesting.

Now that the investigation was wrapping up, she and DS Collins spent most of their time in the station filing volumes of paperwork. And Eastly had the added indignation of officially justifying how she had wilfully destroyed a police car, something that was frowned on at the best of times. But, with no time pressures, it meant she regularly left Fulton police station at five o'clock and walked the long way to her apartment to waste a more time before she arrived home and spoke to her mother.

That phone call never changed. Her mother spent three-quarters of the call recounting in minute detail the events of her day, which were identical to the ones the same day last week. It was a routine embedded in stone and only ever changed with embellishments about the details of people she had bumped into. Eastly got to know the names, relationships statuses, physical descriptions, and job details, of *complete* strangers in the course of the story. It all confirmed a heavy sense that her mother was having a richer life than her daughter.

Eastly stared at the sad range of microwave meals in her freezer, unable to decide which bland one would accompany an evening watching *The One Show*. Her phone rang, and she snatched it up without looking at the caller ID. The hope that it was the Guv with another tragic case to keep her busy was dashed when she didn't immediately recognise the voice. It took her tired mind a few seconds to realise it was PC Kevin Fenton. As he spoke, her eyes strayed to the badminton racket propped under the coat rack. She listened to Kevin's proposal, then slammed the freezer shut.

"I have a better idea..."

She told him her plan, and thirty minutes later she was running out of the door, looking forward to a dining experience she'd wanted for a while. Nando's wasn't the place to eat alone. And for once, she didn't have to worry about that stigma.

Raymond Collins was still at his desk. After Eastly had left, he had taken down most of the mugshots and maps. Everything had been diligently entered into the police computer, including his reports, which were peppered with embarrassing typos. At least cleaning those up would waste a few extra days.

Once he'd submitted the case, there would still be plenty of things for him and DC Eastly to do. He'd already been told about a rash of bicycle thefts around the area and sightings of a large black cat that witnesses swear was an escaped leopard, although the only photograph Raymond had seen looked like a small tabby sprinting across a field.

Once again, he dreamed of a position on a large force, tackling cases with nationwide implications. And maybe, just maybe, they'd even involve a gun or two. Just to spice things up. He saw an email had arrived from DS Hamper, which he quickly deleted without reading it. If the swanky MET detective wanted anything from him, then he could pick up the phone.

On the staff noticeboard, he remembered that a few people were heading to a pub quiz tonight. He used to enjoy pub quizzes with his mates, but since moving to Fulton, he hadn't been in touch with them as often as he'd like. So, a quiz with folks from the station could be fun. Or enjoyable compared to staying in alone...

But they were the people he saw every day, and they had formed their own cliques. Raymond felt that the time for forming new friendship groups was in your twenties into your thirties, when people partnered up and new pools of friends formed. Then people got married from their thirties into their forties, by which time you were stuck with the pools you had already formed. That was it for a social life. Raymond was certain that in his fifties, there was no hope of making new friends. Those chances had passed. He would have to make do with what he had. He'd toyed with dating on Tinder, but it wasn't the best place for a copper to hang out.

Feeling glum, he scrolled through his phone contacts and stopped at Judith's number. She annoyed the hell out of him. But she also made him laugh, and life was generally interesting when she was around. But at seven o'clock on a Thursday, she was probably busy.

Raymond Collins turned his computer off. As the last person to leave the office, he also turned the lights off. He allowed his stomach to set plans for the evening. First, a portion of curry and chips to eat in the chip shop. Then he'd hunt down a good film or TV show to watch.

At least he could say his life was regular.

Maggie whirled the tea in her cup before tasting it like a wine connoisseur. Finally, she swirled it around her mouth before swallowing it and gave Judith a nod.

"Not too bad. PG Tips."

On the other side of her kitchen table, Judith Spears nodded, despite feeling highly unimpressed. "I don't see this skill developing to have much of a future."

"Oh, I tell you now, Fabian is a man who loves his tea. He has teas from every corner of the planet. And he is taking me now to a tea-tasting day for the paper!"

"Riveting. I imagine they are like wine-tasting days but without the fun."

"Ah, Judith. You need to see beyond these four walls."

"Don't get me wrong, I'm thrilled that you and Fabian are doing well."

"*Officially courting.*" Maggie wagged her eyebrows. "There, I said it."

"Congratulations. He's a lovely man."

"He will be when I've finished with him," growled

Maggie. "Although having you as my friend doesn't make my life easy with him. He's more than a little irked that you drove a train through his station."

Remarkably, the tough old engine had suffered relatively minor damage and a preliminary insurance inspection indicated that it could restore it back into shape. The only issue Herbert Holland was wrestling with was whether he should bother. With no station at Denzel Green, no carriage, and a dysfunctional Rail Society, he was unsure what to do next.

"I'll remind him it wasn't me," said Judith diplomatically. "I was the one who had been kidnapped and was facing certain death. I went through this with him when he tried to interview me for his paper."

"Telling him to sod off upset him."

Judith shrugged. "I prefer to remain an international woman of mystery. What can I say? I'll make it up to him. If the PG Tips is that good, maybe I can add it to his collection."

Maggie shot her a sarcastic smirk. "I'd like you two to get on and not quibble like this."

"I promise I shall indeed," said Judith, determinedly slapping her palm against the table. "In fact, I am going to invite you both around for a superb meal."

Maggie's eyes narrowed suspiciously. "The old Judith I knew would never do that without an ulterior motive."

Judith clasped her hand against her chest. "Maggie, you should know at any time I have at least *two* ulterior motives in play."

"Oh?" Maggie's interest was piqued.

Judith's gaze fell to the table for a long moment as she assembled her thoughts. "Your new/old beau has carved himself a very interesting position between being mayor and newspaper editor."

"Yes," Maggie said, the cogs visibly working through her mind. "That's the other thing I like about him, aside from his tea fetish."

"Then I would be very interested in telling you both a story. About me."

Maggie's eyes narrowed as Judith leaned conspiratorially closer.

"This is not like you."

"I think some things may be catching up with me and I may need a little help from you both."

"What sort of things?"

Judith pursed her lips. "How about this Saturday evening you both come around, and maybe learn a secret or three?"

Also by Sam Oman

MURDER BY INVITATION

(book 1)

A DOSE OF MURDER

(coming soon)

SAM OMAN
presents a JUDITH SPEARS mystery

A Dose of MURDER

Printed in Great Britain
by Amazon